Deadly Reigns IV

The Saga Continues

A Novel

By

Caleb Alexander

Copyright 2012

1

This book is a work of fiction. Any references to historical events, real people, establishments, organizations, or real locales, is intended to give the fiction a sense of reality and authenticity. All other names, characters, places, and incidents are either the products of the author's imagination, or are used fictitiously.

ISBN: 978-0-9826499-8-5978-0-9826499-8-5

Published by Golden Ink Media

Cover Design: Oddball Designs
Printed in the United States of America

Deadly Reigns IV

Deadly Reigns IV

Chapter One

"Fuck!" Elizabeth turned away from the decapitated bodies and vomited. She had been an FBI Agent for more than two decades, and yet, she had never seen anything like this.

"Senorita, are you okay?" Eduardo Gomez asked her. Gomez was the regional head of the Mexican Federal Police. It was his agency that was in charge of the discovery, and the recovery. He had known Elizabeth Holmes for more than fifteen years, and considered her not just a colleague, but a friend.

"I'm getting too old for this shit, Eddie," Liz replied, wiping her mouth. She lifted the white surgical mask back to her face, but it did little to dissipate the stench of the bodies lying in the trench below her. It was a stench worse than burning flesh or rotting meat, worse than putrid swamp water, or raw sewage, it was a warm radiating stench of decaying remains that permeated not only the air, but seemed to seep into every fabric, every fiber, every pore of every individual within a five hundred yard radius.

"What kind of sick fucks are we dealing with?" Grace Moore asked, while peering down into the unearthed mass grave.

The bodies in the grave numbered in the hundreds. Well

over five hundred, to be more precise. Bus loads of passengers killed by the cartels in revenge for the killing of one of their leaders. The body count not only included civilians, but kidnapped Mexican soldiers, dozens of Mexican law enforcement officers and agents, and many members of rival cartels. Elizabeth and Grace, as well as numerous other U.S. officials were present, because three of the bodies belonged to Americans.

The manhunt to find and hopefully recover alive, Border Patrol Agents Charlie Herrera, and Mike Rivera, as well as El Paso County Sheriff Jimmy DeWitt, had consumed the American public for weeks. The President had promised to find the agents and bring them home, members of Congress had promised and reassured a stunned American public that they would provide whatever resources the FBI and the Mexican authorities needed to bring their fellow citizens home alive. The world media had become fixated on the event. And now, the Mexican Federal Police, responding to an anonymous tip, had found the Americans buried in a mass grave in a field outside of Juarez, Mexico, along with hundreds of others. The American population was shocked. And they would be even more disturbed in the days and weeks ahead, once they learned the details of the find. All of the bodies inside of the mass grave, had been beheaded.

Tears flowed from Grace Moore's eyes. She was tough. A well tested FBI veteran who had been through the fire many times throughout her life, but she had never seen anything like this. Sure, she had dealt with numerous drug lords and mafia scum throughout her career, but never had she witnessed anything so brutal, so heartless, so sadistic. Many of the victims inside of the pit had been bound, with their hands tied behind their backs. In other words, they had been executed in cold blood.

"Is it them, Frank?" Elizabeth asked, peering down into

the mass grave. "Is it our boys?"

FBI Agent Frank Hawk, dressed in an all white protective jumpsuit with a gas mask covering his face, peered up at Special Agent in Charge Elizabeth Holmes and nodded. He turned over one of the bodies he was standing over. The headless body still had its Border Patrol uniform on, along with the Agent's name tag.

Liz wiped away a tear that was slowly rolling down her cheek. "Let's get them out of there, Frank. Let's get them into the ambulances and take Charlie and Mikey and Jimmy home."

There were numerous FBI agents inside of the pit, along with numerous members of the Mexican Federal Police. They were stepping on bodies trying to recover their agents first, while at the same time, trying to preserve any forensic evidence that may have been left.

An FBI Agent approached Elizabeth with a secure Satellite phone. "Ma'am, it's the Director."

Liz grabbed the Sat phone. "Sir?"

Director Mueller cleared his throat. "What's the deal, Liz? The President is waiting for my phone call."

"Bob, I'm sorry," Liz told him. "We haven't ID'd them positively as of yet. We'll do the DNA once we get them to the morgue in Juarez. But we're pretty sure it's them. Bob, they still have their uniforms on."

"God, Liz," the Director declared, sounding crestfallen. "What kind of people would do this?"

"They're monsters, Bob," Liz told him.

"Congress is going to want blood," The Director told her. "Members of the House and Senate are already calling this narco terrorism, and are pressing the Attorney General to declare it such. They want to use some of the Nine-Eleven statutes on the books to justify going after these thugs with our military."

"Bob, Mexico is a sovereign country," Liz cautioned.

7

"So was Pakistan," the Director countered. "They are going to want blood. The American people are going to be up in arms over this."

"You caution the President when you give him the news, Bob," Elizabeth told him.

The Director exhaled. "Is it true what they are saying, Liz? I mean, the initial reports? Were all of the victims decapitated?"

It was Elizabeth's turn to exhale. "It appears so."

"Ours boys?"

"Yeah, our boys too," she said softly.

"Get them home, Liz," the Director told her.

"The Mexican government is going to want us to verify their identity by DNA, before we transport them across the border."

"Fuck that!" the Director exploded. "They don't get to play games here! Not this time, not on this one! You bring those boys home! I want them on American soil, tonight! If they have a problem with it, we have elements of the Texas National Guard already along the border, remember? They were participating in the search for our people. You call General Franklin, if they try to stop you from crossing that border, you got that?"

"Bob..." Liz said softly, trying to calm the Director.

"Liz, the President is pissed. The Congress is even madder. And even more upset, are the American people. I have to call the President, and inform him that three of our citizens are dead, decapitated, and decomposing in a mass grave in Juarez, Mexico. How do you think that phone call's going to go?"

"About as well as this one, I supposed."

"Sorry, Liz," the Director said more calmly. "Things are just fucked up right now."

"It's shit duty everywhere tonight, Bob."

"I know. I'm sorry. Just get home, Liz. Get those boys home, and then you get home. I need you here in Washington, Liz."

"You need me to sit behind a desk as head of the Office of Integrity and Compliance?" Liz asked sarcastically. She had been promoted. And she hated her promotion. She wanted to stay in the field, even if it was as a Special Agent in Charge of a field office. She would rather have that than sit behind a desk in Washington. But she couldn't resist her promotions any longer. She had been given a directive, either up or out. Accept her promotions, or retire. And life without the Bureau is a life she didn't want to contemplate. So, reluctantly, she accepted her latest kick upstairs.

"You could have said no," the Director told her.

"And retire?" Liz huffed. "No thanks."

"See you in a few days, Liz," the Director told her.

"Bob, be careful," Elizabeth warned. "When the townspeople gather their pitch forks and work themselves into a frenzy, it's up to us to provide some clarity and bring some sanity to the situation."

"Ten-four," the Director acknowledged. "That's why I need you here."

"Soon enough."

"Soon enough," the Director acknowledged, before disconnecting.

Liz tossed the Sat phone to one of her agents, and turned to watch as the bodies of the Border Patrol agents were gently lifted out of the open pit and placed on gurneys. A waiting ambulance with its lights flashing, backed closer to the pit. In the distance, the lights from the international news media began to grow brighter as more and more members flocked to the scene. The Mexican police formed a snaking human barricade to keep them as far back from the exhumation as possible.

9

Grace moved closer to Liz, and almost clasped her hand as they watched the bodies of the agents and the sheriff being placed inside of the ambulance.

Liz turned toward Eduardo Gomez. "Eddie, we're taking the bodies across the border tonight. I just heard from the Director of the FBI. Don't fight us on this one."

Eduardo nodded. He understood the sensitivity of the politics surrounding what had happened. And he had been around politicians long enough to know when to stay out of the way and let events take their course. There would be grave ramifications for this, he knew. He just didn't know how bad things were going to get. Mexican cartels had kidnapped a United States Sheriff, and two United States Border Patrol agents, brought them across the border, tortured and beheaded them, and then dumped their bodies in a mass grave. The American people were going to be up in arms once the full story came out. And no matter how much they wanted to hide some of the details, on events such of these, the details always got out. This had the potential to be extremely bad for his country, and he was not going to make it worse by playing bullshit political games at this time. The bodies of those two agents and the sheriff, were still in uniform, with their name tags visible. He wouldn't dishonor them by forcing them to go to a hospital in Juarez for a DNA examination.

"I am releasing the bodies into your custody, Liz," Eduardo told her." He was a police officer as well. The American's just wanted to take their countrymen back home, so they could bury them with the honor they deserved. As a fellow law enforcement officer he understood the meaning of such things.

"Thanks, Eddie," Liz said, shaking his hand. She peered at the other bodies that were being brought up from the pit. "Your men?"

Eduardo nodded. "Twelve of them. Plus ten soldiers, and

four local cops."

"I'm sorry, Eddie," Liz told him. It was so easy to get caught up in the American aspect of the situation, that one could forget the devastating losses that the Mexican police forces and the Mexican people had suffered. "I'm so sorry."

"We're going to get those bastards," Eduardo told her. "I'm going to do whatever it takes."

Grace gasped, turned toward Liz and started weeping. The Mexican police were now bringing up the bodies of young children. One of the bodies was that of a little girl, whose dead arms was still clutching a doll. A headless doll. It was a grim joke, and a sadistic action by some inhuman cartel murderer. The US and Mexican recovery teams were all breaking down into tears, while anger flashed across their faces.

"Liz, get me the fuck outta Juarez," Grace told her.

"Sorry, baby, but we have a job to do," Liz replied softly.

Grace watched as the technicians loaded the little girl in the back of a coroners van. She was furious. The child, was little Damian's age. And if these monsters would do that to her, they wouldn't hesitate to hurt her son. Grace turned. She found her legs going wobbly and her stomach growing queasy.

"Grace!" Liz cried out, steadying her friend.

"Are you okay, *senora*?" Eduardo asked.

Grace steadied herself and nodded. She wished that she was back in the States chasing big time drug dealers and mafioso drug lords. This was a duty that she hated. Being Liz's deputy chief of station was a great promotion, but it came with dealing with bullshit like this. And things were certainly to get worse. Not only had Liz been promoted, but so had she. Liz would be leaving for Washington, while she would be leaving for Houston. She was going to be the Special Agent in Charge of the FBI's Houston field office. She would have dozens and dozens of agents and supporting personnel working for her. It was a great promotion. It would also place her in

Texas, close to her son, who was now living with his father permanently. Although ambivalent about being so close to Damian once again, those feelings were super ceded by the fact that she would be able to spend so much more time with her son. And her son, was her entire world.

"Grace?"

"Yeah, Liz?"

"Are you okay?"

"I'm okay," Grace nodded. I just need some water. I need to get away from here for a minute.

Liz nodded.

Grace turned to head to a vehicle to take her down the road to a trailer that the FBI had set up as a command post. There, she could sit down and drink her water. Far away from the stench of the pit. No doubt, the diseased air would contaminate her water if she tried to drink some there. No, she would go to the command post, lie back on the sofa, and collect her thoughts. She turned and stared at the coroners van that contained the remains of the little girl holding the doll. What kind of sick fucks did that, she wondered? What kind of sick fuck decapitates a little girl's doll, and then the little girl herself? What kind of sick fucks would cut Dora's head off?

Grace took a step, and that's when she heard the shouting in Spanish from the pit. And then she heard the loud click. And then she felt the explosion that ripped through the air.

Grace, Liz, and all of the others standing above the pit flew through the air, as the massive blast radiated from out of the pit. The agents, officers, and workers inside of the pit were disintegrated instantly.

Grace hit the ground next to Liz. She reached out and grabbed at her friend's hand, not knowing whether she was dead or alive. She could see that Liz's face was blackened, her hair was melted away, and she was burned over much of her body. Grace didn't know how bad she was hurt. She felt nothing but numbness. Her ears were still ringing internally from the blast, so she couldn't hear anything around her. Her body was stiff, and she found that she was unable to move. She continued to direct her hand to reach out to Liz, but was finding that it was taking forever to actually get to her. Grace quickly became exhausted, not realizing that the blood draining from her body was causing her to slowly lose consciousness.

Her last thoughts before she blacked out: Those sick fucks had placed explosives beneath the dead bodies at the bottom of the pile.

"Damian..." Grace murmured. She was not calling out to her son Lil Damian, but to his father. "Kill... them... Kill... 'em...all."

Deadly Reigns IV

Chapter Two

Desire Dents was all go, no slow; high speed, high caffeine, and high drama. She was CNN's newest piece of eye candy. She was every man's fantasy. She had enough chocolate in her blood to get White men's blood rising, *and* she was mixed with Cambodian, so Black men fell all over her long, silky hair, Asian eyes, and high cheek bones. Her accent was educated valley girl, which allowed her to appeal to middle America. She was petite in stature, which allowed the network to dress her size zero body in the latest fashions, turning her into not only a fashion icon, but a walking, talking, new stream of ad revenue. Designers threw money and clothing at the network, in hopes of having her wear their brand on television.

Desire hailed from all over. She was military brat. The product of a Cambodian mother, and African American father. She was born in Germany, lived in Japan, Turkey, Italy, and all over the United States. She was a hard charger, like her gun ho father, and an overachiever like her math professor mother. Desire entered Harvard at the age of sixteen, graduated at twenty, and had completed grad school by the age of twenty two. She had a Master's degree in communication, as well as BA's in mass communication and journalism. She was a network's wet dream.

"Get the camera up!" Desire ordered her crew. "C'mon,

let's go! Let's go!"

The camera crew groaned. Being assigned to Desire was the worst gig in the studio. Camera crews dreaded being assigned to her, and there was a running joke amongst them. Whenever assigned to Desire, call your wife and kids and say goodbye, just in case it's the last opportunity you would have to do so. To the executives, Desire was a hard nose, hard charging, investigative journalist. To camera crews, she was dangerous, reckless, and sometimes foolish. She charged into bank robberies, shootings, and bomb threats like she was Superwoman with a microphone and a cape. It's okay if she wanted to get herself killed, but why her entire camera crew, they often wondered. Today, was just such a foolish operation.

"Is that thing on yet?" Desire demanded.

The cameraman held up his fingers and began the countdown. "We go in five, four, three, two, one. We're on!"

"Hi, I'm Desire Dents reporting live from the Texas border," Desire turned for dramatic effect, allowing the camera to pan the desert like landscape just behind her. "Today, we have learned that the President of the United States has just ordered the Texas National Guard to take up positions along the US-Mexico border, thus militarizing the border between the two countries for the first time in over a century."

The camera showed thousands a U.S. Soldiers in camouflage marching into positions across the desert landscape. They were accompanied by hundreds of camouflage Humvees, in a scene reminiscent of the American invasion of Iraq.

"This is a dramatic escalation of the war on drugs, and comes on the heels of the greatest act of narco-terrorism in our country's history," Desire continued. "Only days ago, the bodies of two US Border Patrol agents, and the Sheriff of El Paso County, were found in a mass grave just outside of Juarez, Mexico. This, after a massive two week manhunt for them, which ultimately proved heartbreaking. It was during the retrieval of those American law enforcement professionals that the act of narco-terrorism was committed, resulting in the loss of more than twenty four FBI agents, two State Department officials, thirty Mexican Federal Police officers and agents, the Mexican Deputy Minister of Justice, and several international journalist, including two of my colleagues here at CNN. It was a devastating loss felt throughout the international law enforcement and journalistic communities."

The camera panned across the landscape, again showing American soldiers on the march.

"The President has stated that he will go after the narco-terrorist responsible for this heinous act, and that the US-Mexico Border is effectively closed until further notice. The word the administration officials used, was quarantined, which means they will be searching each and every vehicle seeking to cross into US territory. This will result in massive delays at the international crossing, effectively shutting down the border. The reason for this, is to stop the violence from seeping over onto the US side, administration officials declared. And as you will remember, those American law enforcement officials were kidnapped from the American side of the border, and then spirited into Mexico, where they ultimately met their brutal demise. This is Desire Dents, reporting for CNN."

The cameraman held up his fingers and performed a backwards countdown. "Three, two, one, we're off."

Desire exhaled and lowered her microphone. "Good, let's get to the truck, get the feed to the station, and then head over to the Texas National Guard command post. I want to see if I can get an interview with General Franklin."

The cameramen peered at one another and shook their heads. They both thought the same thing without either having to speak. Here she goes with that bullshit again.

REIGNS FAMILY RANCH

The entire family was gathered at the family's 25,000 acre South Texas ranch. Today was a somber and celebratory occasion. It was Lucky' fifth birthday party, and it was also the week of Angela's death five years ago. The family gathered to support Dante, and to show Lucky that despite not having a mother, she still had plenty of family that loved her and that would be there for her. The entire ranch had been turned into one giant Toy Story 3 fantasy land.

Blown up castles dotted the party area. Pony rides, giant Disney merry-go-rounds, bouncers, and water slides, shared space with a full petting zoo. Actors dressed in Toy Story character costumes walked around performing for the numerous children in attendance. On the main table, sat Lucky's near life sized Toy Story 3 cake, consisting of all of the main characters. Dante had pulled out all stops with this birthday party. And with each passing year, it appeared that he tried to top the previous year, in order to compensate for Angela's absence.

"A beautiful, party, Dantito!" Consuela exclaimed, while peering out of the kitchen window into the massive backyard

"Thanks, Consuela," Dante said.

Detecting a hint of sadness in his voice, Consuela turned toward him. She knew Dante well. In fact, she practically raised Dante, Damian, Princess, and their other siblings. She had worked for the Reigns family since before the kids were born. They viewed and respected her like a second mother as well.

"What's the matter, Dante?" she asked. "And don't you lie to me!"

18

Dante shook his head. "Nothing."

"This has to do with Angelina, no?"

Dante shifted his gaze toward the ground.

" Every year. Every single year, I watch you go through this. You tear yourself apart, because she's not here. I watch you spoil that beautiful little girl of yours, trying to make up for the absence of her mother." Consuela placed her finger beneath Dante's chin, and lifted his head so that their eyes could meet. "Listen to me, *mijo*. Angelina was a beautiful woman, and a wonderful wife to you. And she would have been a *fantastico madre* to Little *Lucquita*. But, Dante, *Angelina* is gone. And you can't make up for her absence by buying things for that precious little girl. She doesn't need toys, or games, or animals, she just needs you. Right now, you're all she knows. You're her everything. And to her, you're her whole world, and that's good enough to her. And if it's good enough for her, it should be good enough for you."

"I know," Dante said peering down again. "But, she needs her mother. She didn't get a chance to even know her."

"*Dantito* ! Listen to me!" Consuela said sternly. "*Angelina's* death, was not your fault. Put that out of your head, right now! It was not your fault. And you can't spend the rest of your life blaming yourself, or wondering what if. You have a baby to raise!"

"I know."

Consuela snapped her fingers in his face. "Consuela didn't raise no punks. Snap out of it!"

Dante laughed. "You were around my mother waaay, too long!"

Consuela and Dante shared a long laugh.

" Mijo, don't you worry about *Lucquita* not knowing her mother," Consuela continued. "The way you look into that little girls face, tells her all that she needs to know. That you loved her mother, *con todos tu corazone*. With all your heart."

19

Dante smiled, leaned forward, and kissed Consuela on her cheek before walking out of the kitchen.

"Dante, c'mere!" Damian called out to his brother.

"What's up?" Dante asked, walking into the family room, where Damian, Princess, and Emil were gathered. Their eyes were fixated on the television, where CNN reporter Desire' Dents was reporting from the border.

"Damn, she's fine!" Dante said smiling.

"Ain't she though," Damian agreed. "She can interview me anytime."

"If you agree with them, I'm going to cut your dick off," Princess said to Emil, without taking her eyes off the television.

Behind her back, Emil nodded to Damian and gave the thumbs up. The brothers laughed.

"What the hell's she blabbering about now?" Dante asked.

"The headless bodies that the Cartel booby trapped in Mexico, is fucking things up," Princess told him. "The President is pissed, and he dropped the hammer. He's completely closed the U.S.-Mexican border."

"Not only that, he's militarized it," Damian added.

"You're fucking kidding me?" Dante asked.

Emil shook his head.

"Nothing is going to get through," Damian told him. "Abso-fucking-loutely-nothing."

"And Cedras has Colombia all fucked up with his little takeover moves," Dante added. "What the fuck?"

"That's what we're all wondering," Princess told him. "What the fuck. The Commission is going to panic like school girls getting their cycles on prom night."

"Ugggh," Emil said shaking his head. "Couldn't you have used another analogy?"

"Oh stop," Princess said, dismissing him. "You like

20

bloody pussy."

Damian and Dante both stared at Emil, who was shaking his head no.

"Okay, too much information, sis," Dante told her. He turned to Damian. "What the fuck are we going to do?"

"First, get with our people in the House, and at Justice, and see how long this shit is going to last," Damian told him. "Time for them to earn all that money we've been shoveling to them. Second, we check our inventories. We should be fine for a while."

"Three months," Princess told him. "We can ride this out for three months. After that, we're dry. And during that three months, while everyone else is running out, and getting cut off, prices are going to go through the roof."

"Okay, so we all agree, shit is going to get bad," Damian asked rhetorically.

"Real bad," Emil added.

"Let's put out feelers and start seeing where else we can buy from." Damian told them.

"Panama? Bolivia? Honduras? Costa Rico?" Princess asked.

"All of them," Damian said, lifting an eyebrow and exhaling.

"In the meantime, get rid of those worried faces," Dante told them, wrapping his arms around Damian and Princess. "We have a birthday party to attend."

The four of them headed out of the family room, with Damian turning and peering back at the television. He knew how bad things were about to get.

Deadly Reigns IV

Chapter Three

"Hey Liz," Nathan said, clasping her arm as he seated himself at the head of the large conference table. They were at the FBI's Washington D.C. Headquarters. Today's briefings were one of many that had been held since the border crisis. Nathan had slept little in the past week.

"I'm fine," Liz told him. She was in bandages. And using a cane. She had checked herself out of the hospital just the previous day, against her doctor's orders, took a flight to D.C., and was now attending a meeting on the very cartels that almost took her life.

"You know you shouldn't be here," Dave Wellborn told her. Dave was the new Special Agent in Charge of the San Antonio office. Nathan's old job. His territory also included the South Texas border regions.

"I'm fine, Dave," Liz said, shrugging off his concerns.

"Liz, you're walking with a goddamn cane!" Nathan told her. "We all know you're tough, you're an excellent field agent, and *you* of all people in law enforcement, have nothing left to prove. I want you back in a hospital, Liz. Is that clear?"

"Nathan, I need to do my goddamn job!" Liz snapped. "There's a young lady laying in a hospital bed in El Paso, Texas right now because of *me*. I took her down to Juarez with me. There are dozens of other agents that I served with, many of whom were under my command, that would give anything

23

to be able to see their families again. I have to be here. I have to get those son of a bitches. Even more so, I'm *armed* right now. And neither you, nor anyone else in this goddamned building, could drag me away from this table right now."

Several agents walked into the room and joined them around the conference table.

"Gentlemen, I believe that most of you are familiar with each other," Nathan told them, after clearing his throat. He frowned at Liz and leaned in toward her. "Our little discussion isn't over."

Handshakes were exchanged around the table.

"Hector, how's your mother?" Elizabeth asked, ignoring Nathan.

"She's great, ma'am," Agent Hector Villa answered. Hector was one of Liz's trainees back at the academy. He was an veteran field agent now, with more than twelve years of service. Fluent in Spanish, he was a fast riser within the Bureau. He had spent the better part of his career going after MS-13 Drug Gang members in California, and in their home country of El Salvador.

"And that sister of yours?" Liz continued. "Is she still in Afghanistan?"

"No, ma'am," Hector said, "She's in Okinawa now."

"Good," Liz smiled. "Jose, how's Rosa?"

Agent Camacho nodded. "She's good."

Agent Jose Camacho was another Spanish speaking agent brought into the Bureau during the height of the drug war. A former Border Patrol agent, Jose joined the Bureau after his brother was killed in the line of duty tracking down illegal entrants. Frustrated at the bureaucracy that kept his agency's hands tied, Jose decided to join the FBI and go after the drug dealers and their human drug mules another way. He had infiltrated three different cartels, and had been instrumental in bringing down some of the highest profile cartel bosses ever.

Jose was one of the Bureau's super stars.

"I told her to divorce your ass," Liz told him.

"I know," Agent Camacho answered. "Good thing she didn't take your advice."

"Good for who," Liz smiled. "For you, or for her?"

"Shit, for her!" Camacho declared.

The Agents around the table broke into laughter.

"For those of you who weren't aware, Agent Daniel Lopez here, is now the Special Agent in Charge of the El Paso field office," Nathan announced.

Agent Lopez nodded at those arrayed around the large conference table. He also was a Spanish speaking agent, though not of Mexican decent. Agent Lopez was actually born to parents of Colombian ancestry. He found his way into the bureau after serving in the U.S. Army special forces. After eight years in the military, and after obtaining his Bachelors degree while serving, he found himself gravitating towards law enforcement. Perhaps it was him running away from his family's criminal activities, or from his crime infested neighborhood. Whatever it was, he was now another rising star within the Bureau.

"Congratulations!" Frank Hawk told him.

"I wasn't aware," Liz said, surprised.

"Congratulations, Danny!" Dave Wellborn said, slapping Agent Lopez across his back.

"How many of the current Special Agent's in Charge have been trained by you, Liz?" Frank asked with a smile.

Frank was another lucky one from Mexico. He had left the pit only minutes before the explosion, and was on his way to the command center when the booby trap went off.

Liz paused and thought for a few seconds. "All, except for maybe seven of them."

Nathan shook his head. "That's a damn shame, Liz. You've been doing this shit for *way* to long."

"You're telling me!" Elizabeth smiled.

Nathan turned to Daniel Lopez. "So, what the hell is going on in Mexico?"

Special-Agent-in-Charge Lopez shook his head. "Complete chaos. All of the cartels are at war with one another. The old school cartels are being hammered by the new ones. The ex Mexican special forces have formed their own cartel, and they are taking no prisoners. They are killing people like it's going out of style."

Elizabeth nodded solemnly. "I heard about the new beheadings."

"Which, ones?" Agent Camacho chimed in. "The ones in Juarez, the ones outside of Mexico City, the ones in Vera Cruz, or the very latest ones just across the border?"

"All in the last week!" Hector Villa added.

"Hector is our chief law enforcement liaison in Mexico City," Nathan announced.

"Embassy duty!" Bob Ritchie blurted out. "Blah! I hated that shit with a passion!"

"Been there, done that!" Dan Pendleton agreed. "Three fucking years in Islamabad. The worst three years of my life!"

"Those sons a bitches just executed fifty people in cold blood," Agent Camacho told them. "This, after the second bus load of killings. This, on top of the five hundred plus bodies in the mass grave just across the border. Over five hundred!"

"*Jesus!*" Nathan said, leaning back in his seat.

"The agents in my office are running around like chickens with their heads cut off," Lopez told them. "There is too much to be done. Missing persons, disappeared persons, bloody cross border violence. We are *overwhelmed*."

"All of the law enforcement agencies along the border are feeling the same thing," Nathan said, throwing up his hands. "I just sent you more agents, more resources, more everything. Hell, pretty soon, your drones, will be bumping into the border patrol's drones, and the military's drones, and they'll start knocking each other out of the sky. I've sent you everything that I can send for now."

"Pull agents from Dallas, Oklahoma City, Kansas City," Lopez pleaded.

"I can't!" Nathan told him. "I already pulled too many agents from those offices and sent them to New Mexico and Laredo. I can't pull agents from Shreveport, or anywhere in Mississippi, because they're all in New Orleans. Gentlemen, *everyone* is feeling the pinch."

"Remember, fighting crime is not the hot thing do to anymore," Frank Hawk said sarcastically. "You have to be fighting terrorism to get money from Congress these days."

"Pull some of those gumshoes from the financial crimes division and send them to the border," Agent Villa said, frustrated.

"After the Wall Street meltdown?" Nathan asked, lifting an eyebrow. You let the press get wind of that, and they'll eat our lunch. "So, what are the chances of this shit spilling over into the U.S and turning into a full blown cartel war on *this* side of the border?"

Agent Lopez shook his head. "Who knows. They haven't been that bold yet."

"They were bold enough to kidnap two border patrol agents and a Sheriff," Liz reminded them.

"Yeah, but this is pretty much a Mexican thing," Agent Villa declared. "The cartels are warring amongst themselves *big time*. They are fighting to control the Mexican drug trade. Too many power vacuums have been opened up, and they are all rushing to fill them. The kidnapping, was way out of line for them. Even they are starting to realize how big they fucked up."

"Nothing's getting through," Agent Camacho added. "The trade is basically frozen. No one is making any money, and the dope is just piling up, or getting burned by rival cartels."

"How's that going to play out on this side of the border?" Elizabeth asked.

Agent Camacho shook his head. "It's not going to look good."

"What do you mean by that?" Wellborn asked.

"The war between the Mexican cartels is getting bloodier with each passing week," Villa answered. "And it's only going to get worse. The drug supplies into this country are going to be seriously interrupted."

"That's not a bad thing!" Wellborn said, enthusiastically.

"Actually, it is," Elizabeth informed him. "A restricted supply, means drastically higher prices on the streets. And if prices on the street sky rocket, then you can best believe that things are going to get a lot more violent on the streets here."

"Why?" Wellborn asked.

"Because, just like anything else, the less you have, the more valuable it becomes," Liz explained. "The more valuable something is, the more people want it, and the more they'll be willing to do in order to get it."

"In other words, people are going to kill for cocaine," Nathan said flatly. "And our friendly neighborhood American cartels? What's going to be there next move?"

"The Commission?" Dave asked, now in his element. "They also deal with Colombian suppliers. I imagine, they'll just shift their purchases to Colombia more."

"But remember, things in Colombia aren't settled," Bob Ritchie reminded him. "Colombia is also going through a transition. There is no clear leader or leading Cartel as of yet."

"But the American cartels and mafias will just buy from whoever is selling," Dan Pendleton declared.

"And what's that going to do to the Mexican cartels bottom line?" Nathan asked, smiling. He already knew the answer to most of these questions. He just wanted his agents to *think.* "What is going to be their reactions to losing tens of billions in revenue?"

"You think they'll react violently and lash out into the U.S.?" Dan asked. "But it'll be their own fault that the American cartels had to buy from somewhere else."

"Mike, you've been quiet over there," Nathan said, prodding his former son-in-law. "How is this cocaine shortage going to affect the American drug organizations?"

Michael Rogers peered down the table toward his ex father-in-law. "I'm in agreement with Bob and Dan. They'll just go shopping elsewhere. Colombia, Bolivia, maybe even Panama and Venezuela."

"So, what should be our next move?" Nathan smiled. "The President is pissed, Congress is pissed, and the Attorney General is pissed. We all lost a lot of good people last week. We have to come out of this meeting with a plan, people. The Director wants to be able to walk into the White House with a plan when he meets with the President."

"Operation Interdicting Fury," Elizabeth smiled. She opened a folder sitting on the table in front of her. She had been waiting for this moment. It was her chance to hurt those bastards where it counted the most to them. She was going to destroy the cartels, by ending the drug trade.

"We coordinate with the Coast Guard and the Navy, and we step up searches and interdiction on the high seas." Liz continued. "Gentlemen, this drug war presents us with a unique opportunity. We know exactly where the drugs are coming from. It's the eighties all over again, but this time, we have more satellites, and lots of spy drones and other intelligence assets at our disposal. We can really make a difference."

"I knew you would have something up your sleeves, Liz," Nathan told her with a smile.

Elizabeth handed Nathan a copy of her plan, and passed

other copies around the table to the other agents. "It's simple, Nathan. We turn our intel assets on Colombia. We know every ship leaving there and what its destination is, and we inspect all ships coming from Colombia either on the high seas, or once they enter U.S. territorial waters, or once they dock at American ports. Again, we bring in the Coast Guard, the Navy, the NSA, The DEA, and Customs, and shut down the cocaine supplies coming into this country."

"I thought you just said that things would get extremely violent?" Dan asked.

"It will at first," Nathan smiled. "But only while someone has cocaine to jack. Once *no one* has any cocaine, then the violence will fall precipitously."

"We are forgetting one thing, gentlemen," Michael told them. "If there is no more cocaine, won't people just turn to other drugs?"

"Some," Liz conceded. "But most won't. Junkies have drugs of choice. A lot of people will go without, and hopefully, eventually go without it long enough to get the monkey off of their backs and quit."

"Big gamble," Mike told her.

"Not really," Liz replied. She was thinking the one thing that Michael wasn't. That crack was a drug for minorities, heroine and meth was not. She was going to bust up the cocaine organizations, end the crack epidemic, and bring hope to her community. Hope that it hadn't had in a long time. She knew that Nathan was thinking the same thing. This was the opportunity that they had been waiting for. And for her, it would be doubly sweet. Helping out her people, while getting revenge against the cartels.

"Liz, I'm going to go over your plan, and then get with the Director," Nathan told her. "I need you to stay over in Washington an extra day so that we both can meet with the Director. He's going to have to know everything in order to present this plan to the president."

"No problemo, Nathan," Liz told him. "I thought you wanted me back in the hospital?"

Nathan ignored her. "Anything else?"

Heads around the table shook.

"Okay, here's how we play things," Nathan told them. "We hold the line and keep an eye on Mexico and the war over there. I'll see if I can get the Director to get with the Attorney General, and have them press the White House for more agents on the Border. More Border Patrol, more resources for local law enforcement to hire and get assets into the field. I'll get with my counterpart in Mexico and coordinate with him, and see if we can get increased Mexican assets on the border as well.. And last but not least, we use the war in Mexico to squeeze the cocaine out of this country, and to strike a major blow to the cartels. With less money to buy weapons and influence, the Mexican police should be able to contend with them. I'm sending out an action memo to the relevant field offices and other law enforcement agencies, informing them to get ready to implement Liz's plan. We are going to dry up the cocaine supplies in this country gentlemen. We are putting all of the drug organizations out of business. Permanently!"

Florida

Emil's men opened the door to the warehouse, and raced inside. They quickly surrounded the men inside, who instantly knew that they were outgunned. Their own security men laid it down without a fight. Emil strolled through the warehouse door looking like a Perry Ellis model in his three thousand dollar double breasted suit, and six hundred dollar Perry Ellis leather wingtips. He glided up to the conference table, where the four men were seated, going over plans and smoking thick Cuban cigars.

"What is the meaning of this?" David Vargas demanded. He rose from the table at which he had been seated.

"Sit down," Emil said firmly.

"What are you even doing in Florida?" Ricky Vargas asked. "You can get killed showing up in other people's territory uninvited. "And with a bunch of soldiers."

Emil's men had the warehouse on lock down. They stood in their business suits, holding assault rifles and keeping a watchful eye on the bodyguards of the men around the table.

"I believe that I have an open invitation from the boss of this state, to show up anytime that I wish," Emil told them.

"She's not here, asshole," Pedro Sanchez told him.

"I know that," Emil said. He leaned over Ricky Vargas, and lifted a piece of fruit off the table. He bit down into the the pear. "Which brings me to my question. What are four of her under bosses doing having a secret meeting in a warehouse, way out in the middle of nowhere?"

"None of your fucking business, *Puto!*" Ricky Vargas told him.

"That's where you're wrong," Emil smiled. "When four assholes threaten the woman I love, then it is my business."

"The woman you love?" David Vargas sneered. "You mean your boss, don't you?"

The Vargas Brothers, and Pedro Sanchez shared at laugh.

"Actually, she's your boss, and my fiancee," Emil told them. "Which means, that makes me your boss as well."

David Vargas spit at Emil's shoes. "Never, monkey!"

Emil shook his head. "Now, David, why'd you have to go and do that?"

"What the fuck do you want?" Pedro Sanchez asked.

32

"Nothing," Emil told them. "There's nothing that you can give me."

"Then why the fuck are you here?" Ricky Vargas asked.

"I'm here, to break up this little conspiracy, and squash you like a bug, before it even gets started," Emil answered.

"Conspiracy?" David Vargas held out his hands. "What conspiracy? We're just four friends having lunch together."

"That may work in a court of law, asshole," Emil told him. "But I ain't the law."

Ricky went for his weapon, and the fourth man at the table, Chavo Martinez grabbed him, turned his own weapon on him, and shot him in the face.

"Motherfucker!" David Vargas screamed. He jumped up from the table. and Chavo turned his dead brother's weapon against him, and shot him in the chest. David Vargas flipped back over his chair, and landed on his back.

Pedro Sanchez's eyes where bulging out of his head. "What the fuck?"

Emil shook his head. "Not everyone is a fucking traitor. Chavo, here, is extremely loyal to the Reigns family, and to Princess in particular."

"You sold us out for a bunch of niggers!" Pedro shouted to Chavo. "Your own *gente*? *Que Paso, Carnal?*"

Chavo rose from the table. "You ain't my people, you Cuban piece of shit. I'm from El Salvadore!"

Chavo lifted the gun and aimed it at Pedro. He put three bullets in Pedro's chest, and another three bullets in his face. By the time he was finished, the barrel of the 9mm Beretta was smoking.

"Thanks for calling me," Emil told Chavo.

"No problem," Chavo told him. "You talked to Princess?"

Emil nodded. "She sends you her gratitude. You've been loyal to her from the very beginning. Back when she was at war with her brothers, trying to take over the Reigns family."

Chavo laughed. "Those were the good old days."

Emil smiled, and patted Chavo on his back.

"I wish I could have put a bullet in Dante's face," Chavo told him.

"Well," Emil shrugged. "Now, the family is all back together again. So, don't worry about that."

"So," Chavo nodded toward the bodyguards of the men he just killed. "What are we going to do with them?"

Emil turned and stared at them. "Whatever you want to do with them."

Chavo stared at the men. "They were just following orders. They're foot soldiers. And they have families."

Emil shrugged. "I'm heading back to Georgia tonight. It's your show. Princess says that you're in charge. She wants you to wrap up all the conspirators. The men I brought with me are all loyal. You can use them to take out the under bosses who've gone bad."

Chavo nodded. He turned toward the bodyguards. "Any of you have any problems with what just happened?"

None of the men spoke.

"Good," Chavo continued. "If you are loyal to me, and loyal to Princess, then come with me. Any of you who feel like you can't roll with us, then you can leave now."

The bodyguards stared at one another, and none of them moved. They weren't stupid. They knew that if they headed for the door, they would be slaughtered once they stepped outside. Besides, moving from a dead boss to a living one, was the nature of the business. They had families to take care of.

Chavo nodded toward the dead bodies. "Grab the bodies, put them in the trunks, and get rid of them. Take them to the swamps."

The bodyguards lowered their arms, and jumped into action. They immediately began to gather up the bodies of their former bosses.

Emil extended his hand, and Chavo shook it.

"If you need me, I'll be in Georgia," Emil told him.

Chavo nodded. "I can handle this shit. I just have two more motherfuckers to kill, and this shit is over. The rest of the bosses are loyal."

Emil twirled his finger in the air, signaling for his men to wrap things up and go. "We are out of here."

"Give Princess my love," Chavo told him.

"Will do."

Deadly Reigns IV

Chapter Four

The meeting was to take place at the Palladium, the newest casino off the Las Vegas strip. It was designed to be bigger than the world famous MGM Grand, but to not step on that casino's toes, or draw any attention away from the Vegas flagship. At 750,000 square feet, the Palladium was the largest casino in the world. What set it apart from the other massive mega gaming houses, was that it was less of a showpiece, and more of a complex. With 5000 gaming machines, some 1000 poker tables, some 50 different restaurants and bars, and over 5000 hotel rooms, it dwarfed the next largest casino in the world, by a large margin. What kept the Palladium off the map of the high rollers, was that it was designed to be an extremely kid friendly establishment. With Universal Studio characters running around, a massive water park, and theme park housed in the center of the complex, it was secretly a cash cow. Parents got to feed their gambling addictions, while kids got the amusement park rides, and the chance to interact with all of their favorite movie characters. And the casino, was owned in part by Palladium Investment Group, an investment front for the Old Ones.

Don Graziella Biaggio waddled his way into the meeting room, and plopped his wide, fat body down at the chair that had been reserved for him at the head of the large conference table. His weight had taken its toll on his knees, and the gout he now suffered from only served to complicate matters even more. Asthma was now a factor, and his inhaler shared a medicine pouch with a half dozen other pills. The Don's lifestyle had taken a toll on him. Too much alcohol, too much tobacco, too much pasta, too much bread, and no exercise, had him in the condition he was in now. He was so fat and in such bad shape, that he wheezed slightly when he talked.

"Don Biaggio!" Tito Bonafacio exclaimed, as he entered into the room. Don Bonafacio was in much better shape than his counterpart. He had lost weight, and maintained a slim figure and healthy diet. His doctor ordered him to get fit, or die, after his second heart attack, and the Don had taken her orders to heart. He cut a stunning figure in his dark grey, pinstriped, Brioni suit and matching fedora.

"Don Bonafacio!" Biaggio exclaimed. He and Tito Bonafacio were the only ones left of the original old dons. The others had met their death during the war with the Reigns family, and that upstart Commission they belonged to. And now, there were all of these new faces seated around the table. Bambinos, Biaggio thought, taking in their faces. They were babies. At least to him, and his eighty years on this earth. None had the experience, the wisdom, nor the treachery that came with age. They were all wet behind the ears, and they had the audacity to seat at the table with him as equals. He would show them.

Don Bonafacio and Don Biaggio embraced. They acted as if they were old friends, from the old country, despite the fact that they had many competing interest, and each had tried to kill the other in the days of their youth.

Biaggio kissed Bonafacio on each of his cheeks, greeting him in the proper Sicilian way.

"What a pleasure to see you, old friend," Biaggio said, with an exaggerated smile.

"It is such a wonderful blessing to have an old friend,"

Bonafacio replied. The two men embraced once again, and then Bonafacio made his way to the other side of the table, where he pulled off his cap and seated himself.

"Tito, you know everyone?" Biaggio asked, waving his hand around the table.

"Some, but not all," Bonafacio replied.

"Please, allow me to perform the introductions," Biaggio said graciously. "To my right, is Don Amedeo Esposito. Don Amedeo is now the head of the Pancrazio family."

Don Amedeo cleared his throat. "It is now the Esposito family," he said, correcting the old don. Amedeo was sensitive to such matters.

Don Amedeo had served Don Pancrazio loyally for thirty years. He was his most loyal and trusted adviser, and his most loyal and trusted under boss. For many years he had borne the brunt of much ridicule, as people often referred to him as Don Pancrazio's chauffeur, or Don Pancrazio's messenger boy, or the Don's bodyguard. In reality, he had been much more than that. He knew all of the old Don's business, and because he had served the old don loyally, he felt that it was his right to move up into the old don's spot. It was too bad that he had to fight the old don's sons for the territory, and for control of the family. His years of service to the don had paid off. He had learned the don's ruthlessness, while the don's spoiled kids were off in boarding schools, and skiing in Colorado and Utah, or shopping on Rodeo Drive and Worth Avenue. They proved to be no match for Don Amedeo, and eventually had to flee for their lives to Florida. Out of respect for his old boss, Don Amedeo didn't pursue them there. He would let them live out the rest of their lives in peace, so long as they kept their asses in Florida. In they tried to return to New York, then all bets were off.

"Excuse me," Don Biaggio said to Amadeo. "The Amedeo Family."

Bonafacio and Biaggio exchanged glances. They were both thinking the same thing. How dare this glorified messenger boy correct a true don. Neither one of them would forget it. And soon enough, they would put him in his place, and bring their old friend's kids back from Florida to run the family that they should have rightfully inherited.

"Don Giuseppe De Luca to my left, now controls what used to be the Cinzia family," Biaggio continued.

"It is still the Cinzia family," De Luca declared, showing respect to the don's, and to their old friend's memory. It was a big contrast to Amedeo. Biaggio and Bonafacio both decided that they liked De Luca. Both knew him well. He was a made man, from a old Sicilian family. His great grandfather was head of one of the original five families. His grandfather was one of the most honorable, and beloved dons that ever exist. His father had been a stand up guy, who lost his life at a young age in a mob war. And no one in the De Luca family, had ever turned snitch, or informant, or put on a police uniform. The De Luca's were mafia royalty. And this young De Luca was much welcomed in their circle. Hopefully, the De Luca family name would restore some of the old luster of the five families. The De Luca's were true warriors. When they went to war, they battled to the last man. And when it came to peace, they always kept it, and never broke their word.

"And of course, we all know Don Lombardi!" Don Bonafacio declared happily.

Don Claudio Lombardi was another new don with a illustrious family name. The old Lombardi family was one of the original five families as well. The original Carlito Lombardi actually went to prison instead of ratting on his colleagues, and was then deported back to Sicily, where he became the head of his family's Sicilian branch. The remaining Lombardi's eventually departed New York for Vegas, Chicago, and Hollywood, leaving a power vacuum that was eventually filled by the Cipriano family. And now, the Lombardi's were back, taking over for the Cipriano's, to whom they were related. It would be good to have a Lombardi back at the head of one of the five families as well, Don Biaggio thought.

"How have you been, uncle?" Claudio asked Bonafacio. The two were not related, but calling the old don 'uncle', was a sign of respect.

"Well, my son," Bonafacio replied. "I've been well. And your father?"

"Dad's doing as well as can be expected," Lombardi answered.

"Alzheimer's," Biaggio exclaimed. "What a terrible disease!"

"God, take my soul," Bonafacio exclaimed, shaking his head. "Is there anything I can do?"

"You asking about him, and having him in your hearts is enough," Lombardi told them.

Amadeo shifted in his seat, growing impatient. He peered at his Patek Phillip watch, and cleared his throat. "Gentlemen, if you don't mind..."

"Yes, of course," Don Biaggio said, taking control of the meeting. "Time is money, so we can just get right down to business."

Don Biaggio and Don Bonafacio exchanged knowing glances. They were both thinking the same thing. Amedeo Esposito was an uncultured animal. No time for the exchange of pleasantries, no social graces, no knowledge in the art of politics. He wouldn't last long. Don's who came in so brash and who were always in a rush, were the Don's who didn't last long. They were gone in a flash of the pants. In there business, patience was not just a virtue, but a dire necessity. It kept one alive.

"Gentlemen, we are here today, to discuss the situation in Mexico, and with this Commission as they call it," Don

Biaggio started off. "As you all know, the unpleasantries across the border has cause a great disruption to some of our activities."

"I can't get nothing in!" Don Esposito said forcefully. "Nothing! The Niggers are traveling all the way to Philly to get there fix! I'm losing money day and night."

Don Lombardi leaned back in his seat, and pressed his finger tips together. "Perhaps it's time to get out of those types of operations. Perhaps it's time to return to the things that we all used to do, and leave the other stuff to the people who do that better."

Don Bonafacio smiled. He knew exactly what Lombardi was getting at. They should leave the low life drug dealing to the Niggers and Mexicans and their fucking low life commission. It was a point he had brought up many times in the past.

"What are you talking about?" Esposito told him. "I make millions off that shit. Millions. No way I'm giving up the dope."

Lombardi disdained Esposito. He was a Lombardi, while Amedeo Esposito was nothing more than a glorified driver who had taken over his old Don's family, and ran out the old Don's sons. He was a usurper, nothing more. A smack peddler, who belonged guarding a craps table. That's as high as he should have risen. That's about as high as he would have risen in the old days.

"What I'm saying, is that it's not worth the life of one Sicilian," Don Lombardi told them. "Not one. Let's go back to the old ways. Let's go back to the days of our fathers and grandfathers. The days of honorable men."

"What?" Esposito laughed. "Busting up union heads for not paying us a percentage? Running liquor out of Canada? What are you talking about? This ain't the Nineteen Twenties anymore. Things have changed. The money is in the dope, and I ain't giving it up."

Don Bonafacio nodded slowly. While he himself had argued Lombardi's point many a times in the past, he was now making a fortune on Cocaine, Heroine, Ecstasy, and other illicit drugs. Plus, he had gained territory from the deaths of Don' Pancrazio, and Don Cipriano. He was no longer inclined to leave the drug business behind.

"We have other ventures gentlemen," Lombardi said, peering around the table for support. If Amedeo wanted to battle the Blacks for the dope trade, then that was his business. He was a businessman, and his family was about business. They were going to make money as efficiently, and quietly, as possible.

"No, you're family has other ventures," Amedeo corrected him. "Some around this table are more fortunate than others."

Lombardi wanted to laugh in Amedeo Esposito's face. The idiot had taken over the family, and run the kids out of town. He got the loyalty of the old Don's soldiers, and even the loyalty of most of the old Don's under bosses and capos. He got the drugs, the prostitution, the gambling, the unions, and all of the illegal businesses. But the kids ran to Florida, and they got all of the Don's legitimate businesses. They got the Don's casino interest, they got the Don's legitimate businesses, they got all of the old Don's stocks, bonds, real estate holdings, and business ventures. And more importantly, they got his cash, his accountants, and his lawyers. Stupid ass Amedeo got the soldiers, and the small shit, while the kids escaped with hundreds of millions in cash and assets. And they ran to Florida under the protection of not only two of the most powerful old Sicilian families ever, but also with the blessing and protection of Princess Reigns, who controlled Florida for The Commission.

"Your requirements are well understood, my friend," Don Biaggio said to Don Esposito. "We are not going to abandon anything hastily."

"So, what are we gonna do about the Mexican situation?" Don Esposito asked.

Don Giuseppe De Luca cleared his throat and spoke up. "What can we do about it?"

"At this point, little," Biaggio answered. "Like everyone else, we'll have to ride it out. Unless, we can establish an alternative source."

Don De Luca smiled and leaned forward. "I have heard much about this "Commission' as they call it. In the days of the De Luca's this thing would have never been able to take hold. The De Luca's would have fought against its existence to the last man. But now that it is here, perhaps it is time to show it who we really are."

"Spoken like a true De Luca," Bonafacio smiled.

"What do you have in mind?" Don Biaggio asked, with his own smile spreading slowly across his face.

"First, I think we should fight fire with fire," De Luca continued. "This Commission is a baby, an infant. We have been at this longer than any other organization on Earth. Our existence spans all the way back to the Collegium of Rome. And yet, we have allowed these babies, to take over. The families have been playing checkers, while this Commission has been playing chess. They have been out thinking The Families at every turn. Perhaps it time that we too begin playing chess."

Don De Luca pulled out a fat Cuban cigar, lit it, and blew rings of smoke into the air. "This Commission gets its drugs from Colombia, no?"

Don Bonafacio nodded.

"Perhaps we too, can make friends in Colombia," Don De Luca said with a smile. "Perhaps we could even make friends, with their friends"

Smiles slowly spread around the table.

"You are suggesting we deal with the Colombian dogs?" Don Esposito asked.

"I am saying, that perhaps their Colombian friends, would like to make new and better friends. Reliable friends. Not friends who keep going to war with them and with each other. Everyone understands business," Don De Luca explained.

"I like it," Biaggio said, nodding.

"I like it too, my friend," Bonafacio added. He leaned in. "How do we make it happen?"

"We send a message to Colombia," De Luca told them. "Set up a meeting. We kill several birds in one stone. One, we secure our drug supplies. Two, we give the Colombian's a reliable source here in the states. Three, we get strong, while this Commission gets weak. According to my sources, the Colombian's are refusing to sell to this Commission, until this Commission accepts their authority."

"And will these same Colombians try to assert their authority over us?" Esposito asked.

Biaggio shook his head. "The animosity between The Commission and the Colombian's stem from the fact that the Colombian's are the ones who helped to set up and organize The Commission, and then The Commission turned around and bit them, once they were strong enough. The Colombian's will deal with us based on respect and mutually beneficial business opportunities."

"So, we will have the dope, while this commission will have none?" Esposito asked, while nodding. "I like that. Perhaps we can even get Philly back. And keep those Goons outta our backyard."

Don De Luca leaned back in his seat once again. "I hear that they are expanding."

"Those *Moolies* are trying to set up a territory in Jersey," Esposito declared. "Jersey! Can you fucking believe that?"

"We cut a deal and got them out of New York," Bonafacio

45

told them.

"We draw the line in Jersey," De Luca declared. "As far as I'm concerned, Jersey is New York, and Jersey is off limits. They set up a seat on their commission for Jersey, and try to take over the state, we go to war, is that clear? And when I say we go to war, we go to war until the last man."

Nods slowly went around the table.

Biaggio and Bonafacio exchanged glances. Each man's heart was filled with joy. They finally had some balls seated around the table once again. The Old Ones were back.

"They're already in Philly!" Esposito told them.

"We can't do anything about Philly at this point," Biaggio admitted. "They are too deeply rooted in. Too many Niggers in Philly. They are too strong."

"For right now," De Luca said. "But we have just as many Italian's in Philly. We can eventually contest the city, and the rest of the state. But for right now, we get big. We recruit, and we bring in real soldiers. Soldiers from the old country as well."

"And we make contact with the Colombians," Bonafacio added.

"My family has no connections, no asset in Vegas," Esposito told them. "We got foot soldiers here in New York, but not the cash to build and sustain an even larger army. We need in."

"In?" De Luca asked with a smile. "In what?"

"In on Vegas," Esposito declared. "We need for the other families to move over and make room at the trough. The Esposito family needs to eat. We need to buy in to some of the casinos, some of the construction businesses, some of the contracts."

"Why would we do that?" De Luca asked.

Esposito shot De Luca a look that could kill. You fat fuck, Esposito thought.

"Even if we were inclined to move over, you don't have the cash to buy in," Lombardi said flatly.

"Let me worry about my family's finances," Esposito declared. "You make room, and I'll get you the money."

The other dons around the table exchanged glances. Each wondered what Esposito was up to, and how he would get his hands on such an enormous sum of money. It made them nervous. Desperate men did stupid things, and stupid things often cost the people around them their freedom, and sometimes even their lives. None of them wanted to be around Esposito. They thought him desperate and dangerous. He was a RICO indictment waiting to happen.

"Old friends, let us discuss these matters further, at a later date," Bonafacio declared. "Much has been said, and much has to be contemplated. Let's move on contacting the Colombian's, and let us move on restoring the glory and the power of the Old families."

The dons all rose. Each lifted his wine glass off of the table, and held it up in a toast.

"To the families," Biaggio toasted.

"To the families!" the others repeated.

"*Cent' anni!*" Bonafacio declared.

"*Cent' anni!*" the other repeated.

They toasted that the old families live another one hundred years.

Baton Rouge, Louisiana

Anjounette was sitting in the park with Dajon, watching her step children, Lil DJ, and Cheyenne, play in the playground. Dajon was busy fiddling with his iPad, while Anjounette waiting patiently for her cargo to arrive. She spied the massive black eighteen wheeler pulling in to the parking lot of the park.

"I'll be back in a flash, Sweetie," Anjounette said, kissing Dajon on his cheek. She rose from the park bench, and headed for the trailer of the eighteen wheeler.

The truck was new, painted all black, with Tibbideaux Freight Lines painted in big, bold, steel gray letters on the side. A silver knight was also painted on the side of the truck, as it was the company's logo. Tibbideaux Freight Lines was supposedly as trust worthy, and reliable, as the ancient knights of old. TFL was a company that her late husband started, but never really paid much attention to. It was only after Dante killed him, and she took control over all of his assets, that the trucking company prospered and grew meteorically. Anjounette poured tons of her drug proceeds into the trucking company, hiring new drivers, buying new rigs, opening up warehouses, purchasing the latest in data and tracking software and equipment, and really turning a company of ten trucks, into a corporation of more than five hundred trucks. She had built one of the largest shipping and freight companies in the nation, and she was proud of it. And although her last name was now Reigns, she kept the name Tibbideaux not only on the side of her trucks, but on all of the businesses that she took over from her late husband Rene. She was going to build these companies for her children, and leave them something that they could be proud of. Her children had their father's last name, and so she was building for them a Tibbideaux empire. All that ever mattered to her, was the safety, well being, and prosperity of her children. She would do anything to expand their holdings. And that was why she was here today.

Anjounette strolled up to the rear of the truck, and one of her men opened up the rear of the trailer for her. Another provided her with a ramp to walk up, and she strutted into the back of the truck in full command of all that surrounded her.

At the front of the trailer, two of her men were holding the Vice President of Gulf Operations for BP by his arms. Another one of her men, was holding her favorite pet on a leash, trying to restrain him. Anjounette walked up and took the leash.

"His name is Popeye," Anjounette told the oil executive. "He's an eighteen foot long saltwater croc, and he weighs in at over half a ton. We feed him chickens everyday. Well, at least not for the last three days. I wanted him to be extra hungry, and a little bit pissed when the two of you met."

"What... what is this about?" the exec asked, stammering out his question.

"This is about my hungry little croc, and about your influence on the contracts that BP has been awarding for Gulf cleanup," Anjounette said with a smile. She knelt down, and stroked Popeye's back. The massive crocodile shifted and tried to hiss. Anjounette's men had and thick band across the croc's mouth, preventing him from opening it. They also had blinders over his eyes, trying to keep him somewhat docile.

"The contracts are awarded by a board who accepts the best bid!" the executive shouted. "I have nothing to do with that!"

Anjounette nodded. "Oh, you have more influence than you know. BP has a seat on that commission, and that BP vote, is the vote that I need to put me over the top. So far, that asshole has always voted against me, and I've watched billions of dollars in contracts go to other companies. That stops today."

"I can't influence his vote!" the exec screamed.

"You're the Vice President in charge of Gulf Operations," Anjounette said calmly. She held out her hand, and was handed a pair of scissors. "Perhaps BP needs a new VP for its Gulf Operations. Someone with a little more stroke. Someone who's willing to use that stroke to help a friend."

Anjounette placed the scissors around the band that was holding the croc's mouth shut, and cut it. The croc's mouth flew open, and he let out and ear splitting snarl.

"Dinner time," Anjounette said with a smile.

"No!" the exec shouted. "Wait!"

"What was that?" Anjounette asking, cupping her hand around her ear.

"I'll meet with him!" the exec said, eyeballing the massive croc nervously. "I'll do it."

"I want my cut of that massive multi-billion dollar clean up fund, do you hear me?" Anjounette asked. "If I don't start getting contracts awarded to my clean up company, my construction company, and my entertainment company, then my men will once again be inside of your home, waking you up in the middle of the night, telling you to come with them. And the next time, we won't meet inside of a truck, Mr. Vice President. The next time, it'll be during Popeye's feeding time, and you'll be inside of his pen. Do you understand what I'm telling you?"

The oil exec nodded.

"Good!" Anjounette placed her scissors into one of her men's hand, turned, and headed for the exit at the rear of the trailer. "Take that son-of-bitch back home. And get somebody to hose out my truck. He pissed himself!"

Chapter Five

Dante walked down the steps of the Reign's family's private Gulfstream jet and climbed in the back of the waiting limousines. He had not only twenty five Reigns family bodyguards, but another one hundred Bahamian police and paramilitary escorts along with him as well. The police motorcycles would clear the route to the hotel, ensuring that his already short trip would be even shorter. Inside of the limo, Dante turned to the Reigns family's most trusted adviser, the Honduran killer, Nicanor Costa Mendez.

"What's the deal?" Dante asked.

"Same shit, different day," Nicanor told him. "Your security is tighter than the Prime Minister's. We have paid off all of the police, the military, and we have an alternate plan waiting just in case. We also have boats waiting on either end of the island, as well as a helicopter that can land and get you out of here at a moment's notice. But, with what we paid, it won't be necessary. The military and the police are all deep inside of our pockets.

Dante peered out of the window, and took in the exotic scenery, and the beautiful iconic shape of the Atlantic resort hotel.

"If I have some extra time, I may want to take a swim with the dolphins," Dante smiled.

"Somehow, I can't imagine that in my head," Nicanor

laughed.

Dante examined the police motorcycles zipping by, escorting his convoy to the resort.

"These guys are really stupid," Dante declared.

"Why?" Nicanor asked. "I thought it was a great idea to meet here. I got to come down, set up security, lay on the beach, scuba dive, relax. Hell, you need to meet here all the time."

Dante laughed. "No, I'm saying. They really think that this makes them safe. As if I couldn't kill them all here anyway."

Nicanor laughed.

"They didn't want to meet in the States," Dante continued. "They demanded that we meet on neutral territory. Far away from the arm of the Reigns family. Someone needs to tell them that the only place our arm can't reach is in space."

"Don't say that too loud," Nicanor told him. "These scary assholes will demand to meet on the moon."

Dante laughed.

The limo pulled up to the resort, and security opened up the limo door for Dante. He took in the scenery. The entire lobby of the resort hotel had been cleared for his arrival. There was nothing but security police, his men, and Bahamian paramilitary forces inside of the lobby.

"The meeting is in a specially configured Presidential Suite on the twenty fourth floor," Nicanor said, waving his arm toward the elevator. "Our men are already in position. The hallway is cleared for your arrival, and everyone is already in the room waiting for your arrival."

"Good," Dante nodded. "Hey, did you already hit the Pyramid water slide?"

Nicanor smiled and nodded. "Oh, yeah!"

"Fucker!" Dante told him.

Nicanor laughed.

Dante stepped into the elevator and proceeded upstairs to the meeting.

"Was it fun?"

"Oh yeah," Nicanor nodded.

"Did you swim with the dolphins, Nic?"

"I can't tell a lie," I was too scared.

"Bullshit!" Dante laughed.

"Some of those dolphins look pretty damn big," Nicanor explained.

"You, the most merciless killing machine in the world, was afraid of Flipper?"

"Hey, fuck you," Nicanor told him with a smile. "Some of those damn dolphins are six feet long, and they ALL have teeth. Plus, they're like the smartest mammals in the world."

"Scary mother fucker!" Dante told him.

"Okay, I can't wait to see you hop in the water, bad ass!"

"I will," Dante told him.

The elevator door opened, and Dante's face changed from a smile, to a scowl. It was business time. The security escort walked him to the door of the room, swiped the card key, and opened the door for him.

"I'll be right outside," Nicanor said. He winked his eye at Dante. "You want the room dead, you hit the button, and then hit the floor."

A smile briefly returned to Dante's face. "That won't be necessary. Killing all of these assholes, would just mean we would have to take over more fucking territory. And Damian would throw a hissy fit. We're trying to get out, remember?"

Dante gave Nicanor a knowing wink, and Nicanor laughed. The family had been trying to 'get out' of the drug business for the last eight years.

Dante turned and walked into the room.

"Well, glad you could fucking join us, Dante!" Barry Groomes of Arkansas told him.

"Nice to see you too, Barry," Dante said, exhaling. He could already tell what type of meeting it was going to be. He nodded at his cousin Brandon, who was in charge of Maryland, and his cousin Josh, who was in charge of Pennsylvania.

Princess winked at Dante, and he winked back. Princess was here, because she was the head of Florida, and her fiancee Emil was also present, as the head of the State of Georgia. Anjounette, squeezed his forearm and smiled. In addition to being married to his brother Dajon, Anjounette was also head of the State of Louisiana, a position she gained when Dante killed her husband and spared her and her children. Julian Jones of Mississippi chunk Dante the deuces and nodded 'what's up'.

Princess was seated at the head of the table. Anjounette was seated at the other head. So Dante was cool with taking a seat in the middle of the table. He took a seat in between Jamie Forrest of Tennessee, and Steve Hawk of Kansas.

"Hey, Steve," Dante said smiling. "Hey, Jamie."

"What's up, Dante," Jamie replied.

"Dante," Steve said, nodding.

"Now that we're all here, can we get down to business," Adolphus Brandt of Colorado asked.

"I'll start off by asking what everyone is thinking," Cesario Chavez of Arizona declared. "What the fuck are we going to do about our dope?"

"Exactly!" Raphael Guzman of Oklahoma chimed in. "We're fucked. This fucking war in Mexico is going to be the end of us!"

"Let's not get our panties in a bunch," Princess smiled.

"That's fucking easy for you to say!" Malcom 'Baby Doc' Mueller of Alabama countered. "The Reigns family has what? A sixty, maybe ninety day supply? You can ride it out until the border reopens and shit settles down. The rest of us are fucked!"

Dante was surprised that Malcom had that information.

"We're not as well off as you think we are," Princess declared. "Remember, what we have in stock, has to supply Texas, Maryland, Pennsylvania, California, Nevada, and Florida."

"As well as your lap dogs in Georgia, Mississippi, and Louisiana," Chacho Hernandez of New Mexico added. Chuckles went around the table.

"Fuck you!" Julian Jones of Mississippi shouted. He was Damian's ace, but he hated being thought of as a Reigns family stool.

"And don't forget you have to supply the parts of my territory that your people have stolen and taken over!" Raphael Guzman told them.

"And mine!" Chacho added.

"Can we get over this, and deal with the issue at hand?" Dante told them.

"Get your fucking people outta my state, Dante!" Chacho shouted.

"You're like a broken record, Chacho," Dante smiled.

"You think it's fucking funny?" Barry Groomes asked.

"You too, Barry?" Dante asked with a smile.

"Fuck you!" Barry shouted.

"Okay, let's get this shit out of the way right now!" Dante told them. He turned toward Chacho. "You want Hobbs back, is that what this is about?"

"Yeah, and I want all of your people out of Santa Fe, and all of the towns in and around Hobbs!" Chacho said forcefully.

"Okay, done," Dante told him.

"Bullshit!" Chacho shouted.

Dante slapped his hand against his forehead and begin laughing. "Got damn, I give you what you ask for, and you're still tripping? Can't win for losing with you, Chacho."

"Because we all know that the Reigns family is full of

shit," Baby Doc told him.

"Why would you just pull out of those territories after all these years?" Chacho leaned in and asked. "Why would you just give them back, and ask for nothing in return? Ain't nobody stupid, Dante."

"All you had to do is ask me nicely," Dante said with a smile.

"Fuck you!" Chacho told him. "I'm tired of your fucking games!"

Dante leaned back in his chair and exhaled. "You want those territories back, you can have them. On one condition."

"Okay now, here we go!" Chacho shouted. "Here comes the bullshit! I knew there was strings. I knew you were up to something!"

"You can have them back, if you promise peace," Dante told him. "And our people who were loyal to us in those territories, are not to be touched. No retaliation against the people who worked for us who live there, you got that? You kill even one, and we're going back in to Hobbs in full force, is that understood?"

"That's it?" Chacho asked suspiciously.

"Peace, and no retaliation, and no bullshit across our Texas border," Dante told him.

"That's it?" Chacho asked. "No money, no other spots, no dope in exchange, just peace, and a guarantee not to touch your people's head?"

Dante nodded. "That's it."

"If you're serious, then you got a deal, Dante," Chacho said. He couldn't help the smile that spread across his face.

Dante eyed Princess. She nodded slightly toward Raphael Guzman of Oklahoma.

"You want your shit back too, Raphael?" Dante asked.

"You giving me the same deal?" Raphael asked.

"We got a lot of good and loyal people in Oklahoma,

Raphael. Especially in Tulsa, Oklahoma City, and Lawton,"
Dante told him. "I got a LOT of people in Tulsa, and we OWN
Lawton and Altus."

"I want all of Oklahoma City, and all of the other
territory," Raphael told him.

"And Lawton? Dante asked. "What happens to Lawton
and Altus?"

"You can fucking keep those shit holes!" Raphael smiled
like a giddy child.

"And what do we do about Tulsa?" Dante asked.

"Power sharing?" Raphael suggested. "You keep dealing
with the Blacks, and I'll take the rest."

"You control your people," Dante told him. "No bullshit,
no violence against my people. We stay to our shit, your
people come back in, and they stay to their shit."

Raphael smiled and nodded. "Deal."

"You're being mighty generous today, Dante," Barry
Groomes told him.

"Barry, you can have all of Little Rock, and all of
Arkansas," Dante said cutting off the conversation. "Just don't
fuck with the people who were loyal to us while we were there,
you got that? No retaliation. You guarantee that, and we'll
pull out completely."

"Deal," Barry said, smiling.

"Okay, so will you cut the fucking Santa Claus routine so
we can get down to business?" Adolphus told them.

"Yo, I wouldn't take those deals, y'all," Baby Doc told
them. "There's more to it than what it appears. Why in the
fuck would y'all trust a snake that done bit y'all asses plenty of
times?"

"Shut the fuck up!" Anjounette told Baby Doc.

"So, Santa Claus, what are we going to do about the
dope?" Steve Hawk asked.

"What can we do?" Emil asked. "Any suggestions?"

"I hate to be the fucking village idiot here, but the solution is obvious," Raphael told them. "We go back to Colombia."

"Fuck that!" Julian said, shaking his head. "Bowing back down to those motherfuckers? Do we really want to do that?"

"What else is there?" Adolphus asked.

"That would mean accepting Cedras as the head of this Commission," Princess told them. "That means that Cedras sends a representative here, to sit at the head of this table, and tells us what to do. Our families aren't our own anymore. Our prices are set in Colombia, not by us. That means that whatever Cedras says, goes. If he tells one of us to give up territory, then we have to do it. Are you ready to bend over and take that again? We got rid of *El Jeffe* for you. We did that! And now you want to put an even worse mother fucker in charge?"

"And don't forget that after you bend over and let him fuck you, you still have to send him ten percent of your profits," Dante reminded them. "So, not only do you pay him for the dope, but after you sell it, you have to pay him another ten percent of what you made."

"Where else are we going to get dope from?" Chacho asked. "Keeping ninety percent of something, is better than having a hundred percent of nothing!"

Arguments broke out around the table.

"Wait a minute!" Dante told them. "Just wait a minute!"

The debates around the table subsided and all eyes turned to Dante.

"Let me go to Mexico, and see what I can do," Dante told them.

"See what you can do?" Adolphus asked. "You've gone from playing Santa Claus to Ghandi the peacemaker? Jesus Christ Himself couldn't end that fucking war in Mexico. Those Cartels are going to kill each other off. They are in it to the last man!"

"Yeah, but not all of them are at war," Dante pointed out. "There are other Cartels that have product to move, who aren't at war."

"Yeah, the dope is not the problem," Raphael told him. "The closed border is the problem. So even if you could find a Cartel to supply us, they can't get the dope to us."

"Leave that to us," Dante told them.

"Bullshit!" Baby Doc shouted. "We listened to you before, and that's what got us in this predicament. You got us to switch to Mexico for our supply, and look what happened? You're the ones who were constantly beefing with *El Jeffe*, killing off every representative that he sent here! You did this shit! I'm tired of following you down the fucking rabbit hole to La La Land!"

"You want to suck Cedras' dick, then go right ahead!" Princess told him. "No one's stopping you, big boy! I always took you for a peter puffer anyway!"

"Fuck you bitch, I got your peter puffer!" Baby Doc stood, and started unbuckling his pants. Chacho and Raphael, and Jamie grabbed him.

"Naw, man!" Baby Doc protested. "I'm tired of laying down for them. We should have all went after their ass when they killed my homeboy Big Rook out in Cali!"

"It was business," Dante told him.

"No it wasn't!" Baby Doc shouted. "You killed him cause you felt like he disrespected you! Like you're God or something. You fed him to a fucking whale! Fuck you, Dante! Fuck you! I'm disrespecting you! So come after me! Come after me, mother fucka!"

Dante peered up at Baby Doc. "You flying back home?"

"Fuck you, Dante!" Baby Doc shouted. "I ain't scared of you!"

Dante waved his hand around the room. "You think that because we're in the Bahamas, that I can't get to you, is that it?"

"That's what I'm talking about!" Baby Doc shouted. "You don't run this shit! You want to go to war when a muthafucka get in your face and get under your skin. That ain't business! You ain't as cool, calm, and collected as you want everyone to think, Dante! You front like you got all the answers, acting like you got everything together, but you don't! You don't know shit!"

"We need to stop this!" Adolphus shouted. "This going to war all of the time, has to stop. Taking over territory that belongs to another member has got to end!

"We need to discuss the second major issue that we came to discuss," Jamie Forrest told them. "We need to expand the Commission, and we need to go back to having a rotating chairperson for our meetings. We need to meet at least once a month like we did back in the day."

Steve Hawk waved his hand around the table. "Look at this shit! It's like a Reigns family reunion here! You have Princess as the head of Florida, you have Brandon as the head of Maryland, you have Joshua as the head of Pennsylvania, Dante is representing Texas, Anjounette is now a Reigns by marriage, and Emil is engaged to Princess. We need new blood. More diverse blood."

"We've been discussing Commission expansion for the last five years!" Princess told them. "Every time things don't go someone's way, they bring up expansion."

"You have too many votes at this table," Adolphus declared. "A vote would not even be fair."

"I don't care about expansion," Dante told them. "Didn't I just give Raphael his territory back? Didn't I just give Barry his territory back? Didn't I just give Chacho his territory back? The Reigns family doesn't care about territory."

"And may I remind this Commission, that we all agreed on Josh taking Pennsylvania, especially Philly, so that we could be in a position to strike at the Old Ones in New York."

"Okay, we remember, but now we need to bring in more voices and new members," James Speech declared. "And while you're in a generous mood, why don't you have Brandon pull his men back to Maryland, and out of Hampton Roads."

Brandon shook his head and smiled. "Ain't gonna happen. This is my family. I control it from Baltimore. D.C. is mines, and so is Hampton Roads."

"I vote to bring in North Carolina, West Virginia, Ohio, South Carolina, Kentucky, Michigan, Indiana, and Wisconsin," Steve Hawk said, lifting his arm in the air.

"And I also vote, that Nevada, California, and Florida get their own heads to sit at this table," Baby Doc said, lifting his arm.

Adolphus, Cesario, Barry, Chacho, Raphael, Jamie, Steve, and James all lifted their arms in the air.

"There you have it," Dante told them. "You have a majority. "New members and new states will be admitted. Do you know who from those states we're are going to seat?"

"We'll do it that same way that we've always done it," James announced. "We'll get the strongest organization in the state, help them organize and consolidate, and bring them in."

"All that is fine, but you aren't taking Florida away from me," Princess told them. "I went to war, and I took it over, and I killed Don Alemendez fair and square. And I did it with my own family, with no help from my brothers, remember."

"That's right, you were trying to kill your brothers at the time," Adolphus said snickering. He winked at Dante.

"We can seat someone for Vegas," Dante told them. "We'll give up Vegas. The only reason we even took Vegas, was because Fat Freddy was in bed with the Vegas and New York families, remember?"

"And California?" Baby Doc asked.

"We're keeping California for right now," Dante declared.

"Why?" Adolphus asked.

"Because it's like Texas," Dante explained. "It's too profitable, it shares a border with Mexico, and it gives us access to a lot of soldiers."

"As a matter of fact, we don't even give a fuck about Pennsylvania," Princess added. "We can seat someone to take over Pennsylvania. The only thing we want is Philly. We give up all of Pennsylvania, and we keep Philly. Brandon can run Philly from Maryland. That way you can seat another person on The Commission if it makes you happy."

Nods of approval went around the table.

Adolphus leaned back in his seat and frowned. "What are you up too? Why are you giving up so much territory?"

"We don't want it, and we don't need it," Dante told them. "We have Texas, and California. Brandon has Maryland, D.C., and Philly. Princess has Florida. My sister-in-law is in charge of Louisiana, my soon to be brother in law is in charge of Georgia, we're happy."

"Okay, we've solved that issue, but now for the main issue," Steve told them. "We still don't have any dope."

"And why are we talking about seating new members on the Commission, when no one has any dope?" Raphael asked.

"Give me a chance," Dante told them. "Let me see if I can get the water back on."

"One month," Adolphus told him. "You have one month. After that, we cut a deal with Cedras, is that understood?"

Dante and Princess exchanged glances. They would simply kill whoever Cedras sent, once the situation in Mexico was resolved.

"Deal," Dante told them.

Baby Doc shook his head. "All you muthafuckas are crazy. You can't make a deal with the devil. Never trust the fucking Reigns family. Someway, somehow, these snakes are going to fuck over all of us. All of you, mark my word.

"Oh, Malcom, get your panties out of a bunch," Princess

said with a smile.

Deadly Reigns IV

Chapter Six

The Bio One headquarters was now a two hundred acre, ultra modern, glass and steel complex. The complex was composed of some one hundred buildings, occupying a park like setting filled with water features, and colorful flora. The buildings themselves were a study in modernity. The glass buildings were structured in such architecturally astounding ways as to appear structurally impossible to comprehend. Glass buildings twisted and spiraled and intertwined with one another, while others jutted out of the manicured landscape like crystals popping out of the Earth. The campus had won numerous awards for its architectural design, and had been featured in just about every architecture, design, and landscape magazine on the planet. The Bio One campus and its adjacent level one trauma center and hospital were Damian's pride and joy. He had named the hospital part of the complex the Asa Yancey hospital and trauma center, while the research and teaching part of the hospital facility was named after none other than the legendary Dr. Charles Drew. The complex also included the Benjamin Banneker scientific research center. It was in the Banneker Center where today's critical meeting was being held.

"C'mon in, Damian," Tommy Voight said, holding open the door for Damian to enter the conference room.

Damian knew that it was bad. His chief business attorney

was waiting for him in the hall, while his chief attorney, Cherin King, was in deep discussion with Adrian Andrews, his criminal attorney. Why his criminal attorney was at a Bio One business meeting, was an enigma. A disturbing one at that. He was sure he would find out sooner rather than later. Attorney's loved to give the bad news first.

"Hey, Damian!" Kayla Marin said, smiling and waving at him. Kayla was Bio One's attorney. Actually, one of them. Her law firm, Marin, Lynch, and Malveaux represented Bio One. And the fact that Paula Lynch, and Diane Malveaux were also present, meant really bad news. All of the partners were present, along with their army of junior partners, junior attorneys and legal assistants.

"Hey, Kayla!" Damian walked to where Kayla was standing, wrapped his arm around her waist and kissed her on her cheek. "You're looking fine as always."

Kayla pushed his hand away. "Boy, stop."

Kayla was a no nonsense sister with a degree from Harvard Law. She was a class behind Damian at Harvard, but her reputation preceded her. She was fierce, and feared. She wasn't a pit bull in a skirt, she was more like a shark with lipstick. She ate people alive in a courtroom.

Damian kissed Paula on her cheek. "Paula you looking pretty jazzy too."

"Don't play with me Damian," Paula told him.

Paula was the methodical one. If Kayla could tear a person a knew asshole by always having a trick up her sleeve, and by being able to break a witness or a defendant down in a courtroom or at a deposition of business meeting, then Paula could destroy them with her laser like focus and robotic precision. She was always calm, cool, collected, and precise. She was a surgeon inside of the courtroom. And her preparation was second to none. It was as if she knew exactly what the other side was going to do, and had the evidence already on hand to counter their moves. She was also a Harvard Law grad.

Damian wrapped his hands around Diane Malveaux and pulled her close. "I'm not letting go."

"Damian!" Diane said, eating up the attention.

"Girl, what have you been doing?" Damian said, leaning back and taking in Diane's new svelte figure.

"Getting my J-Hud on!" Diane gushed. She spun around so that Damian could examine her new figure.

"I see!" Damian smiled. "You look fantastic!"

"I lost over sixty pounds!" Diane declared.

"Wow!" Damian exclaimed. "But you messed up, you know that?"

"Why?"

"You lost some of that fat booty!"

"Boy!" Diane slapped him across his arm. "Stop!"

"I told you, I didn't want you to lose not an ounce of that big juicy booty," Damian said smiling. "You trying to get one of them White girl figures. And you know I don't roll like that. I like 'em thick! Corn bread fed!"

The ladies laughed.

"Get your ass over to this table," Kayla told him. She was the lead partner for the Bio One account.

Damian seated himself at the head of the table. Cherin King, his lead attorney kissed him on top of his head and then seated herself next to him.

"Was that the kiss of death?" Damian asked with a smile.

Cherin exhaled, and smiled back. The other attorneys seated themselves around the table, while their assistants and junior attorneys stood behind them waiting for orders.

"What is the deal?" Damian asked.

"You want the bad news, or the worst news?" Kayla started off.

"Give me the worst news," Damian said.

"You could go to prison," Adrian Andrews, his criminal attorney declared.

"What for?" Damian asked.

"If things get bad, and public pressure builds on the government to do something, you could be held liable," Paula Lynch told him. "Not personally liable, but liable as board chairman."

"For what?" Damian asked.

"That's a worst case scenario," Adrian added. "And highly unlikely. But, we just wanted to give you the worst possible scenario first."

"The worst possible scenario for what?" Damian asked again.

Cherin exhaled forcibly. "Damian, it appears that RD-221, and its derivative, RDX-214, do not work as advertised."

"What!" Damian rose. "How is that possible?"

Kayla pointed toward Damian's chair. "Sit down, and calm down."

Damian frowned, and slowly reseated himself.

"You want to call in the scientist?" Tommy asked.

"I can explain it to him," Kayla declared. "I went to Harvard."

"I thought those drugs went through human trials!" Damian said. "During the animal testing phase, which lasted years, the drugs proved successful with no re-occurrence, no regression, no re-viralization, no nothing!"

"Damian, calm down," Paula told him.

"Calm down? Paula, I can't calm down!" Damian turned to Kayla. "What do you mean they don't work?"

"I didn't say they don't work, I said they didn't work as advertised," Kayla corrected.

"As advertised? If they don't work as advertised, then they don't work! What kind of word games are we playing here! We advertised those drugs to cure AIDS, and to cure Cancer!

If they don't do that, then they don't work!"

"Damian, the drugs do not cure those diseases, it severely suppresses them," Kayla explained. "In the case of RDX-214, it suppressed the virus to the point of non-existence, it boast t-cell count, and it boast the human immune system. It allows a person's body to fight off diseases and viruses on its own. However, once you stop taking it, the virus slowly regains strength. RDX-214 is still the best drug out there. No side effects, no residual damage, nothing. It knocks the virus off its feet and puts it on its deathbed, it just doesn't kill it off like we thought it did."

"How did we miss this?" Damian asked.

"It suppressed the antibodies to the point of non detection," Kayla explained.

"Damian, here is the silver lining," Tommy Voight explained. "RDX is still the best AIDS drug on the market. The doctors love it, the patients love it, and they'll keep on prescribing it."

"We're in trouble, because we pushed it as a cure, and it wasn't," Paula explained. "We're already changing that up. We're completely revamping the warning and our ads to reflect this."

"Have we notified the FDA?" Damian asked.

"Not yet," Cherin told him.

"That's the next step," Damian ordered.

"You need to get your war chest together," Diane told him. Of all the attorneys present, Diane was the master strategist. She was like a chest grandmaster in the courtroom. She could see ten moves ahead. "You're going to need to settle lawsuits."

"We're going to get sued, even though it's still the best treatment out there?" Damian asked sarcastically.

"That's the world we live in," Kayla told him. "And, the FDA will want to sue us, and the people who contracted HIV, after they slept with a partner who thought that they were cured. Those lawsuits are going to be massive."

"What are we talking?" Damian asked. He could feel a knot forming in his stomach.

"In the billions." Cherin told him.

Damian closed his eyes and leaned his head back. He was reeling. Billions in lawsuits. A massive FDA fine."

"Here is the deal," Kayla explained. "It's still the best treatment, and the best viral suppressor on the market. Nothing is going to change that. The FDA is going to stop us from selling it for a while, and they'll want knew studies done as a viral suppressor. They'll balk and throw a tantrum, but at the end of the day, RDX-214 still gives patients a quality of life that they've never had before. We have that on our side."

"And, we still have the fact that we can pull from Energia Oil," Tommy told him. "The revenues from Energia Oil are through the roof right now. Another thing we can do, is offer a Bio One stock offering."

"Take Bio One public?" Damian asked. It was a nightmare to him. He had worked his entire adult life thus far, building Bio One into a privately own pharmaceutical monster. And to have to give up even the smallest amount of control was like driving a stake through his heart.

"It may be the only way to save it," Paula said. "It depends on how massive the fines, and how much the lawsuits amount too. We won't know yet. This is all worst case stuff, Damian."

"Okay, keep moving in the direction you're moving in," Damian told them. Change the marketing, change the labels, and notify the FDA. Get me a couple hell-a-fied PR people working on the damage control. We can't appear to be the bad guys. We just have to look like the idealistic guys, the guys who really wanted to make a difference and do something good in the world. People won't fault us for being idealistically stupid, but they won't forgive us if they think we pushed this out with false advertisement to make a profit off of AIDs and cancer patients. Got it?

Nods went around the table.

Damian peered at the army of assistants standing behind the attorneys. "This does not get out of this room, is that clear?"

Nods went around the table again.

Damian rose and exhaled forcibly. "Stack 'em, pack 'em, and rack 'em. Let's get on this. This is an all hands on deck emergency."

*****

"Well, well, well, if it isn't Princess Tiana"

Princess removed a cucumber from her eye and peered up from her lounge chair. Upon seeing who it was, she placed the cucumber back over her eye. She was wearing an avocado cream mask, and lying next to the swimming pool at the Reign's family ranch, with a towel wrapped around her hair. Her body was on display, filling out a tiny two piece bikini.

"What the hell are you doing here?" Princess asked.

Julian Jones seated himself on the lounge chair next to hers. He leaned back, allowing the sun to strike his muscular bare chest. His sandals fell to the ground next to his chair, and he lifted his small round, Armani sunglasses and peered over at Princess, taking in her luscious curves.

"Got a call from Cherin," Julian told her. "She told me to fly down and hang out with Damian for a few days. Maybe take him golfing, or fishing, or sailing or something. I guess she wants me to be there for him, get his mind off of something."

Princess smiled. "Awwww. You flew here to be there for

71

your BFF in his time of need. Isn't that sweet. You two just need to fuck and get it over with."

"Fuck you, Princess."

"I'm just saying, it's acceptable these days. Same sex marriage is allowed in about ten states now."

"That is really funny," Julian said, pulling his shades back down over his eyes. "You should try out for Comedy Central. The way you used to eat pussy back in the day, I'm sure you could come up with a whole slew of gay jokes."

Princess smiled. Julian wasn't one to take shit. He was so much like Damian, that it was as if they had been separated at birth. Except Julian was way finer than her brother. He had smooth chocolate skin, and naturally wavy hair, along with a pair of big chocolate brown eyes that made a bitch cum just from staring at them. She lifted the cucumber over her eye, and peered at him again. She wanted to check out his hot body, and she caught him staring at her body and checking her out as well. She could feel a tingle in a place she shouldn't be feeling a tingle in. Julian was her big brother's best friend. And was almost like an older brother to her as well. He was definitely off limits.

"What are you staring at?" Princess asked.

"Just wondering how someone so fine, could be so fucking evil."

Again she smiled, lowered the cucumber slice back over her eye and laid back in her lounger. "So, you examining my soul?"

"Nah. A soul examination would involve me sticking a prob inside of you. Deep inside of you." Julian laughed.

"Nigga, you ain't hung like that."

"Princess, I'll make a grown woman jump up and go to church."

Princess laughed. She had to. She loved cocky men. They turned her on. And Julian was cocky. And he was powerful. He had his own state, his own soldiers, his own money. Self made men were like an aphrodisiac to her. They got her juices flowing.

"Yeah? Well I've jumped up and ran to the church house to pray that a nigga get a clue. Or at the very least, five more inches."

This time Julian smiled. "Damn, five more inches. Five more inches would put me way off the ruler."

Princess swallowed hard. She silently pleaded with herself to stop the conversation, but couldn't. And she damn sure didn't want to ask the next question she found herself asking. "How much off the ruler?"

Julian laughed. "Way off the ruler, little mama. Way off the ruler."

Princess had to shift in her lounge. She found herself crossing her legs.

"How long you gonna be in town?" she asked, changing the subject.

"Couple a days."

She shook her head and exhaled. "You don't have to report to Damian what was said at the meeting. Me and Dante will brief him in just fine."

"I'm not here for that," Julian said. "I am my own man. A real man, you know what I'm saying? Then again, maybe you don't."

"What's that supposed to mean."

"I'm just saying. You probably don't know what a real man is like."

"Fuck you, Julian," Princess said, lifting her middle finger. "Is that supposed to be a shot at Emil?"

"Pretty big rock on your finger," Julian said. "Why so big? Is he trying to make up for something?"

"Don't worry about that!" Princess said forcefully. "Me and Emil know how to bring the cops knocking."

"You and Emil, huh? Funny you didn't just say Emil. He needs help, huh?"

"He needs help? Julian don't make me deflate your little ego."

"Deflate my ego? You can't deflate my ego."

"Oh yeah? You talking about Emil, and how much of a man you are, but you wasn't such a big man, when Baby Doc was running your ass out of Mississippi. Remember, I had to step in and spank Baby Doc's ass."

"Well, for one, I would have handled that shit in due time. And two, what about your man and his punk ass needing you to send him men from Florida to get Georgia back under control. A couple a more months, and them Savannah niggaz would have had his ass in a shallow grave on one of them islands."

Princess smiled.

"I can handle my shit, baby girl. Trust and believe that. What about your fiancee?"

"You're not going to get a rise out of me with that bullshit, Julian. So get off my man."

"I ain't on your man. Don't want to be on your man. It's you I want under me."

"You couldn't handle this."

"Princess, I would go so deep that I would give you chest pains. And I would fuck you so hard you would cry and beg for mercy. And I would fuck you so long, you wouldn't be able to walk straight for days."

Princess whimpered slightly.

The sex talk, along with examining her body, made blood flow into Julian's penis. His dick was hard and he wanted her to see it. He rose from off of the lounge.

"All this talk about me fucking the shit out of you, is making me have to jump into the pool and cool off."

Princess pulled off both cucumber slices and sat up. Her eyes immediately shot to Julian's bulging shorts. Upon seeing what he was working with, she gasped. She hadn't had a horse dick inside of her since she killed her husband Marcus. She could feel herself creaming.

"When you ready for a real man in your life. One with power in the bed, and out of the bed, get at me. When you ready to be fucked like I was drilling for oil, get at me. When you ready for me to sweat your little hair do out, and when you ready to scream and holler and beg for dear mercy, then get at me."

Julian dove into the swimming pool, and Princess laid back down on the lounger, thinking about what she had just seen. The length and thickness of Julian's dick was unlike anything she had seen before. She could feel him deep inside of her. She could imagine digging her nails into his back as he stretched out her pussy. Princess bit down on her bottom lip, and creamed in her bikini again.

Deadly Reigns IV

Chapter Seven

Dante was met on the tarmac at General Heriberto Jara International Airport in Vera Cruz, Mexico by an armed escort consisting of members of the Yucatan Cartel. The cartel had sent some two hundred men to provide security for their guest, to insure that his arrival went off without a hitch. They had an additional two hundred men along the route from the airport to the grand cathedral where the meeting was to take place.

Dante climbed inside of the waiting armored black Escalade for the short drive to the cathedral.

"You ready for this?" Nicanor asked.

"I hope that I am," Dante said, peering out the window, and taking in the grand Spanish colonial architecture. "I never realized this place was so beautiful."

"Beautiful, yes," Nicanor agreed. "Violent, yes. It's a shame."

"Angela would have loved this place," Dante said softly. "She loved Spanish architecture. She's the reason I built that damn mansion out in Cordillera."

"Beautiful place," Nicanor said softly. "What are you going to do with it."

"Sell it," Dante told him. "I can't imagine living in it now."

"Why not?"

"Too big," Dante said. "Too empty."

"Be a great place for Lucky to grow up," Nicanor said. "Show her all of the touches and the love that her mother put into building it. Maybe even give her a little piece of her mother to hold on to."

"Never looked at it that way," Dante told him.

The Escalade pulled up to the *Virgen de la Asuncion*, a massive, white, 17th century domed Cathedral that was nestled in the historical center of the city. The architecture was awe inspiring.

"Wow," Dante whispered. He turned toward Nicanor, as the convoy came to a stop, and the security men opened up his door. "Here?"

Nicanor shrugged his shoulders, indicating that he did not know.

Dante climbed out of the SUV and was escorted inside of the Cathedral. Upon entering the nave, he dipped his fingers in bowl of holy water near the door, and made the sign of the cross on his head and body. He then proceeded to the rear of the church, where he knelt down, clasped his hands in prayer, and began to pray. He was Catholic through and through.

"I thought it best that we meet here," a voice said from behind.

Dante lifted his head from prayer and turned. It was Don Benito Yanez, head of the Yucatan Cartel. The Don was dressed in a dark gray Brioni suit with thin white pin strips. He had a white button down shirt, and a matching gray tie. His appearance took Dante by surprise. He had expected to see the Don dressed in a white linen suit, or some other gaudy mafioso attire. This Don looked professional. More like one of the old Italian Dons, than one of the usual Latin American cocaine monkeys that he was used to dealing with. Dante rose.

"Don Yanez," Dante said greeting him. He extended his hand, and the Don gripped his hand with a firm shake.

"Call me Benito," the Don said, with a disarming smile.

Dante knew that behind the Don's smile, was an army of men that numbered in the thousands. Don Yanez's family was the largest of the Yucatan Cartel, and because of this, he had been made head of the Yucatan families. Which basically meant that he spoke for them.

"Thank you," Dante told him. "And you may call me Dante."

Don Yanez smiled and bowed slightly. "Come, my friend. We can speak freely here in the back of the Cathedral. The Mexican authorities have many operatives, and much technological know how, yet, they will not bug a Cathedral. Not here, not in such a devoutly Catholic country."

Dante nodded.

"Besides, I own the police as well," the Don laughed. "So, tell me, what do you think of our lovely little church?"

Dante peered around the massive structure. Stained glass, hand carved wood, marble floors, solid gold trim, carved travertine statues of various saints; all of it conspired to make the massive Cathedral a masterful work of art.

"I think, that this is one of the most beautiful Cathedrals that I have ever laid eyes on," Dante told him.

The Don smiled. "I hear that your family is devoutly Catholic. And that you have given millions to Catholic charities over the years. All of the Bishops, Arch Bishops, and priest speak very highly of your family."

Dante nodded. "We try to give back to The Church. My parents raised us to be charitable. The Church does so much good, and it is an honor to be able to give to it whatever it needs, whenever we can."

Again the Don smiled. He motioned toward a church pew once they reached the rear of the church, indicating that he wanted Dante to take a seat. "That is why I took this meeting with you, Dante. Your family's good and charitable works, speak volumes about you."

Dante took a seat in the pew. "Thank you."

The Don seated himself next to Dante. "So, tell me my friend, what is it, that I can do for you?"

"There is a great disturbance along the border," Dante started. "And this disturbance has made it extremely difficult to trade between my family, and other families in Mexico."

The Don nodded. He understood everything that Dante was saying. "And because of this great disturbance, the border has been closed."

"Yes, the closed border is one thing, but also the discord in Northern Mexico has grown to the point where trade is no longer possible."

"Ahhh, I see," Don Yanez nodded. "And so, since your family can no longer trade with the families of the North, you want to trade directly with us."

"If that is possible," Dante told him.

"Anything is possible," the Don told him. "The question is, why would we do such a thing?"

"Trade between our two organizations would be mutually beneficial, and extremely profitable," Dante told him.

"We're not starving," the Don told him. He leaned back and crossed his legs. "What you are asking, could potentially cause your former trade partners to become jealous of our new relationship. Why would we risk hostilities with anyone, when we don't have to? We are at peace here on the Yucatan Peninsula, and we would like to keep it that way. We are businessmen, and we like to stay under the radar, and do things peacefully, and quietly."

Dante nodded. "And that is why we are coming to you, Don Yanez. You do business the right way. You do business the way we want to do business."

"And yet, if the border hadn't been closed, you would have kept doing business with the organizations in the north."

"Their proximity to us, made it convenient."

"Marriages of convenience, always result in jilted lovers, and unhappy relationships," the Don told him. "What happens once the borders reopen? What happens to your new lover? Do you jilt us, and run back into the arms of your old *amor*?"

Dante and the Don shared a smile.

"No," Dante said shaking his head. "We feel like this would be a match made in Heaven. We feel that the Yucatan families, are our true soul mates."

The Don laughed. "I have to take this marriage proposal back to the other families of the Yucatan."

Dante nodded. "I know."

"And even if they saw the benefit of such a marriage, how do you propose to kiss your bride? Northern Mexico will still be violent, and the borders will still be closed. How can we get our trade goods to you?"

"That is what we will have to figure out," Dante told him. "I just needed to know if your family would be willing to trade with us. Once I had that answer, I was going to work on the second part of the situation, which is, getting your trade goods back to America."

The Don rose from the pew. "I will get back to you in a couple of days."

Dante rose. "Thank you, my friend."

The Don turned to leave, and then paused and turned back toward Dante. "I hear the Reigns family likes to kill their suppliers."

Dante's heart skipped a beat. He was in Mexico, surrounded by hundreds of soldiers from the Yucatan Cartel. All he had was Nicanor, and a handful of men back at the airport guarding his private jet. The question had taken him completely by surprise.

"Uh, no," Dante answered. "We had great difficulties with our former trade partner in Colombia."

"He was an asshole," Don Yanez said with a smile.

"Hopefully, our relationship will be much better."

The Don turned and walked out of the Cathedral. Hundreds of his men left with him. Nicanor walked into the Cathedral and strolled up to Dante. The Don's message had been very clear. They weren't going to put up with any bullshit. And they weren't *El Jeffe*, or none of them other motherfuckers. They were the real deal, and it would be war.

"I talked to Chuchi and Johnny," Nicanor told Dante.

Dante lifted a surprised eyebrow. Chuchi Espinoza was Don Benito's killer. He was to Don Benito, what Dante was for Damian. While Johnny Talamantez was the Don's fixer, and right hand man. He knew everything, and his opinion mattered to the Don. He was one of the Don's chief counselors.

"What are they saying?" Dante asked.

"Johnny says they are going to do it," Nicanor told him. "They don't know how they are going to get the shit to us, but it's pretty much a go."

An enormous smile spread across Dante's face. If Johnny said it was a go, then it was go.

"Let's get back to the airport and get the hell outta here," Dante told Nicanor.

"I'm with you on that!"

*****

Princess stepped out of her house and peered around, taking in her surroundings. Even though she had a dozen men standing outside of her home providing security, she still wasn't one to get caught slipping. She always felt that her ultimate safety and security was up to her. She strutted to her waiting heavily armored black Infiniti QX 56, and started to

82

climb inside. The whine of a high pitched V-12 motor caused her to stop and stare down the street.

The black Lamborghini Aventador revved its engine several times, as it rolled down the street toward her home. Her bodyguards placed their hands on their weapons, while a couple of them tried to force her to climb inside of the armored SUV for safety. Princess refused. No assassin would roll up in brand new Lamborghini in broad daylight and try to kill her. That car was just too beautiful to get shot up.

The Lamborghini pulled up to the driveway and the scissor type door on the driver's side flipped up. Julian sat behind the wheel staring at her with a great big grin.

"You want to get your shit shot up, Julian?" Princess told him. "Just keep on pulling moves like that."

Julian waved his hand, dismissing her. He nodded toward his passenger seat. "C'mon, girl. Come and take a ride on the wild side."

Princess placed her hand on her hip. "Now, why would I go anywhere with you?"

"Because you like me, and because you think I'm fly," Julian said, with his electric smile. "Because you find me irresistible, and because you're dying to have a real man in your life."

Princess shook her head and smiled. "I have a real man, and I'm not going anywhere with you Julian. I have to..."

"Meet your brothers," Julian said, finishing her sentence. "I know. C'mon, I'll give you a ride to Damian's."

"He won't get jealous seeing us together, will he?" Princess asked, lifting an eyebrow. "I mean, I wouldn't want to step on my brother's toes."

Julian smiled and nodded. "See, there you go with that gay shit again. Lil Momma, you running and hiding, and using that as a front, 'cause you know you can't handle this snake I got between my legs."

"I have a car," Princess told him.

Julian revved his engine. "Yeah, but not like this one. Having a car, and having a *car*, are two different things. Girl, come get your ass in this Lamborghini. Dante called, his plane is landing as we speak."

Princess exhaled.

"I won't bite," Julian told her. "Not unless you want me to."

Princess turned to her bodyguards. "Follow."

She handed one of her men her briefcase,and walked around to the passenger side of the Lamborghini. She opened the scissor door and climbed inside.

"Nice," she said, running her hand over the leather stitching.

"You talking about me, or the car?" Julian asked.

"The car."

Julian shifted his Lamborghini into gear, and started off toward Damian's. "When are you going to stop playing games with me?"

"What?" Princess asked. "Where the fuck is all of this coming from, Julian? Tell me that? Why all of a sudden, do you want to make me one of your little conquest? Have you gone through all of the bitches in Mississippi or something?"

Julian laughed heartily. "What makes you think it's anything like that? What makes you think I'm just trophy hunting?"

"Because, you know I have a man, and you know that this can never go anywhere between us."

"Where does it have to go?" Julian asked. "Why can't it just be."

"Oh, you wanna be fuck buddies?" Princess asked. "I'm not in high school or college anymore, Julian. And neither are you."

"Which makes it even better. You will have a man on the

side who can give you everything your little heart desires. Who can make love to you all night, and treat you like a Princess all day. A man who can protect you, who will love you and cherish you, and who will always be there for you."

Princess turned, stared out the window of the Lamborghini and smiled. "I am a Princess. I can already buy anything that my heart desires. I am already well protected. My fiance already cherishes me. And, he can make love to me all night if I so choose. So, it appears that you have nothing to offer me, that I do not already have."

"I can offer you meat," Julian said with a smile.

Princess burst out in laughter. "You are fucking crazy."

"But you love me though."

Princess turned and stared out of the window once again. Julian was the perfect man for her, she thought. He was so self confident and sure of himself. He was a man's man, and that was something that was lacking in a lot of men she came across. She was always the boss, or the one with the money and the power. Even now, she could crush Emil if she wanted to. While Julian, on the other hand, would be more difficult to crush. He had a large family, that he had built on his own, and he was worth some $600 million dollars, that he made on his own. He had crushed all enemies and all opposition in his state, and he dealt with his adversaries ruthlessly. He was truly a man after her heart. And he was fine ass hell to boot.

Princess thought about the dangerous game that Julian was playing. If Emil found out, it would be bad blood between the two. It may even cause Emil to do something stupid, like make a play on Julian. And whereas Emil had a larger family, because he controlled Georgia, Julian's family was a lot more hardcore. His men were hungry, and that made them straight up killers. She doubted if Emil could take on Julian, which meant she would have to come to his aid. And then the Reigns family would be at war with Julian, and then Julian's friends on

The Commission would come to his aid. Shit could get way out of hand. All because Julian wanted some Princess pussy.

Princess knew that she would have to stay away from Julian, and stop the game that he was trying to play. She wanted to fuck him, if only just once, to see if he could really work that massive snake between his legs. But she had to think about the cost and consequences of such actions. No, it was too dangerous, she thought. She stared out the window, as he pulled up to the gate at Damian's estate. She needed to leave his ass alone.

Chapter Eight

Dante strolled into Damian's office to find his brother seated behind his desk, tapping away at his computer.

"I'm fresh off the plane, bro," Dante told him. "What's so important that I had to come here straight from the airport?"

Princess strutted into the office. "What's the deal?"

Damian waved to the two large leather wing back chairs on the other side of his desk. "Have a seat."

Princess and Dante both seated themselves, and exchanged knowing glances. They knew that it was bad news by the look on Damian's face, and by the fact that Cherin, Damian's chief counsel, had called Julian to Texas to hang out with Damian for a few days. They both leaned back in their seats and crossed their legs, bracing for the news.

"Well, I'll give it to you straight, with no chaser," Damian told them. "We are in trouble. A lot of trouble. Bio One is going to face massive lawsuits."

Dante and Princess exchanged glances.

"What's going on, Damian?" Princess asked.

Damian leaned forward in his seat, clasped his hands and placed them on his desk. "It appears, that Bio One's new wonder drugs, aren't so wonderful after all."

Dante leaned back in his chair. "Shit!"

Princess shook her head. "How bad is it?"

"It's going to be pretty damn bad," Damian answered.

"The lawyers think that Bio One is going to take a massive hit financially. In order to settle all of the lawsuits. I mean, there are things we can do. We can have the lawsuits joined in a class action suit, and try to settle them all at once, with one massive settlement. But it's going to damn near bankrupt us."

"Bankrupt?" Dante asked, lifting an eyebrow. "How the fuck can we be bankrupt?"

"It's going to take every penny that Bio One has in the bank to settle this thing," Damian explained.

"And what about our other companies?" Princess asked. "We still have our entertainment group with our casinos, our construction company, our restaurant chains, and don't forget about Energia Oil."

Damian exhaled, and stared Princess in her eye. "Energia Oil, is the second biggest corporation we own, after Bio One. However, it is maxed out in its capital outlays. We spent massively buying up potential oil fields in Africa, and going after oil contracts off the coast of West Africa. Every penny Energia Oil is taking in, is going to maintain the company, and into the exploration of the new fields. Energia will survive, but they can't carry us until some of our endeavors pay off."

"And Reigns Entertainment Group?" Princess asked, lifting an eyebrow.

"The entertainment group is good," Damian told her. It's generating plenty of revenue. We're not going to be out on the streets. But remember, we have an enormous family to take care of. Also, we can't just depend on entertainment revenues. When the economy goes south, so does the entertainment business. We don't want to be caught with our pants down like that. We took a massive hit with this last recession, and The Reigns Entertainment Group is just now starting to recover from that mess."

"And Reigns Construction?" Princess asked. Deep down inside, she was wondering if Damian had mismanaged the family's legitimate businesses.

"Reigns Construction is okay," Damian told her. "We got some decent contracts during the stimulus, but the stimulus contracts are all fulfilled. And with the Republicans controlling the House of Representatives, you can bet your ass that there will be no more stimulus money. They are acting like bitches, and refusing to fund any new construction projects. We had our eye on California's high speed rail project, as well as the D.C. to New York high speed rail project, and several projects here in Texas. They are all on hold."

"Which leaves my side of the family business," Dante said. "I can get us all the money we need, once we clear up our little supply situation."

"And how is that coming along?" Damian asked.

Dante shrugged. "The boys on the Yucatan are willing to play ball. But, it's a question of logistics. How are we going to get it here. Also, their message was very clear; no fucking around. They're willing to say fuck the border cartels and do business with us, but it better be good business. They are not into all of the killing, the violence, the attention, or any type of bullshit."

"Which brings us to another issue," Damian told them. "I want all beefs settled. No more bullshit."

"We settled that shit at the Commission meeting," Princess told him. "We agreed to pull out of everyone's territories in exchange for peace, and for the safety and security of the people who were loyal to us."

"We need to settle the beef with the Old Ones as well," Damian told them.

"We crushed them," Dante said with a smile. "They aren't a threat anymore."

"They are always a threat," Damian told him. "The Collegium has been around since the days of Ancient Rome,

89

and will always be around. Never underestimate them."

"I can get us all the money we need, Damian," Dante said with an evil grin. "I'll take two hundred of our soldiers, hit up a Don, and have them transfer all of their money into an account in the Bahamas before I kill them."

Damian smiled and shook his head. "Yeah, and that's good for a couple of million."

"A few hundred million, if I hit the right muthafucka!" Dante shot back.

"A few hundred million," Damian smiled. "That would have to be a big time Don. A Don who is going to have a lot of protection. And after you kill him, then the war is back on in full effect. I don't want to risk any of our people getting killed over money. A few hundred million would be nice, but in the long run, the price in blood, and family, is not worth it."

"So then what?" Dante asked.

"First, we make peace between Minister Malaika, and the Old Ones," Damian explained. "Then, I'll focus on handling this lawsuit. You will focus on a solution to our distribution problem. And Princess will run the day to day operations for the family. Dante, I'll also need you to manage the pull back operations for the family. I want to keep Texas, California, Maryland, and D.C. We are also keeping Hampton Roads in Virginia, and we're keeping Philly. Tell Anjounette that Louisiana is now hers. She is no longer a Reigns under boss. She is now in charge of Louisiana in her own right, with her own family."

"And Jersey?" Dante asked with a smile.

Damian shook his head. "I don't know. I want to keep an underground presence in Jersey. Jersey is too lucrative, and it also allows us to strike at the Old Dons in New York if we need to.

"We can do that from Philly," Princess told him.

Damian nodded. "Keep New Jersey in limbo for right

now. We'll see how things play out in the future. But in the meantime, we are pulling back from all the other territories that we took."

Dante shook his head. "I don't understand your logic. We need money, but you're giving up lucrative territory?"

"Yeah, let someone else have to worry about supplying that shit for right now," Damian told him. "We don't have the inventory to supply half the damn country. We give up those territories, and we let someone else worry about them. That will extend our supplies for Texas and California. We have to keep Texas and California happy."

Princess and Dante both nodded. They understood the strategy.

"I hate giving up Memphis," Dante said. "Memphis was a major supply of soldiers for us. And now, it's going to be a major supplier of soldiers for someone else."

Damian shrugged. "We still have D.C. and Maryland to supply us with soldiers for the East Coast. Besides, Princess has Florida, Emil has Georgia, and we still keep a small army in Jersey. We'll be okay in the East. Besides, between Texas and California alone, nobody can match us in manpower. We'll be okay if a major war comes."

Dante and Princess rose from their seats.

"Are we going to be okay?" Dante asked

Damian leaned back in his chair, and peered out of his office window. "I believe so. I'm going to damn sure do everything that I can to try. I just need you to get the water turned back on, and get the wet flowing again."

Dante nodded. He turned and he and Princess left Damian's office. In the hall, Princess turned to her brother.

"What do you think?"

"I think that it's worse than he's actually letting on," Dante answered.

"Worse than Bio One going bankrupt?" Princess asked,

lifting an eyebrow.

Dante nodded. "Bio One is his baby. Energia Oil can't save us because all of its money is tied up. The Entertainment Group is just now cranking its revenues back up. The construction company is scrambling for new projects. And the worst of it all, is that we can't get any fucking dope into the country to make up the difference. We got a lot of people to pay. A lot of soldiers, a lot of politicians, a lot of police officers, workers, and everybody else. It's pretty bad."

"What are we going to do to fix the situation?" Princess asked.

"The Yucatan Cartel has the dope, it's a question of getting it in," Dante explained. "We shifted all of our damn resources and connections to the inland ports. We became so focused on getting those eighteen wheelers full of dope through the border checkpoints, that we neglected all of our other entrance points."

"Are you proposing that we go back to using ships?" Princess asked.

"It may be our only way," Dante told her.

"The Coast Guard is going to have a field day interdicting those ships," Princess shot back. "We don't have enough Customs people, or DEA on the payroll anymore. And don't forget, if it starts coming in by ship, then that makes Louisiana more powerful, that makes Georgia more powerful, that makes Mississippi more powerful, and that make Alabama more powerful. Do we really want to let Baby Doc get that kinda money and power?"

"We may not have a choice!" Dante told her. "But at the same time, it reduces Chacho and Cesario's power in Arizona and New Mexico."

"It also reduces our power and influence in Texas. We had it set up, so that all drugs come through Texas. We could tax that shit, step on it, redistribute it, and pretty much control the entire country's drug trade and pricing, from here. Going back to the ships, means Portland, Seattle, the Gulf States, and the East Coast ports are all back into play. We lose power and control."

"Sis, Texas has ports," Dante reminded her with a smile. "We can run that shit through Texas, Louisiana, California, and Florida, and still control it. Remember, we are keeping Maryland, and Hampton Roads as well. Damian is not stupid, we still control most of the ports in the country."

Princess exhaled and shrugged. "Make it happen. But mark my words, that bastard Baby Doc is going to cut a separate deal with one of the cartels, and he's going to try to make Alabama a major distribution route, giving him unlimited cash. He's going to have the money, and the soldiers, and he's going to be damn near uncontrollable. I can see it now, we're going to end up having to kill his ass."

"Then put it in place," Dante told her. "Get the shit set up perfectly right now, so that when the time comes, we can spank his ass real good."

Princess nodded, and turned to leave.

"Hey, Princess!"

Princess turned back toward Dante.

"One more Gulf State we didn't talk about," Dante told her.

"Which one is that?" Princess asked, thinking that he was talking about either hers, which was Florida, or Emil's, which was Georgia.

"Mississippi," Dante said flatly.

"What about it?" Princess asked, swallowing hard. She felt a small lump in her throat.

"I saw you ride in with Julian," Dante told her.

Princess shrugged. "And?"

Dante lifted an eyebrow and tilted his head to one side. "Don't."

"Don't what?"

"Don't play this game," Dante told her. "We don't need this right now."

"What are you talking about?"

"I know Julian," Dante told her. "And I know what kind of men you like. We can't afford for you to play this game right now. You're engaged to Emil. The last thing we need, is for our relationship with Emil to go south, because you wanted Julian as a play thing."

"Dante, I'm a grown ass woman!" Princess told him. "So, if there was anything going on with Julian, it would be my business, and my business alone. Understand?"

"What I do understand, is that you're playing a dangerous game," Dante told her. "And if Emil gets caught up in his feelings, you'll have a war between Georgia and Mississippi, two of our families strongest allies on the Commission. We don't need them at each others throats. We all need to be unified right now. Besides, when two states go to war with one another, a lot of people die. Men with children and wives to take care of. Don't orphan a lot of children, because you wanted an intense fuck."

Dante stared Princess in her eye, and then walked past her.

Princess stood in the hall, thinking about what he had just told her. His message was clear. He wasn't going to let it happen. But did that mean he would kill Julian, or did it mean that he would kill her?

Chapter Nine

Chama Gaucha's was an upscale Brazilian steak house on the northern part of the city. The restaurant served upscale Brazilian style steaks, in an all-you-can-eat format. Waiters brought different cuts of select steaks, lamb, and poultry to the guest table until they could eat no more. It was at this restaurant that Dallas, Darius, and DaMina Reigns decided to grab some lunch. It was one of their favorite spots in the city, and they were meeting their cousin DeFranz Reigns for lunch.

Chama Gaucha's decor could best be described as upscale. An enormous salad bar ran throughout the restaurant, while a massive wine bar sat against the far left wall. Round tables draped in white table clothes were spaced throughout the restaurant, while Portuguese music serenaded the diners over the restaurant's speakers. All in all, it was a unique dining experience.

"So, what's the deal, cuzzo?" DeFranz asked, as he strolled up to the group and seated himself.

Darius shook his head. "Same shit, different day."

DeFranz nodded at DaMina, and then at Dallas. "What's the haps?"

"That's what we want to know," DaMina told him. "How is Maryland?"

"Lovely," DeFranz smiled. "Maryland bitches are the finest bitches in the world. But they're crazy as fuck!"

Dallas and Darius laughed.

"Boy!" DaMina waved him off. "Why you gotta be disrespectful?"

"I'm just saying," DeFranz said laughing. "They love me, and I love them."

"What about living in P.G. County?" DaMina asked. "Is it really how they say it is? The Black Mecca?"

DeFranz shrugged. "You got some good areas, and you got some areas your ass better not be caught in after dark. Same just like everywhere else."

"They have that long paper up there?" Dallas asked.

"Fool, you're daddy got more paper than any of them!" DeFranz told him. "Why you don't go up there? You're momma up there in D.C. now."

"Are you crazy?" Dallas asked. "My grandpa found out that Damian was my real daddy, and every since then, he be tripping!"

"Yeah, I guess it's kinda fucked up that your grandpa is an FBI agent that's been trying to bust your father for the last ten years," DaMina added.

"And your Grandpa Nathan is now the deputy director of the FBI or some shit like that," DeFranz said laughing. "Boy, your family get togethers are going to be off the chain!"

"So, what are we celebrating?" Darius asked.

DeFranz leaned in and stared at each of them in turn. "We are celebrating, because Brandon wants me to stay on the East Coast, and he want's me to run D.C. for him."

DaMina was taken aback. She hadn't heard this from Damian or Dante. And Mina was high up in the family organization. "Does Damian know this?"

DeFranz shrugged. "Brandon has his own family, and his own seat on The Commission. He runs Maryland, and Philly, and D.C., so he can do what he wants."

DaMina lifted and eyebrow, and exchanged glances with

Darius.

"Actually, Brandon does run Maryland, but he was put there by Damian," Darius told him.

"Man, trick that shit!" DeFranz said, dismissing Darius. "Brandon is his own man. Damn, cuzzos, I thought y'all would be happy for me. "An under boss running a whole city, and I'm only twenty-three? It took me a year and a half. I've only been out of college two years, remember?"

"Congratulations," DaMina told him. She lifted her glass in toast.

"Congratulations, kinfolk," Dallas told him.

"Brandon says that if I do good, he'll move me up to be the under boss of Philly, and then eventually, I can be his number two for the whole show," DeFranz said excitedly.

"Maybe I should head up to the East Coast," Dallas told them. "That way I can take over D.C. when you take over Philly."

"Boy, your grandfather would kill you!" DaMina told him.

"He don't control me," Dallas protested. "I'm a Reigns!"

"And that's why your ass is going to Harvard as soon as you graduate from high school," Darius told him. "Damian ain't gonna play that shit. You're a Reigns, and Reigns go to Harvard."

"Harvard first, and then you can come up to Maryland and learn the business from me and Brandon," DeFranz told him.

"I doubt that," DaMina added. "Damian is going to have his son under his wing, teaching him the legitimate side of the family businesses."

Dallas shook his head. The thought of a future in the boardroom, wearing suits and ties everyday, and having endless meetings, was a future he was desperate to avoid. He thought that he would die of boredom. Sure, every father wanted a son who would follow in their footsteps, but following his father into a corporate lifestyle was not a part of his plan. Sure, he would follow him to hell and back in the other side of the family's business, but sitting behind a desk all day was not for him. He would do his duty and go to Harvard, but afterward, he would make his own path. Damian would just have to understand.

A waiter approached the table bringing another selection of meat on a skewer. This time, is was a choice selection of Alcatra, a tender piece of steak that was cut from the top sirloin. The waiter took his long butcher knife, leaned over DaMina, began slicing her off several cuts of steak that was impaled on a long metal skewer.

"Thank you," DaMina said, peering over her shoulder at the waiter. But something was not right. He was a waiter, and he was serving her from the left, instead of from the right. At an upscale restaurant, the waiters were trained in proper service. The second thing DaMina noticed, was the tattoo on the waiter's forearm, that became visible when his sleeve raised up while he was serving her. It was a tattoo of a spider. But not just any spider, it was a spider that she had seen before. A spider that she hadn't seen in many years though. It was a spider that was stamped into the bricks of cocaine that came from Colombia, back when the Reigns family used to get their supplies from *El Jeffe* and the Colombian Cartels. It was the mark of the Colombian Cartels. The micro hairs on the back of her neck came to attention instantly. What was a Colombian Cartel member doing waiting tables at a Brazilian restaurant in San Antonio? The answer was simple. He shouldn't be.

DaMina watched as four more waiters approached their table with skewers of meat. This was strange also. The restaurant served its meat in courses. First the Picanha steak, next the Filet Mignon, then the Alcatra, then the Fraldinha, and so on and so fourth. The fact that several waiters were bringing different selections of meats to the table at the same time, really alerted his sixth sense. And all of the waiters were carrying skewers of meats, along with giant butcher knives. One waiter, for each person at her table.

"Fuck this shit!" DaMina said. She pulled out her forty five caliber Smith and Wesson, and turned and shot the waiter standing behind her. If she was wrong, then she would have to pay the consequences later. But she knew that she was right. She had been in the business long enough to recognize a set up. Dante had trained her well, and she had risen through the ranks and learned a lot since her days as head of security for the family.

The restaurant erupted in a panic. Patrons began running, ducking beneath tables, screaming, and fleeing the scene. The scene quickly turned into a chaotic mess.

The second waiter rushed up behind Dallas, and ran his blade across Dallas Reigns' throat. Dallas clasped his throat and fell to the floor. DaMina lifted her gun and shot the waiter. A third waiter plunged his butcher knife into Darius' shoulder near the base of his neck. DaMina switched her gun from the waiter she shot, and then put a hole in his forehead. The waiter's head flew back violently, sending blood and brain fragments throughout the restaurant. Darius fell to the ground writhing in pain. He had a twelve inch butcher knife sticking out of his shoulder.

The fourth waiter dove at DeFranz, who was ready. He clasped the waiter's wrist, and the two of them began wrestling for control of the butcher knife. DaMina tried to get a clear shot at the fourth waiter, before noticing movement out of the corner of her eye. She turned to her left, and spied another worker lifting a sawed off gauge. DaMina lifted her forty five, and blew him away. His body flipped back over onto the wine bar. DaMina shifted her weapon toward another worker, but it was too late. She turned toward him in time to watch the knife plunge into her arm.

"Shit!" DaMina screamed out in pain. She also dropped

her weapon.

The knife throwing Colombian assassin threw a second knife at her, this time striking DaMina on the left side of her chest. Dallas Reigns let go of the burning cut across his neck, and crawled beneath the table for DaMina's gun. He reached the weapon just in time. The knife throwing Colombian had lifted his fallen comrade's saw off shotgun, and aimed it at DeFranz. Dallas lifted DaMina's four five, aimed it at the Colombian and squeezed the trigger. The weapon popped, and the Colombian went flying over the wine wine bar with an enormous hole in his chest.

DeFranz, flipped his attacker over his shoulder, seized control of the knife they were struggling over, and then plunged it into the Colombian's mouth. He reeled back, pulled out his forty caliber Glock, and then put a bullet in the top of the Colombian's skull.

"Son of a bitch!" DeFranz screamed. "Motherfucker!"

DaMina made her way up off the floor, and braced herself against a nearby table. She pulled the knife out of her shoulder, screaming the entire time.

"Aaahhh!" DaMina cried out. She tossed the knife onto the floor. "Bitch!"

Dallas rose from the floor. "You okay?"

DaMina nodded. She then braced herself, breathed in and out a few times, and then pulled the second knife out of her chest. "Fuck!"

DeFranz lifted Darius off of the ground. He was in pain. The knife went in deep.

DaMina tossed the knife she pulled out of her chest onto a nearby table, and then made her way over to Darius. She sat him down in a nearby chair. And then yanked the butcher knife out of his shoulder.

"Aaaaahhhhh!" Darius screamed for dear life.

DaMina lifted a napkin from a nearby table, unfolded it,

and tossed the silverware over her shoulder. She took the napkin, folded it, and placed it against Darius' shoulder.

"Hold it tight and apply pressure," she told him.

Darius nodded, and held the cloth against his wound.

"Fuck!" DeFranz shouted. "What the fuck just happened here?"

"We have to get Mina and Darius to a hospital," Dallas declared. "Stone Oak Methodist is just down the street."

D\aMina nodded. She was a soldier, and she could take the pain. But she knew that she needed a surgeon to stop her bleeding, and so would Darius. Dallas wrapped his arm around DaMina trying to help her.

"I can walk," DaMina told him. "Help Darius."

Darius nodded. "I can walk. Just get me outta here."

DeFranz quickly searched the body of the man he tossed onto the table and killed. He had a spider tattoo as well. He pulled out his wallet, and checked his I.D. He peered up at DaMina.

"I already know," DaMina told him. "It's a Colombian I.D."

"How'd you know?" DeFranz asked.

"The spider tattoo," DaMina said, nodded toward the man's arm. "I'm sure they all have it. It's the mark of the cartel."

"Colombia?" Dallas asked.

"I'll explain it later," DaMina told them. "Right now, let's get out of here. We need to get to the hospital. I'll call Damian on the way."

The four of the them exited the restaurant, and headed for DaMina's Range Rover Evoque.

Damian's Residence

Princess strolled into Damian's living room. "What happened?"

Damian lifted a finger telling her to hold on. He was on his cell phone, trying to get more information from DaMina. Dante strolled into the living room.

"It's war!" Dante said angrily.

Damian pressed the off button on his iPhone. "That was Mina. She's still at the hospital. Dallas is going to be fine. The cut across his throat was superficial. Darius is going to be okay. The knife stopped an inch away from his heart."

"And Mina?" Princess asked.

Damian nodded. "She's a soldier. She's tough. You know Mina, she's going to be okay."

"I want to hit those son of a bitches back!" Dante told him. "I want to show them what happens when they draw Reigns blood."

Damian exhaled. "We have to think this thing through. We can't react out of anger."

"They hit us!" Dante shouted. "And they hit us here, in our own backyard!"

"Mina is certain about the tattoos?" Princess asked.

Damian nodded. "They're definitely Colombian's. My boy in homicide confirmed it."

"Cedras?" Dante asked. "That son of a bitch!"

"Dante, calm down," Damian told him.

"We need to teach those motherfuckers a lesson!" Dante shouted. "We need to show them who we are, and what happens when you try to fuck with us."

"We are trying to set up a deal with the Yucatan Cartels, Dante," Damian reminded him. "Don't forget that. They were clear in their instructions weren't they? No bullshit. No wars, no drama. We don't need this right now. Right now, our biggest priority, is to get the dope flowing again. Is that clear?"

Dante shook his head. "This is bullshit. We need to operate from a position of strength. Always operate from a position of strength. Remember that?"

"How can we even hit Cedras right now?" Damian asked. "It took us years to get in position to get *El Jeffe*. Cedras will be expecting us to retaliate right now, and he would see us coming from a mile away! Think, Dante. Think!"

"Damian is right," Princess told him. "Remember, we need to get the dope flowing again. Our financial issues mandate, that getting the dope flowing again, is our first priority. We need to secure this deal with the Yucatan cartels, and if that falls through, we may need to deal with Cedras again. Remember, The Commission is ready to crawl back into bed with their Colombian pimp."

Dante fumed. He was ready to kill. Finally, he relented. "Okay, we'll play this your way. But weakness, only invites more attacks. We sit back and do nothing, and watch our enemies crawl out of the woodwork and try to get at us."

"And we'll deal with their asses," Princess told him. "Just because we are cutting Cedras some slack right now, doesn't mean everyone else gets the same slack. We just don't need any major shit to jump off and scare away the Yucatan drug connection."

Dante nodded. "I'm getting my men ready. And I'm going to start putting together a plan to get with Cedras. And when the time comes, I'm going to personally plant a stick of dynamite up that son of a bitch's ass."

"Just be cool, Dante," Damian told him. "I would much rather you spend your time trying to find a way to get the dope flowing again. That is what your first job should be. Putting things in place, to secure this family's financial future. Without money to pay our soldiers, this family is dead. Remember that."

"I'm not going down without a fight," Dante told him. "Remember that."

Dante turned, and stormed out of the room. Damian and Princess stared at one another in silence. Controlling Dante was going to be hard. Especially now that Reign's blood had been spilled.

Chapter Ten

Damian's caravan of armored limousines pulled up to The Lucky Horseshoe Casino and Resort Hotel in Bossier City, Louisiana. The Horseshoe, as it had come to be known, was a world class casino on the Red River, attached to a twenty five story, gold glass hotel building. The Horseshoe was known for its luxurious suites, with oversized Roman style, marble bath tubs, and king sized beds. It was also known as being one of the premiere gambling destinations in Northern Louisiana. It was at The Lucky Horseshoe where today's meeting was being held.

Damian had called the meeting to settle things between the Old Ones, and his father-in-law. He needed to stop the war and settle things down, in order to send a message to the Yucatan Cartel. He wanted to show them that the Reigns family was about business, and that it was ready to stop the violence and maintain the peace. It would show that they were serious about doing business with the cartel.

The Old Ones had agreed to meet at the Horseshoe, because it was one of their casinos, with their workers, and it was a place where they would feel safe. Damian agreed to set the meeting up at the Horseshoe, because it was located in Bossier City, Louisiana, which was Anjounette's territory. He would have hundreds of men available outside of the casino, in case anything went down. If things went bad, no one was leaving the casino alive. Damian's father-in-law agreed to meet at the casino for the same reason. He knew that the Reigns family controlled Louisiana, and so he felt as if he would be safe there.

Today's meeting was to be held on the twenty fifth floor of the hotel. There was a secret suite that the Old Ones maintained at the top of the hotel for VIP guest, and secret trips by high level family members to check up on their hotel and casino interest. Today, the twenty fifth floor of The Lucky Horseshoe was more guarded than The White House.

Damian's armored Infiniti QX 56 stretch limo pulled up to the entrance of the hotel, and his men jumped out and opened the door for him. Anjounette and his brother Dajon were waiting at the hotel entrance for him. Reigns bodyguards were everywhere.

"Welcome to Louisiana," Anjounette told him.

"Thanks," Damian said, climbing out of the limo, and buttoning up his Brooks Brothers suit jacket. "Is it always this warm."

"You're in the swamps now, bro!" Dajon said with a smile. He hugged his older brother. "Good to see you."

"Good to see you!" Damian told him. "Man, I miss you. We need to visit each other more often. How's my niece and nephew?"

"Big, and getting bigger with each passing day," Dajon said with a smile. "And that little niece of yours, she's just as fast as she wants to be. She's getting into trouble at school for bullying. You know, she's in with the 'in' crowd, so she thinks that she runs the school."

Damian through his head back in laughter. "Man, what did you expect? She's just like her mother. She has her mother's looks and brains, so you knew she was going to be a handful."

"Yeah, and I took her little ass off the cheer leading squad until she gets herself together," Dajon told him.

"Don't be too hard on her," Damian said. "I can remember her Dad acting up at that age as well."

"May you have children that act like you," Dajon said with a good hard laugh.

"Mom's curse," Damian said, joining in the laughter. "That was one of her favorite sayings."

"I miss her, bro," Dajon said, with his laughter slowing fading.

"I do too," Damian said, placing his hand on his brother's shoulder and squeezing gently. "So, what do we have here?"

"The security arrangements are all set," Dajon said, turning to business. We managed to get people on the hotel staff, so we have people on the inside. "You can take up to ten men inside with you. Five can actually go inside of the room, and five can remain outside on the same floor. But again, not to worry, because we have other people on the inside."

"I also have this place damn near surrounded," Anjounette added. "They know that if anything goes down, they'll never make it out of this place alive, let alone to the airport."

Damian nodded. "Well, let's do this."

Anjounette waved her hand, and some of her men opened the double doors for them to enter into the lobby. Damian, Anjounette, and Dajon, along with dozens of their men, strutted through the hotel's marble floored lobby. Patrons inside of the hotel saw the massive mob of Black men in business suits, and cleared a path for them. The sight of thirty Black men in expensive business suits was intimidating to many. Damian made his way to the elevator, which another one of Anjounette's men were holding for them. They climbed onto the elevator and made their way to the twenty fifth floor.

"What are your chances of pulling this off?" Anjounette asked.

"Who the hell knows," Damian said, shrugging his

shoulders. "I'm hoping that everyone is tired of losing men, and money, and wasting resources on a fruitless war that's been going on way too long. Daisalla's death has been paid for with the blood of many mafia dons and many of their men. My read is, the Old Ones are willing to call it quits, it's just going to depend on the old man. If the chief feels like he's satisfied with the amount of blood that's been spilled, then maybe he'll recall all of his damn assassins and end this thing."

Anjounette shook her head. "Sounds like a tough task ahead."

"We'll see," Damian said with a smile.

The elevator door opened, and another one of Anjounette's men greeted them. He waved for them to follow, and escorted them to a nearby suite. Anjounette fixed Damian's tie.

Damian exhaled forcibly. "Wish me luck."

"You're going to need it," Anjounette told him.

Damian turned, and another one of his men opened the door to the suite for him. Don Graziella Biaggio was seated on a sofa inside of the luxurious suite. He rose, when Damian walked into the room. Damian strode up to the Old Don, outstretched his arms, and the two of them embraced. They kissed one another on each cheek, greeting each other in the old Sicilian style.

"Damian, it's so good to see you!" The Old Don said, enthusiastically.

"Don Biaggio, the pleasure is all mine," Damian replied.

"How is your family?" the Don asked.

"Everyone is wonderful," Damian answered. "And yours? How is that beautiful wife of yours?"

"Wonderful," the Don replied.

"Please," Damian said, waving toward the sofa.

Don Biaggio seated himself, and Damian took a seat on the sofa next to him.

"I'm grateful that you agreed to meet with me," Damian

continued.

"How could I refuse?" The Don said. "You call, and I am here. That's what friends do for one another. No?"

Damian nodded. "Of course. And there is no doubt, how deep our friendship runs. Unpleasantries between our families are most unfortunate. Such misunderstandings between friends, should never be allowed to go on for so long."

The Old Don nodded. "I agree. We should put an end to them immediately."

Damian now knew that the Old Ones were willing to make peace. It was only a matter of his father-in-law agreeing to do the same. The fact that the Old Mafia had sent Graziella Biaggio to negotiate for them, meant a lot. He was now the most senior member of the five families, and thus, the most powerful. He spoke, and the others listened. That meant, for the first time, in a long time, real peace between the Old Mafia, and The Commission was possible.

"How are things with your friends?" Don Biaggio inquired.

"Which friends?" Damian asked. "I would like to think that I have many friends, present company included."

"Of course," The Don said, lifting an eyebrow. "I was wondering about how you and your other friends were faring under the present situation."

Damian nodded. "You mean, with the drought across the state?"

The Old Don smiled.

Damian shrugged his shoulders. "Poor farmers always suffer during a drought. its hit the entire country, and farmers everywhere are feeling it. Is it affecting the aquifers up state as well?"

The Don nodded. "Somewhat. But things are more diversified up north. More industry, less agriculture."

Damian nodded. The Don had just told him that they were

feeling the pinch from the drug shortage, but not as much as The Commission was. The Old Mafia had its money in other things. Casinos, gambling, and construction just to name a few. Drugs sales mattered to them, but not as much. They weren't hurting.

"I hear that you have some new friends around the table," Damian asked.

The Old Don leaned back and smiled. "They are old friends, but new to the table."

"Some very prestigious old families," Damian smiled. He loved showing the Don that he knew what was going on within their circle. "You have a Lombardi, and a De Luca at the table again. As well as my old friend, Amedeo Esposito. Congratulations."

"It was necessary to bring in new blood," The Don told him. Reminding Damian that they had to bring these men in, to replace the ones that the Reigns family, and his father-in-law, had killed.

"I have to do the same," Damian told him. "But, how can you replace a sister-in-law?"

Don Biaggio shook his head. "Such animals. Using bombs, and guns, and stupid things like that."

"A drink?" Damian asked.

"Scotch," the Don told him.

Damian waved his hand. And several of the them inside of the suite raced to get the Don a drink. "Rum and Coke for me."

It took the Don by surprise. Damian was not known to be a drinker.

Damian and the Don were quickly handed glasses with their requested drinks. Damian lifted his glass in toast.

"To the day when guns and bombs become a thing of distant memory."

"Here, here," The Don said, lifting his glass.

Damian and the Don drank from their glasses.

"So, have you found a solution to your water problem?" The Don asked.

Damian shook his head. "We are working on it. The water is underground, it's just a matter of getting it to the surface, and then getting it to the crops."

"If there is anything that I can do, my friend, don't hesitate to ask."

Damian nodded politely. "Thank you."

One of Damian's bodyguards pressed his ear piece against his ear. "I'll let him know." He stepped forward and whispered into Damian's ear. "Chief Malaika has arrived."

Damian nodded, and turned to Don Biaggio. "The chief has arrived."

The door to the suite was opened by one of Don Biaggio's men, and Damian's father-in-law, Chief Immanuel Hillel Malaika, Prime Minister of Ethiopia, and member of the Ethiopian royal family, strolled into the room. He was surrounded by hulking Ethiopian bodyguards. Damian rose, and so did Don Biaggio.

"Your Excellency," Damian said, bowing slightly. "May I present, Don Graziella Biaggio."

Chief Malaika sized up the Don, and then extended his hand. Don Biaggio gripped it, and the two men shook hands. The chief then exchanged handshakes with Damian.

"Please," Damian said, waving toward a nearby chair.

The chief seated himself, and crossed his legs. Damian, and the Old Don seated themselves as well.

"I will get right down to business," Damian told them. "I know that everyone is busy, and out of respect for everyone's time, we may as well get everything out on the table. Gentlemen, it is time to end the bloodshed."

"That's easy for you to say, Mr. Reigns," Chief Malaika told him. "You didn't have to bury your daughter."

"I buried my sister-in-law," Damian told him. "In fact, I've buried two of them. And I loved both of them dearly."

"Have you ever had to bury your child?" the Chief asked.

"I have," Don Biaggio told him. "I've buried two sons, two nephews, a cousin, and dozens of men. Not to mention dozens of friends."

Chief Malaika eyed Don Biaggio in a different light. The Don had buried two sons.

"Enough blood has flowed," Damian said softly. "Daisalla was the best of us. And every time I see my niece, I am reminded of how wonderful Daisalla was. And knowing her, and knowing how she was, she would not have wanted a single soul to die in her name."

Chief Malaika stiffened.

"Let us end this today," Damian continued.

The Chief thought silently for several moments. He closed his eyes, and he could see his daughter's face. He knew that she was the best of them. The best of Damian's family, and the best of his own. She would not have wanted anyone to die in her name. The vengeance had been for him, and for him alone. It was to satiate his appetite for revenge. And now, perhaps it was time to stop. It was time to move on. He had a future to look to. He was about to run for the Presidency of his country, and the president of a nation could not have assassins running around killing the citizens of a foreign nation. Such actions, were an act of war. And Ethiopia could not afford a war with the United States. Perhaps it was time.

Chief Malaika faced Don Biaggio. "You lost *two* sons?"

Don Biaggio nodded solemnly.

The Chief did not want to ask how, or whether it was to his men, or to Damian's men, or to some other group. It would not matter. The only thing that did, was that the man sitting across from him knew his pain. He too had felt the pain of having to bury a child. In fact, the Don had felt it twice.

"Perhaps you are right, Damian," The Chief said, clearing his throat. "Perhaps it is time."

"Can we agree, that the war between us, is over?" Damian asked.

Chief Malaika nodded solemnly. Don Biaggio nodded as well.

"Good," Damian told him. "Then, our business here is finished. Chief Malaika, your grandchildren, my niece and nephew, they are not far away. They are wanting to see their grandfather."

Chief Malaika perked up. "They want to see me?"

Damian nodded. "My brother, has told them how wonderful their mother was, and how much she loved them. He has told them so much about your family, about Ethiopia, about their history, and their heritage. And he has told them much about you. And they want very much to see you, and to know about the other side of their family. They want you in their life. Go to them, and tell them about the glorious history of their mother's family."

The smile that spread across the Chief's face was uncontrollable. He had been head of the Ethiopian Intelligence Service, head of the Ethiopian Secret Police, and of their internal security services, but at the end of the day, he was still a man, and still a grandfather. And like all other grandparents, he wanted to see his grandchildren, he wanted to hold them, play with them, tell them stories. He wanted to pass down his family's history to them. They were his link to immortality.

"You have made me the happiest old man in the world today," Chief Malaika told Damian.

"They like ice cream," Damian told the chief.

"Ice cream," the Chief laughed. "Then, I shall buy them an ice cream parlor.

"Cheyenne loves Barbie dolls, and Justin Bieber," Damian added. "Little DJ is into football. American style football. He

113

also loves video games. You may want to brush up on your Madden skills."

The Chief shook his head. "I don't know what your saying, but I will become the best at it!"

Damian rose. And so did the Chief, and the Don.

"Where are my grandchildren?" Chief Malaika asked.

Damian nodded toward one of his men. "They will take you to my brother, who will take you to the kids. They are at a park playing. They are waiting for their grandfather to take them for ice cream."

The Chief paused. "And what if I would not have agreed to peace?"

"They would have still been waiting to see you, and waiting for you to take them for ice cream," Damian told him. "We would not keep your grandchildren from you, no matter what. They are your family, and you have a right to see them. Daisalla would have wanted nothing less."

Chief Malaika clasped Damian's hand and shook it vigorously. "You are an honorable man, Damian Reigns. This, I will not forget."

"Thank you," Damian told him.

The Chief turned, and rushed out of the room to go and meet with his grandchildren. Damian turned back to Don Biaggio.

"This peace is not only between the Don, and the Five Families," Damian told him. "It is also between the Reigns Family, and the Five Families, as well as The Commission and the Five Families."

Don Biaggio opened his arms, and he and Damian embraced. Peace was now at hand.

Chapter Eleven

Dante pulled the reigns back on the black, pure bred, Spanish Andalusian horse that he was riding, and surveyed the territory before him. He was doing something that he hadn't done in years, he was relaxing, and taking a leisurely horseback ride throughout his family's sixty five thousand acre West Texas ranch.

The Reigns family ranch, known to locals as the Double R Ranch, brought back many memories for Dante. The family spent many summers at the ranch. It was the place of legendary Reigns family picnics, birthday parties, and family football games. It was a place of happy times, of massive family cookouts, and beautiful sunsets, and great fishing trips. He could still hear his mother and his aunt's in the kitchen arguing over some small detail from their childhood, he could still see his father and his uncles in the parlor playing pool, and he could still smell his aunt's cold oven cakes. It was the place where Reigns children ran free, where there was not a care in the world, where it was all about family.

The last time he had visited the ranch, Angela was alive. It was the day his father suffered a heart attack after Nathan and the FBI raided the ranch looking for him on a bullshit warrant. A case that he later beat. He ofter wondered if Nathan hadn't come to the ranch that day, would his father still be alive? Was it his fault, in some small way? Those thoughts weighed heavily on him some nights, and even though he would never admit it, he blamed himself in some small way. He wondered what he could have done differently.

Dante snapped the reigns on his horse, and kicked his heals, spurring the horse along. The beautiful black Andalusian moved along in a meandering gait, making its way across the land, down to the massive river that ran throughout the property. It was at this river, where some of the best fishing in West Texas could be found. It was at this river where he had done some of his best fishing, and where some legendary campfire tales had been born. The river, and the ranch for that matter, provided him with so many memories, and so much clarity. Coming here, reminded him of who he was, where he came from, and what life was really about. It reminded him of why he did what he did. It was all about family. And he would walk through hell with gasoline drawers on, to protect his family. It was for his family's safety and well being, that he had spilled so much blood. It was for his family, that he would continue to do so.

Dante dismounted, walked his horse to the river, and allowed her to drink from the cool, running waters. The cool waters from the river were refreshing. Dante pulled an apple from his leather saddlebag and fed it to his horse, while stroking her beautiful black mane.

"Isabella, I miss this place," Dante said, whispering into his horse's ear. "I miss you too, old girl. I miss Angela. And Mom, and Dad. I miss the family. I miss our football games, our barbecues, Aunt Marjorie's lemon pies. I miss it all."

Dante grabbed Isabella's reigns, and led her to his campsite along the banks of the river. His men were gathered around the campsite, finishing up their preparations. A large cow was being turned on a massive spit, just above a nice simmering fire. The beef smelled delicious, and looked even better.

"Food's just about done, boss," one of the men told him.

"Good," Dante nodded. "Our guest should be arriving soon."

One of his men's walkie talkies crackled and came alive. He lifted it, and spoke into it, before turning to Dante. "They're here, boss."

Dante peered into the distance, and could see a small aircraft in the distance, coming closer and growing ever larger. It was one of his family's Agusta Westland AW 609 tilt rotor aircraft. The Agusta Westland 609's were the latest in aircraft technology. It carried nine passengers in sheer luxury, and its two engines tilted up in the air, allowing the aircraft to take off and land vertically, like a helicopter, before tilting once again while in the air, and allowing the aircraft to fly like an airplane. It was the civilian version of the military's V-22 Osprey, and the Reigns family owned twenty of them. The were useful taking off and getting to larger airports from the ranch, and for taking off from the rooftops of Reigns family buildings in the middle of busy cities. They also used them in Africa for Energia Oil executives and engineers, because of the lack of small airfields close to their exploration activities, and for landing and taking off of oil platforms in the ocean. They came in very handy. Today, Dante was using one to bring in some secret VIP guest to the Reigns family ranch.

The Agusta Westland 609's engines titled vertically, and the plane begin to slow. The pilot hovered for a few moments, before slowly descending to a clearing near the campsite. The clearing was close enough for his VIP guest to take some all terrain vehicles to the campsite, but far enough away to not kick up dust or dirt around the camp site, or to allow the aircraft's rotor wash to put out the campfires.

Dante's cooks, began to uncover a hole that they had dug in the ground. Dante could hear the all terrain vehicles making their way to his campsite. Soon, they pulled up, and his guest climbed out. They were members of the Mexican drug cartels that operated just over the border.

"Welcome!" Dante told them.

"*Hola*, Senior Reigns," Galindo Ortega said, greeting Dante with open arms.

Dante and Galindo embraced warmly. Dante them embraced Nuni Nunez, which was Galindo's number two, and main hit man. Nuni was to Galindo, what Dante was to Damian. He was his fixer, his killer, and counselor, and his number two within the family. But mainly, Nuni was his assassin.

"Nuni! *Como esta, mi amigo?*" Dante said, greeting him.

"*Muy bien, carnal,*" Nuni told him. He had just as much respect for Dante, as Dante had for him. Both men knew that the other, was a stone cold killer.

"Antonio!" Dante said, embracing Antonio Vega, the cartel's lawyer, accountant, and money man. He knew where all of the dollars were hidden, and where they were at any given time of the day. He knew where every single gram of cartel dope was, what the street value was, and what the price was at any given spot on the globe at that moment. He was their numbers guy. And Galindo never let him out of his sight.

"Dante, how are you, my friend?" Antonio said, smiling.

"As good as I can be," Dante told him. He waved his hand around the camp fire. "Gentlemen, get comfortable. Can I offer you something to eat? That was some journey you just took."

"Thank you," Galindo told him. He seated himself on a large boulder near the camp fire. "The ride in, was most impressive. I'm going to have to look into getting me one of those."

"Imagine how much we can sneak across the border in one of those," Nuni told him. "Imagine *what* we could sneak across the border."

Dante's chef, pulled a large pig's head from out of the hole he had dug, and unwrapped the foil from around it. He lifted the lid off of a pan revealing a stack of homemade tortillas.

"*Cabesa Puerca!*" Galindo declared, rubbing his stomach. "Got damn, bro, you sure know how to hit a man's stomach!"

Dante laughed. "I thought you'd like it."

"This is just like the old days, back home!" Nuni said excitedly. "Just like my *Papi* used to make!"

The chef sliced several pieces of tender pork off of the pig's jaw, and placed them inside of the tortillas. He added some *picante* sauce, and begin to hand plates of pork tacos to Dante's guest. Another one of Dante's men opened up an ice chest, and handed the men bottles of Dos Equis beer.

"Whew! this is what I'm talking about!" Nuni shouted. "You sure know how to treat a guest!"

Again, Dante laughed. He knew his guest would love an outdoor cookout. They weren't the fancy hotel types who would be impressed by luxury suites, or marble floors. No, they were from the streets of Nuevo Laredo, and they had come up dirt poor. They had risen to power through the drug game, but they were still poor fellows from the hard streets at heart. This, and the fact that just like all American kids dreamed of being cowboys and eating out on the open range, Mexican kids dreamed of being vaqueros and doing the same. He had chosen his meal and setting perfectly.

Galindo wolfed down his tacos. "This shit is good, bro! Got damn!"

"Hell, yeah!" Nuni agreed. "This is even better than what my *Papi* used to make. This shit is tender as a motherfucker!"

Dante was not a pork eater. The chef pulled meat from the cow that was on the spit, and made Dante a beef taco.

"There you go with that bullshit!" Nuni told him. "Let me find out you turned Muslim in the joint, motherfucker!"

Dante laughed.

"I would eat a pigs ass!" Galindo declared. "As a matter of

fact, pass me that fucking tongue!"

Dante's chef, removed the tongue from the pig's head, and served it to Galindo on a paper plate. Galindo lifted the tongue off the plate, and wolfed it down.

"That shit is good!" Galindo declared.

Dante shook his head. "Y'all some nasty motherfuckers."

"That's the most tender part of the pig, bro!" Galindo told him. "What the fuck are you talking about. You don't know what you're missing."

Galindo was the head of the largest border cartel in Mexico. He was head of the Juarez and Nuevo Laredo Cartels. He was also number one on the DEA's most wanted list. The fact that he had sneaked into the United States for this face to face meeting, said a lot. It told Dante that he had something extremely important to discuss, and that he wanted it to go from his lips, to Dante's ears, with no middle men, and no misunderstandings. He was taking an enormous chance being there.

Dante ate his tacos, and washed them down with some bottled water. He was not a drinker, and he definitely needed a clear mind for the meeting he was about to have. It was Galindo's cartel along with the other border cartels, that supplied The Commission with its cocaine. And now that the United States and Mexico had sealed their border, both sides were suffering. The cartels had tons of dope just sitting in warehouses and not being moved, and thus, put at risk, while The Commission was quickly running out of supply. Soon, The Commission would be completely out of supply, and the various members would have to pay its men, its debts, and maintain their organizations using the money they had in the bank. And no one wanted to dip into their bank accounts to pay out millions of dollars each month. While on the Mexican side, the DEA and The Mexican *Federalis* were starting to bust some of the massive warehouses overstuffed with cocaine.

There was simply no way to hide that much cocaine. Also, the cartels were at war with one another, and the war was getting expensive. The fact that they were not making any money from cocain sells, meant that the war between them, was now hitting each of them in their pockets. Everyone was losing, and everyone was becoming more and more desperate. And so, they were here to discuss the situation with Dante.

The men finished their tacos, and sipped from their beers. One of Dante's men pulled out a couple of bottles of high grade Mexican Tequila, and poured the men a cup. Their bellies were now content, and now they had some Tequila to sip on, as well as some beer. It was time to get down to business.

"Well, you know why we're here," Galindo started off. "This border situation has us all fucked up. We're sitting on tons of supply, and you're probably starting to see your supplies dwindle. And according to my sources inside of the Mexican government, no one knows how long the borders are going to stay locked down."

"What about the tunnels?" Dante asked.

Galindo shook his head. "They're good for some, but not enough. In order to run enough dope through the tunnels, we would have to have trucks running constantly out of whatever warehouses on this side of the border that the tunnels connect to. The DEA would be on to that shit within days. No, it appears that we're going to have to ride it out, my friend."

"Ride it out?" Dante asked, lifting an eyebrow. "How can we ride it out? You just said that your contact didn't know how long the borders would remain closed."

Galindo nodded. "What are your contact over here saying?"

"It's not good," Dante said, exhaling. "That little move you guys made, was not a good one. Kidnapping and killing off American law enforcement agents was not smart. Who the fuck came up with that brilliant idea?"

Galindo shook his head. "Fucking idiots in *Matamoros*. Fucking *Tamaulpas* Cartel are some fucking animals. They don't think, they just react. They called themselves sending a message. Well, look at where that fucking message got us."

"Brilliant," Dante said, shaking his head. "So, what's the deal with the other bodies?"

"More idiots sending more messages," Galindo explained. "Someone kills two, the other guys has to kill five, then the first guy has to kill ten, and pretty soon, we're up to busloads of motherfuckers getting beheaded."

"Shit is out of control," Dante told him. "That's what's gotten us into this mess. You guys beefing, and killing busloads of innocent people."

Nuni shook his head. "Nobody's innocent. If it's a busload, then trust me, its the cartel members, and their families that are on that bus."

"Women and children?" Dante asked, lifting an eyebrow.

"Women, but no children," Nuni replied with a sinister smile. "Bitches don't be innocent. Not in Mexico."

"The only way the borders are going to reopen, is if shit dies down," Dante told them. "The violence has to end."

"You are preaching to the choir, Dante!" Galindo told him. "But ending this shit is virtually impossible. Fathers, sons, brothers, cousins, wives, daughters, nieces, and nephews have all been killed in droves. The blood runs deep, and the blood lust for vengeance is insatiable. People aren't going to forget when you've tortured their brother or cousin or son, and then beheaded them. You can't just lift your hands and say peace."

"Then what the fuck are we supposed to do?" Dante asked.

"Wait," Nuni told him.

"Wait?" Dante asked. "You keep saying wait. Wait for what? Wait until our supplies run out? Wait until we're bleeding money trying to make payroll? The Commission is already tucking its tail between its legs and trying to jump in bed with Cedras."

"Tell them to wait," Galindo said.

"I can *ask* them to wait, but I'm only one voice," Dante replied.

"You're the strongest voice," Galindo told him. "We've been in business together for years. And we're in this shit together. Go back to your Commission, and tell them not to jump in bed with Cedras. You tell them not to fuck over us. We won't forget it."

"That sounds like a threat," Dante told them.

"It is," Nuni said flatly.

"Our war is not going to last forever," Galindo declared. "What do you think is going on in Mexico right now? We're not killing each other for kicks. It's a power struggle between the cartels. One cartel has to come out on top. Right now, you have *Tamaulipas* doing what the fuck they want to do, you have *Tijuana* Cartel doing what it wants to do, you have *Juarez* doing its thing, you have *Guadalajara* doing what it wants to do, you have *Sinaloa* doing what it wants to do, and so on and so forth. You get the picture. When everybody is doing their own thing, then you have motherfuckers doing stupid shit, like those assholes in *Matamoros* trying to kill American cops and shit. But trust me, my friend. We are going to come out on top. And when we do, we will remember who was loyal and who was not."

"How long is it going to take before you win your bloody little war down there in Mexico?" Dante asked.

Galindo shrugged. He tossed the Tequila from his cup into the fire, causing the fire to shoot up into the air. "Until all those motherfuckers are toast."

"Dante, do not go to the Yucatan Cartels," Nuni told him. "Wait for us."

Dante smiled. They knew about his recent trip to Mexico.

123

"The Reigns family will do whatever it can to convince the others on The Commission to wait," Dante told them. "How long they will listen, I don't know. Like I said, they are already panicking."

"Make them wait," Nuni said.

"Dante, I want you to understand me, so that there is no miscommunication on either end," Galindo told him. "We make billions of dollars selling our product to your Commission. They go somewhere else, they are costing me and the other cartels, billions. Your country has a thirty *billion* dollar a year drug habit. *Do not* play with our money. They must wait. We will not allow them to go anywhere else."

Dante nodded. He understood. For a brief moment, he thought about killing Galindo and Nuni, but then again, they had flown in under the guise of his protection. If the Reigns family had nothing else, they had their word. But Galindo's message was clear. The Mexican Border Cartels were saying wait, or else. And the or else in this case, meant war.

"Enough business!" Dante declared. "It's time to eat again. Let's eat, drink, and enjoy ourselves, my friends."

Nuni let out a loud Mexican yelp, and started singing an old Mexican vaquero song. Galindo, Dante, and Antonio joined in.

"Your Spanish is still pretty good," Antonio told Dante, in the middle of the song.

"Of course," Dante smiled. "It had better be. I'm from South Texas, remember?"

Antonio placed his arm around Dante, and the men sang even louder. His guest drank, and sang, and ate, and partied throughout the night. Dante faked it with them. His thoughts were on the message Galindo had just gave, and on Damian's instructions to find a way to get the drugs from the Yucatan Cartel into the country. It would most likely be the last night, he would be able to party with Galindo and Nuni, and call them

124

friends. The day would come, when he would have to kill Nuni, or be killed by him. The future was set. And it was set on a massive collision course between the Northern Cartels, the Reigns family, and The Commission.

Deadly Reigns IV

Chapter Twelve

The Alteza was San Antonio's newest and grandest luxury condominium apartment complex. The luxurious residences started on the twenty fifth floor of the world class Riverwalk Grand Hyatt Hotel, and went all the way up to the thirty third floor. The luxurious penthouse suites occupied the very top of the building, encompassing two levels of decadent living. The buildings designers spared no expense.

The penthouse suites encompassed some five thousand, eight hundred, and sixteen feet, and boasted some five bedrooms, and five bathrooms. Each penthouse suite had its very own private three hundred and twenty five square foot terrace, and each terrace had its own private spa.. The Master suite encompassed its own wing on the first level of the residences, and boasted its own private terrace with views overlooking the city. Sharing the first level with the master wing, was a gourmet kitchen, with Bosch and Sub Zero stainless steel appliances, imported granite counter tops, imported limestone flooring, and gorgeous hazelnut cabinetry. The first level also had a formal dining room, a formal living room with its own private balcony, a den with its own private balcony, a breakfast area, and two other bedrooms, each with their own private baths. The second level of the penthouse had two more guest suites, each with its own private bath, a large game room, a large wet bar, a massive upstairs living room, a

loft, and the main terrace. Exotic hardwoods ran throughout
the entire penthouse, with the exception of the kitchen and
baths, where the imported limestone and travertine took over.
The price for all of this luxury, ran into the millions. And it
was at this high rise unit, that Daniella, Bio One's chief
scientist, was holding Princess's bachelorette party.

"Girl, this place is beautiful!" Princess declared, staring
out of the penthouse's floor to ceiling windows. "You can see
the entire city from here."

"Thank you!" Daniella told her.

"Girl, Damian must be paying you something good!"
Kayla Marin added.

"Maybe I should have gotten a PhD in biology instead a
law degree, " Paula Lynch said, joining in on the conversation.

"And where is the third amigo?" Princess asked the two
Bio One lawyers.

"Who, Diane?" Paula asked. "Her ass is over there by the
food. You know where she's going to be at!"

Princess laughed. "Thank y'all for coming."

Kayla leaned in and hugged Princess and kissed her on the
cheek. "Wouldn't have missed it for the world."

Paula leaned in and kissed Princess on her cheek as well.
"I know right. You know we was gonna be here.
Congratulations, sis,"

"Thank you," Princess told them.

The doorbell rang, and all eyes turned toward the door.
Daniella rushed to her door, and pulled open one of the
massive wooden double doors. Stacia Hess Rogers walked into
the apartment. Princess screamed.

"Bitch! No you didn't!" Princess ran to Stacia, and the
two of them embraced. "No you didn't fly down here! Oh my
God! Girl, it's so good to see you!"

"You know I wasn't going to miss your engagement
party!" Stacia told her. "Somebody has got to see your ass

across the aisle, and make sure that pussy stays on lock down."

Stacia leaned in and whispered in Princess's ear. "Bitch, don't you kill this one."

Princess laughed.

"Hey, hey, hey!" Cherin King shouted. She raced up to Stacia and hugged her.

"Hey, girl!" Stacia told her. "What kinda diet are you on? You are looking mighty damn sexy!"

"Girl, I'm back on that damn Atkins Diet," Cherin told her. "Counting carbs, and jogging again."

"You look good!" Stacia told her. "But make sure you don't lose your booty though! You know that Atkins is for them White girls with no booty!"

Princess, Stacia, and Cherin broke into laughter.

DaMina Reigns sneaked up behind Stacia, and placed her hands over her eyes.

"Bitch, I'm too old to play peek-a-boo!" Stacia declared. She turned, and saw DaMina.

"Mina!" Stacia shouted. She and DaMina embraced.

"Watch the shoulder now," DaMina told her.

"I heard about that," Stacia told her. She lowered her voice. "Colombians?"

DaMina nodded.

"Cedras must be out of his fucking mind," Stacia said shaking her head. "What the fuck is he thinking? And why hit Mina and a bunch of kids? What kind of message would that have sent? What outcome would that have garnered. It just doesn't sound right to me. It was too irrational. That move wouldn't have brought Damian back to the table for a deal."

Princess nodded. "My thoughts exactly."

"I'll look more into it when I get back to Washington," Stacia told them.

"I would appreciate that," Princess told her.

The doorbell rang once again, and this time, it opened

before Daniella could get to it. In walked a face that was
unfamiliar to all.

"Is that her?" DaMina asked.

Princess nodded. "Peaces Espinoza, Future member of
The Commission, for the great state of Ohio."

"Get the fuck outta here!" Stacia whispered. "What the
fuck is going on. Girl, you've got to fill a bitch in."

Princess laughed. "The Commission is expanding, and
they are considering offering her the Ohio seat at the table."

"Her?" Stacia asked, with her mouth wide open. "The
bitch has more tattoos than Lil Wayne!"

Again Princess laughed. "She's straight from the hood.
Came up the old fashion way. She took over her boyfriend's
drug trade after he went to the feds. She was a fast learner.
Went from moving ten keys, to a hundred, to a couple of
hundred, and now a few thousand. She's built up quite a little
distribution network for herself in Ohio. She's street smart, but
raw. Really raw. But, Damian likes what he sees. He thinks
that she has what it takes to run the entire state, so he threw her
hat in the ring. I had Daisalla invite her tonight, so that we
could check her out in person. See if I can get a feel for her."

"She's pretty," Stacia declared. "Mixed, I suppose. Her
last name is Espinoza?"

Princess nodded. "Father is a Black Cuban of mixed
decent, and her mother is a Dominican of mixed race."

"So, her father is half Black, half Cuban, and her mother is
half Black, half Dominican?" Stacia asked.

"Something like that," Princess told her.

"She looks young as hell," Stacia added, walking her eyes
up and down the new guest.

"She is," Princess told her. "She's twenty three."

"Twenty three!" Stacia said excitedly. "She practically a
baby! The Commission is going to eat her alive!"

"Don't underestimate her," Princess said. "Remember,

Ohio isn't exactly a walk in the park. She's had to deal with some rough ass animals from Cleveland, Cincinnati, Dayton, Toledo, Columbus, Akron, and Youngstown. And she's dealt with them, with an iron fist. She has bodies on her."

"What?" Stacia declared.

"Word has it, she's cut a couple of guys up with a chain saw, who tried to get away with not paying her," Princess whispered. "She knows the value of sending a message."

"And if she makes it onto The Commission, can she be controlled?" Stacia asked. "That's the million dollar question. Once on board, will she be a friend, or a foe?"

"That's why the bitch is here," Princess said with a smile. "We're going to make her a friend."

Princess walked over to Peaches and greeted her. "Hey, I'm Princess."

"Oh, Ms. Reigns, it's so good to meet you!" Peaches gushed. She sat her refreshments back down onto the refreshment table, clasped Princess's hand and shook it. "Thank you so much for inviting me."

"How was your flight?" Princess asked.

"Oh, that shit was the bomb!" Peaches told her. "I ain't never been on no plane like that before! Damn, y'all rolling big time!"

Stacia smiled. She turned, and spied Anjounette coming down the stairs. "Pretty girl!"

Anjounette saw Stacia, and lit up. "Hey, Mama!"

The two of them embraced.

"Girl, you are looking beautiful as ever!" Stacia told her.

Anjounette flung her hair back over her shoulder. "You know, I try. Not hard, or anything."

"Bitch, please!" Stacia laughed. "I was just being polite."

Anjounette and Stacia laughed.

"Girl, why didn't you let me know that you were coming?" Anjounette asked.

"I didn't think that I would be able to get away," Stacia told her. "I really didn't know until the last minute."

"Does Damian know that you're here?" Anjounette asked.

Stacia shook her head. "No. I'm going to sneak up on his ass and surprise him."

"And you got invited to this bitch by who?" Anjounette asked. "You know I gotta be nosey."

"Naw, bitch, you trying to be messy!" Stacia told her. "I got invite by Daniella! And yes, I know she is fucking with Damian. But it don't matter. He's had plenty of bitches after me, but he still keeps coming back home."

Anjounette held up her hand, and Stacia gave her a high five.

"Okay, I'm just checking," Anjounette said. She turned and spied Peaches. "Uh, who is that?"

"Your fellow Commission member," Stacia told her.

"Get the fuck outta here!" Anjounette said, spitting some of her drink out. "That's the one they were talking about? The girl from Ohio?"

Stacia nodded.

"The bitch has tattoos and a gold grill," Anjounette declared. "Is she a rapper or something!"

This time, Stacia spit out her drink. "Bitch you crazy!"

"Look at the way she's dressed!" Anjounette said. "And listen to the way the bitch is talking!"

"Okay, she's a little street," Stacia said with a smile. "A little rough around the edges. Not everyone grew up like we grew up. Once she's had some really big money for an extended time period, and has traveled a little bit, she'll change. Right now she's a Coach bitch, but she'll be rocking Hermes soon enough. Give her time."

"I hope they don't want me to take her ass under my wing," Anjounette declared. "Just because we're both yellow bitches with long ass hair, don't mean we have to be paired up and shit."

"I don't know, I think she got you," Stacia said with a smile. "Her hair is longer than yours. She's a little cuter too."

"Bitch, not on my worse day!" Anjounette said, shaking her head.

"C'mon, let's go meet her," Stacia said, with devilish grin.

"Damn, you messy!" Anjounette declared.

The doorbell rang once again. Daniella raced to the door and opened it. Two uniformed officers were standing at the door.

"Princess Reigns!" one of the officer's shouted.

The entire party went silent, and all eyes turned to the police officer.

"I'm here to tell you that you are under arrest, until this party is over. You have the right to get your freak on, and nothing you do tonight, can be held against you! Do you understand these rights as I have read them to you?"

The officer ripped off his shirt, revealing a muscular torso. The second officer did the same. They moved inside of the penthouse and Daniella closed the door. The officers went up to Princess, surrounded her, and started dancing.

The ladies began to whoop and holler.

"Is this the one you was telling us about?" Princess asked.

DaMina shook her head. "The Chocolate Slugger! Cause the nigga is packing a chocolate baseball bat! And Mr. Ooou Weee. Cause when this motherfucker's drawers come off, all the bitches scream Ooooo Weeeee!"

Princess clutched the second officer's dick. "Oooo Weee!"

The ladies gathered at the party all burst into laughter.

Deadly Reigns IV

Chapter Thirteen

Dante strolled down the aisles of the grocery store, examining medication after medication. Usually, this was a task that he relegated to one of his household staff, or one of his bodyguards even, but this evening was different. Being at his family's West Texas ranch reminded him of what he had been missing. Being there, brought back thoughts of a simpler life, a life without bodyguards, FBI agents, and cartel assassins. It reminded him of the simple things that he was no longer able to do, like going out for a quick bite to eat on the spur of the moment. Or even being able to make a simple trip to the grocery store. And so, here he found himself doing just that. He found himself taking a quick trip to the local HEB grocery store, shopping for food and medication, and doing it alone. He left his bodyguards in the parking lot. For a brief moment, he even thought about leaving them at home, entirely, but reason won out. He wasn't stupid.

Dante stood before the childrens medications, trying to figure out which one to buy. On the way to the store his cell phone rang, and one of his housekeepers had informed him that Lucky was running a slight fever. He called 'Ask-A-Nurse', and a slight fever was nothing to be concerned about. He was told to give her some Ibuprofen and Acetaminophen, and that he could alternate between the two. He was also told that a cool bath would do her good as well. And so, he now found himself in the medication aisle at the grocery store, befuddled by the sheer variety of offerings.

Dante lifted a box, read the back of it, and then lifted another and examined it as well.

"Those may not be strong enough for you," a voice said from behind.

Dante turned. She was beautiful.

She wore a University of Texas baseball cap, a loose fitting University of Texas t-shirt, and what appeared to be a pair of loose fitting University of Texas pajama pants. Her tiny, well manicured feet, rested inside of a pair of UT flip flops. Despite her baggy clothing, and attempts to disguise herself, she still looked familiar. Dante squinted and stared at her, as he tried to place her.

"I said, you're going to need something a little stronger," she repeated.

"I know you from somewhere," Dante said, eyeballing her suspiciously. He knew that he had seen her somewhere before, but it wasn't in a dangerous way. He wasn't alarmed, just puzzled. And if she had been an assassin sent to kill him, she could have easily done so while his back was turned.

"I get that a lot," she said with a smile.

"So, what are you looking for?" she asked, taking one of the medications out of his hand.

"Children's Acetaminophen, I guess," Dante told her. "And some type of Ibuprofen."

Dante stared at her intensely. He never forgot a face, but couldn't place her. And someone as beautiful as she was, he would definitely remember. She had long, straight hair hanging down from beneath her baseball cap, and he could tell that she was half Black and half Asian. Judging by her skin color, he guessed that she was of the darker Asian variety. Maybe Thai, or Vietnamese, or Philippine. She could tell that he was studying her intensely, so she extended her hand and

136

introduced herself.

"Desire Dents," she said with a smile.

"I knew that I knew you from somewhere!" Dante nearly shouted. "I knew it!"

Desire smiled. "Can you keep it down."

"What are you doing here?" Dante asked.

"Here?" Desire asked, motioning around her. "Shopping for groceries. What else does one do in a grocery store?"

"I know that!" Dante said, shaking his head. "I meant, what are you doing here, in West Texas?"

"You do have a T.V., don't you?" Desire asked with a smile. "I'm only covering the biggest international incident since the war in Afghanistan."

"The border violence?" Dante asked.

Desire nodded. "Oh, so you do have a television."

Dante shrugged.

"And since I was kind enough to introduce myself, I was wondering if you also had a name?"

"I'm sorry," Dante smiled. "Please forgive my manners. It's not everyday that one comes across a celebrity. My name is Dante."

"Dante," Desire nodded. "Well, please to meet you Dante. So, you are out here shopping for children's medication for?"

"For my daughter," Dante told her.

"Ahhhh," Desire nodded. "So, the wife sent you out for medication and groceries, huh?"

Dante shook his head. "I'm not married."

"Oh," Desire said. "Divorced?"

"You sure are nosy," Dante laughed.

"Hey, I'm a reporter, what do you expect?"

"I'm not the story though," Dante shot back.

Desire laughed. "Okay, so give up the goods. Not married. What, are you somebody's baby daddy?"

Dante shook his head. "I'm a widower. My wife passed

away."

"I am so sorry," Desire said, placing her hand on her forehead. "Sometimes, I just don't know when to shut up."

"It's okay," Dante told her. "It's been years. She died in childbirth."

"Not that many years ago," Desire told him. "You're searching for children's medication."

"Five years," Dante told her.

"And you've been raising you daughter alone ever since?"

"That's what fathers do," Dante said with a smile.

Desire nodded. She had new respect for him. She thought him super cute when she first saw him, and now, it appeared that he'd turned out to be a pretty descent guy. A father who had stepped up and was raising his daughter alone.

"Here," Desire said, grabbing a box of Tylenol off of the shelf. She turned it over and read the instructions. "You can give her this. This is Acetaminophen. There's a dosing syringe included in the box."

"The nurse also said something about Ibuprofen," Dante told her.

"That's Motrin," Desire told him. She lifted a box of Children's Motrin from the shelf, and handed it to him. "Did she tell you to alternate them?"

Dante nodded. "And to give her a cool bath."

Dante eyed the medicines suspiciously.

"Do you know what you're doing?" Desire asked.

Dante shrugged. "I think so."

"You need my help?" Desire asked, placing one hand on her hip, and shifting her weight to one side.

"What? Are you going to come over and show me how to give her the medication?"

Desire shook her head. "C'mon, I'll check out, and follow you in my car. You are obviously in over your head."

"You're really going to do this for me?" Dante asked.

138

This time, it was Desire who shrugged. "Sure. You're not some deranged psychopathic serial killer, are you?"

"No, not recently," Dante told her.

Desire laughed. "C'mon."

Reigns Ranch

Desire pulled up to the Reigns Ranch in her Mercedes Benz ML 550 and sat behind the staring wheel for a few moments. She had no idea who the man in the supermarket was, until she pulled up to the gates of the massive ranch. And then, it all came together for her. He had told her that his name was Dante, but not in a million years would she have imagined that he was *the* Dante Reigns, of the infamous Reigns family. She knew of the family's vast holdings and immense wealth. They were the wealthiest Black family in the world. They owned construction companies, entertainment companies, oil companies, and a vast bio engineering and pharmaceutical firm. And last but not least, they were rumored to be part of a major crime syndicate. Of all the people she could have met in the grocery store, what were the chances that she would have met up with a billionaire scion, of an alleged crime family, she wondered?

Desire stared at the massive farmhouse mansion. She was here now, and she couldn't renege on her offer to help him could she? After all, it was all about a little girl inside who needed some medicine. She would do what she came to do, make an excuse, and leave. And that would be that.

Desire exhaled forcibly. She clutched the steering wheel of her Benz SUV with a vice like grip, before finally opening the door and climbing out. Dante was waiting on the massive white columned porch for her.

"Hey," he said with a smile. "I thought you changed your mind for a moment."

"No, I was just wrapping up a call," she said, faking a smile.

"C'mon in," Dante said, nodding toward the door. He opened the front door for Desire, and she stepped inside.

The interior of the mansion took her breath away. The main house looked as though it could have been featured in Gone With The Wind. It was a massive plantation style structure, with massive Doric Columns, a wrap around porch, and an upper balcony, with giant windows clad with black shutters. The interior of the imposing structure, was also true to the Southern architecture that dominated the exterior. Authentic, hand carved moldings, antique hand carved fireplace mantels, giant crystal chandeliers, and Brazilian cherry wood floors were found throughout the home. The impressive two story grand foyer really took her breath away.

"Wow!" Desire said peering around the entrance of the home. "I was not expecting this."

"Really?" Dante asked, lifting an eyebrow. "What were you expecting?"

Desire shook her head. "Not this. Not this Louisiana, Mississippi River, Antebellum style architecture. Wow!"

"I'll show the rest of the house, after I check on my daughter," Dante told her.

Desire followed Dante up a massive, winding, intricately carved staircase, down a long hallway, and into a pink bedroom that could have belonged to Marie Antoinette. The bedroom featured silk wallpaper, white moldings, and an enormous children's bed that was shaped like Cinderella's carriage. Toys were overflowing from the white wooden toy boxes that lined the room, and a massive crystal chandelier provided the lighting for this fantasy land bedroom.

Desire placed her hand to her chest. "Oh my God!"

Lucky sat up in her bed. "Daddy!"

"Hey, baby!" Dante told her. "I heard that you weren't feeling too well?"

Lucky nodded.

Dante placed his hand on her forehead. "You have a slight temp."

Desire stepped forward and placed her hand on Lucky's forehead. "Hey, sweetie. My name is Desire."

"Hi, Desire," Lucky said.

"She does have a slight fever," Desire told Dante. "Here, give me the medicine."

Dante handed Desire the box of Children's Tylenol. Desire tore open the box, took out the measuring syringe, and then opened the bottle. She dipped the syringe into the bottle, and then pulled in the correct amount for Lucky's age and weight.

"This is going to make you feel better, sweetie," she told Lucky.

Lucky opened her mouth, and Desire placed the syringe inside of her mouth, and carefully administered the medicine.

"Are you a nurse?" Lucky asked.

Desire shook her head. "No "

"Then how do you know it's going to make me feel better?" Lucky asked.

"Because, that what it says on the box," Desire explained. "And, your Daddy talked to a nurse, and she told him to give you this, to make you feel better."

"You already have your jammies on," Dante told her. "Did someone give you a bath?"

Lucky nodded. "Sonia and Consuela gave me a cold bath, and Sonia put my jammies on," Lucky explained.

"Good, so you're all ready for bed," Dante told her. He

kissed her on her forehead, and Lucky laid back in bed. Dante placed the cover over her.

"She has a fever," Desire said, pulling the cover off of Lucky.

"Oh, I forgot. Goodnight, Sweetie!"

"Goodnight, Daddy!" Lucky shouted. "Goodnight, Desire!"

"Goodnight, Sweetie," Desire told her.

Dante headed out of the room, and Desire followed just behind.

"She is so sweet!" Desire told him, once out of the room. "She is just so cute too!"

"Thanks," Dante told her. "That's my little angel. I really appreciate you doing this."

Desire waved him off. "Don't mention it. And after seeing her, it was well worth the ride. She really is precious, Dante."

Dante nodded. "I know."

"I could really go for a cup of coffee right now," Desire told him. Seeing Dante interact with Lucky had changed her mind completely. He wasn't some spoiled rich guy, or some player type, or just some baby daddy taking care of his child on some random weekend. The love she saw in Lucky's eyes, told her what kind of father he was, and thus, what kind of man he must be. She decided that she could stay for some coffee, and perhaps get to know him a little more. If nothing else came of it, at least she would have a contact within the Reigns family, if a story ever necessitated it.

"You are talking to a coffee maestro," Dante said with a smile. "I am the man, who could put Starbucks out of business if he chose to."

"You sure do a lot of talking."

"I can back it up," Dante told her. He nodded for her to follow. "The kitchen is this way."

Desire followed Dante back down the winding staircase, down another hall, and into an elaborate country kitchen. The kitchen looked as if it should have been on the cover of every kitchen and bath magazine in the country. It had custom blue stainless steel Viking Appliances, blue agave gemstone counter tops, custom white cabinetry, hand painted blue and white Talavera floor tiles, hand painted blue and white Talavera tiles with copper inserts as a back splash, and an enormous Marie Antoinette Swarovski Crystal chandelier over an equally enormous center island. Even the ceiling was decked out with authentic hand carved wood beams, with white and copper ceiling tiles spaced in between.

Desire stopped at the kitchen entrance to catch her breath upon seeing the room. Dante strolled up to the counter, and started searching the cabinets. Desire folded her arms, shifted her weight to one side, and smiled in amusement, while watching Dante search.

"That's what I thought," Desire said, after watching Dante search for several moments. "You have no idea where anything in this kitchen is. Your house keepers make the best coffee in the world, is probably what you meant to say."

Dante laughed. "Okay, you got me."

Desire strolled into the kitchen, and walked right up to a corner shelf that had a roll up appliance bin beneath it. She pulled up the door, and pulled out a coffee machine.

Dante smiled sheepishly. "I knew it was there all along."

Desire laughed and nodded. "Sure you did."

One of Dante's men walked into the room. "Boss, we have a visitor."

"A visitor?" Dante asked, lifting an eyebrow.

"All the way from San Antonio," his man told him.

Dante turned to Desire.

Desire waved her hand. "I got this. Go and handle your business."

"Thanks, babe," Dante told her. By instinct, he leaned over and kissed her on her cheek, and then hurried into the living room. He didn't realize what he had done until after he had left the room. He was puzzled by his actions. Had he become so comfortable with Desire in that short period of time? Her helping him with Lucky, and then her going into the kitchen and knowing where everything was, and fixing him coffee while he handled business, reminded him so much of Angela. Desire served to remind him of how much he missed her, of how much he missed having a woman around him to take care of him, and to provide the softer side to his iron core. She was real cool, her actions tonight had proved that. And he had vibed with her instantly. He wasn't used to being in this position. Not since Angela. He wasn't used to feeling this way about a woman. For the first time in years, he actually felt like a school boy with a high school crush.

Dante strolled into the formal living room of the mansion, to find Kevin Reigns sitting in one of the Queen Anne wing back chairs.

"All hell, he said a visitor from San Antonio!" Dante told him.

Kevin stood, and he and Dante embraced.

"I told him to say that," Kevin explained. "He said you had a guest, and I didn't want anyone to know that I was here."

"What's up?" Dante asked. He waved his hand at the chair Kevin had been seated in. "Have a seat, kinfolk."

Kevin shook his head. "Naw, I won't be staying long."

"Won't be staying long? Kev, it's a six hour drive back to San Antonio!"

"I'm heading to the airport in Midland once I leave here," Kevin explained. "I'm heading to Dallas, and then on to Vegas."

"Vegas?" Dante asked, lifting an eyebrow.

"To get some men for you," Kevin explained. "I'm pulling

144

some guys from Dallas, and from Vegas, and then heading to Frisco to wait for you."

"Why am I going to Frisco?" Dante asked.

"The Frisco under boss doesn't understand the concept of loyalty," Kevin explained. "He still doesn't realize that California now belongs to the Reigns family. He's calling secret meetings, trying to build up support, and trying to get the other under bosses to support him in a bid to take over the state."

Dante shook his head. "Stupid asshole!"

"The message from Damian was simple," Kevin said matter-of-factly. "He wants it to be public, and he wants it to be messy. He wants everyone to understand that California is without question, a Reigns family state. Just like Texas, just like Florida, California is ours."

"No second chances, no warnings, just a message," Dante said with a smile.

Kevin shook his head. "Uh-un, he sent me personally, to tell you face to face, he wants it public, and he wants it bloody. He wants everyone to understand that there is no difference between California and Texas, as far as we are concerned."

Dante nodded. "Well, then, I guess I'll see you in a day or two."

Kevin extended his hand, and Dante shook it. "I'm outta here."

"Later, cuzzo."

"Later."

Deadly Reigns IV

Chapter Fourteen

"Here we go again," Princess said, standing outside the door of the conference room. She smoothed out her DKNY skirt, and tugged on the matching black DKNY jacket to straighten it out as well. "I'm so tired of this shit."

DaMina nodded in agreement. One of Princess's men opened the door to the conference room, and Princess and DaMina strutted inside.

The conference room was on the tenth floor of Chicago's famed Conrad Hotel. The Conrad Chicago resided at one of the most prestigious address on Chicago's famed Magnificent Mile. It was located in the historic Chicago landmark, the McGraw-Hill Building. Being located on The Mag Mile, as it was known locally, meant that the patrons had access to some of the finest restaurants and luxury shopping in the world. It was no secret, that Chicago had more 5 Star restaurants, than any other place on the planet. The Mag Mile was also home to an abundance of world class shopping. Everything from Bloomingdales to Neiman Marcus, from Saks Fifth Avenue to Nordstrom, from Barney's New York to Cartier. A walk down the street would showcase store fronts from Escada, Bulgari, Chanel, Vera Wang, Jimmy Choo, Harrry Winston, Prada, Ralph Lauren, Marc Jacobs, Hermes, Gucci, Louis Vuitton, Giorgia Armani, Salvatore Ferrragamo, Ermenegildo Zegna, Brroks Brothers, Burberry Hugo Boss, Yves Saint Lauren,

Juicy Couture, David Yurman, and Tiffany & Co., just to name a few. And patrons paid heavily for this access. Only movers and shakers held events and/or rented rooms at the Conrad. It was the place where today's Commission meeting was being held.

"Welcome!" Adolphus Brandt of Colorado told her. "As usual, you're late."

"Sorry, I had a hang nail," Princess replied. "Are you going to send me to the principal's office?"

"If the rest of us can be here on time, then what makes you think you're so special?" Cesario asked.

"Are we really going to spend more than ten seconds taking about my tardiness?" Princess asked.

"It's not about your tardiness," Barry Groomes of Arkansas told her. "It's about the Reigns family thinking that it can do whatever it wants."

"Are we going to go through this again?" Princess exhaled. "Did we or did we not, just give all of you back your territories? Didn't we withdraw our men without asking for a single concession?"

"Look, we are not here for all of that," Emil said, stepping in for his woman.

"Right, we're here to discuss Commission expansion," said Raphael Guzman of Oklahoma. "Which according to the vote we took before you arrived, is a done deal."

"Oh really?" Princess asked, lifting an eyebrow. She walked to a an empty chair, and seated herself in between Emil and Julian. "You've already voted?"

"We have," Jamie Forrest of Tennessee said with a smile.

"And you voted for expansion?" Princess asked.

"We did," Steve Hawk of Kansas told her.

"And did we also decide which states were to be admitted?" Princess asked.

"We did," James Speech of Virginia told her.

"And did we decide which people we were going to admit from each of the states that we are going to admit?" Princess asked.

"We did," Jamie Forrest said with a smile.

"The Reigns family recommended certain people for certain seats," Princess told them. "I hope that you gave weight to our recommendations."

"Your recommendations were given their proper consideration," Adolphus said with a sly smile.

"Don't play with me," Princess snapped. "I promise you, if you admitted a bunch of people hostile to the Reigns family, they are never going to be seated at this table."

"How the fuck you figure that?" Malcolm 'Baby Doc' Mueller of Alabama asked. "You don't have that kind of juice anymore, sweetheart. Ain't nobody at this table sweating your threats. It's only a matter of time before the entire Reigns family is living in a shelter and eating in a soup kitchen."

Princess recoiled. "What? I believe that you are sadly mistaken."

"It's no secret about Bio One, *Puta!*" Chacho Hernandez of New Mexico told her. "Everyone knows that your family is in trouble. And everyone knows that a bunch of blood sucking lawyers are going to take all of your fucking money."

"No money, no soldiers," Cesario said with a smile. "You're in big fucking trouble, little lady."

"I'm not," Emil told them.

"Ain't nobody worried about your soft ass," Baby Doc said, laughing.

"Apparently, somebody has told you motherfuckers something wrong," Princess told them. "If you think that the Reigns family is weak, then make a move. We've spanked all of your asses before. Remember that."

"We don't have to make a move, all we have to do is sit back and wait," Chacho said with a smile. "The lawsuits are going to do, what most of us haven't been able to do. They are going to eat your ass up."

"Don't bet on it," Princess told them. She was frustrated. They knew too much, and they were talking too much shit. Worst of all, she didn't have a comeback. Bio One was in trouble, and the Reigns family's finances were in dire straight.

"Another issue that we've taken up while you were dealing with your hang nail, was about the situation in Mexico," Adolphus told her. "My sources tell me, that there is no end in sight to the closing of the borders, or to the Cartel's war amongst themselves. We have to get the water back on. We've decided to take Cedras up on his offer."

"Gentlemen, the last time we met, you agreed to give us some time to work things out," Princess told them.

"We did," Barry Groomes told her. "And that time has now expired. We need to make a move right now. This Commission can not wait on your experiments or hopes or wishes any longer. We need dope, Cedras has it, and he says that he can get it to us."

"You want to go back to kissing Cedras's ass?" Princess asked. "Is that what you really want to do?"

"I think that you don't like the idea, because Cedras will get the dope to us through the ports, which means that he no longer has to go through Texas like the Mexican's did," Baby Doc told her. "And I have a port. And I'm sure Cedras would love to be able to come through my port, and cut your asses off."

"Things have changed," Cesario said with a smile.

"We wait, you get weak, we get stronger," James Speech of Virginia told her. "Your days are numbered."

"You want to kiss Cedras's ass, go right ahead," Princess told him.

"We've already voted," Adolphus told her. "It's already a done deal. This Commission is once again in bed with

Colombia. You don't like it, leave the Commission."

San Francisco, California

Corey 'Boss Hogg' Ross, was the master of all he surveyed. He was the king of Northern Cali, and most certainly of the Bay Area. He was the Reigns family's under boss for the Frisco area. But even more than that, he was the head nigga in charge of his own family. He had been doing this shit for the last fifteen years, and he considered himself at least equal to Marion Rook. If that fucking Dante hadn't killed Marion, then he would have. He had plans to take over all of Cali from Marion, before that idiot went and got himself killed. He had the soldiers, the organization, the loyalty of his men, and the personal skills to run the entire state. And now, it was his time to shine.

Corey sat back inside of his Escalade and surveyed the streets of Frisco. Everything was quiet, and peaceful. Everything was the way it should be. All of the stars seemed to have aligned for him of late. He had secured the loyalty of the under boss from Oakland, as well as a solid commitment from the boss of Sacramento. The LA under boss was his chief rival, and had his own designs on the state. He too, was trying to secure the other under bosses commitments to back him up if he decided to take the state away from the Reigns family. And then there was that fucking suck ass in San Diego, who was completely loyal to the Reigns family. He had Northern and Central Cali, and if only he could work something out with his rival in LA, then all of California would be his. He would just kill off that stool in San Diego and replace him with his own man. Everything depended on getting LA in line. But what would that cost him, he wondered? What could he put on the table that would make LA fall in line behind him?

Boss Hogg was so deep in thought that he didn't see the massive green garbage truck racing toward the Escalade that his bodyguards were riding in. The garbage truck took out the lead car in Boss Hogg's caravan, totally incapacitating or killing everyone inside.

"Oh shit!" Boss Hogg shouted. His first thought was that it was an accident, but then his street sense kicked in, and he immediately grabbed his pistol.

A beige Ford F-150 Dual axle work truck, slammed into the chase car in Boss Hogg's caravan, taking it out. Men in dark suits poured from inside of the F-150, and the garbage truck. Armor piercing rounds took out the fortunate few of his men who had survived the crash.

"Go around!" Boss Hogg shouted to his driver. "Get the fuck outta here! It's an ambush!"

An armor piercing .50 caliber round tumbled through the front windshield, taking the driver's head off. And then, one by one, the tires on the Escalade that he was riding in, were taken out. He could feel the car shift each time a tire was deflated. And then, he saw him.

Dante Reigns walked calmly toward the disabled black Escalade, with several of his men following just behind him. Seeing Dante, told Boss Hogg that it was all over. Everything that he had worked for all of those years, was now about to end. But, he wasn't going out without a fight. He still had his . 50 Caliber Desert Eagle clutched in his hand. At the very least, he was going to put a bullet in Dante.

And massive explosion rocked the Escalade, nearly flipping it over. The rear door opposite of where Boss Hogg had been sitting, was completely blown off its hinges. The massive explosion had also disoriented him, and caused him to drop his pistol.

Reign's soldiers pulled Boss Hogg from the opening where the rear door used to be.

"Hello, Corey!" Dante told him.

Corey tried to struggle, but two of Dante's largest men were holding him by his arms.

"Fuck you, Dante!"

"Corey, today is your lucky day," Dante said with a sinister smile. "Today, is your great going home day. You're about to meet Sweet Jesus. Or, the devil, if your life's not right. Either one, I want you to ask him about loyalty when you get there."

"Loyalty?" Corey sneered. "What does the Reigns family know about loyalty?"

"Oh, we're loyal. We're loyal to each other."

"Coming from the man who tried to kill his sister? The only thing you motherfuckers understand, is money."

"This coming from the man who is about to die, because he wanted more of it?" Dante asked, lifting an eyebrow. "Greed, Corey, is one of the seven deadly sins."

"Fuck you, Dante!"

"No, fuck you, Corey!" Dante pulled out a pistol, and aimed it at Corey's face. He was about to squeeze the trigger, but then lowered his weapon. "I always liked you, Corey. I always thought that if anybody would betray us and try to make a move against us, it would be those son of a bitches in L.A."

"California is not yours," Corey told him. "Cali, should be run by a Cali nigga. How would you feel if Texas was run by a Cali nigga? You wouldn't take that shit!"

Dante nodded. "You're right, in some twisted federal penitentiary kinda way. But this ain't the joint. And this ain't about a hood, or a turf, or who controls what. This is about money, Corey. Lots of it. Do you have any idea how large the California drug market is? We are never going to give this place up."

Boss Hogg nodded. "You will, one day. Mark my words. Somebody from Cali is going to take it from you. You won't have a choice."

Dante shook his head. "Too bad for you, that today, is not that day."

Dante lifted his weapon and put a bullet in Corey 'Boss Hogg Ross's forehead, causing his to drop instantly. Another one of Damian's men approached with an ax. Dante took it from him, handed the man his pistol, and then gripped the ax tightly.

"Sorry, Corey, but Damian wanted it bloody." Dante swung the ax, sending Corey's head tumbling away from his body.

"Jesus!" one of Dante's men cried out.

Dante shrugged, and handed the man the bloody ax. "At least I killed him first. I could chopped his fucking head off while he was alive."

Three white Infiniti QX 56 SUV's wheeled around the corner and stopped just in front of Dante and his men. Dante surveyed the scene before climbing inside of his getaway transportation. Damian wanted to send a message, and he wanted it bloody. He was leaving ten dead bodies on the streets of San Francisco, one of them without a head. The other California under bosses would surely get the message.

Chapter Fifteen

Today's meeting was being held at the massive Bio One headquarters campus on the outskirts of San Antonio. The lawyers had requested that the meeting be held there, after consulting with several Bio One scientist and researchers. Today's briefing would be an update on the corporation's legal woes, as well as a technical explanation from the scientist, biologist, chemist, and physicians on what went wrong with the failed drugs.

Damian strode into the conference room and took his seat at the head of the long conference table. "I won't make this long and painful for anyone. I hate long drawn out meetings myself, so I guess we can just jump right into it. I presume that everyone here knows each other, so, I'll turn the meeting over to Bio Onc's lead attorney, Diane Malveaux."

Diane nodded at those arrayed around the conference table. "I am Diane Malveaux, Bio's One's lead attorney for this case. These are my partners, Paula Lynch, and Kayla Martin. And I'll just go around the table and introduce everyone again, just in case some of us aren't familiar with each, or have forgotten who's who. To my right, is Adrian Andrews, Damian's personal defense attorney, to his right is Cherin King, Damian's chief legal adviser, and to her right, is Thomas Voight, Damians' personal business attorney. Of course we all know Mr. Reigns, and to his right, is Dr. Daniella, head of the biology lab here, and then we have Dr. Y'honatan Levi, chief biologist, and one of the top molecular bio physicist in the country. Then we have Dr. Benjamin Klein, chief virologist, and one of the leading HIV researchers in the country. Next to Dr. Klein, is Dr. Hannah Rosenthal. Dr. Rosenthal is another distinguished virologist and mircrobiologist. And then we have my girl, my ace, my sister from another mother, Dr. Judith, Bernstein. We call her D.J., for Doctor Judy. D.J. is a microbiologist, hematologist, immunologist, pathologist, and every other ologist that you can think of. D.J. has more degrees than a thermometer, and we are fortunate to have her here. She is also the director of our BSL-4, bio safety lab here in town. To her right, is Dr. Cabot Van Der Groot, Ph.D. Economics, Bio One's Executive Vice President, and Chief Financial Officer. To his right, is Dr. Helga Strasser, another brilliant economic and business mind. She is Bio One's Deputy CEO. And with those introductions done, I will turn it over to my colleague, Kayla Marin to brief us on the legal situation as it currently stands."

Kayla cleared her throat. "Good morning everyone. I am Kayla Marin, partner in the law firm of Marin, Lynch, and Malveaux, and as stated early by my partner, we represent Bio One. As you all know, we are in the middle of a group of lawsuits concerning the drugs, RDX-214, and RD-221. To the point, we are facing an enormous catastrophe on the legal front. That's the bad news. I always like to get the bad news out up front."

Laughter went around the table.

"Now with that said, let's talk about some of the positive developments and issues surrounding the case," Kayla continued. "My partners and I were able to get the lawsuits joined into one class action suit, which is a plus. This means we don't have to fight thousands of tiny lawsuits all at once. We can just focus our efforts at fighting one big one. So, that's a positive. Two, no one has died from the administration of the two drugs, which is always a plus. The drugs continued to act as, and be utilized as viral suppressants, and do a tremendous job as such. Our biggest challenge, is that some idiots marketed those drugs as a cure, instead of marketing them as a suppressant. However, like all of the drugs in the suppressant class, doctors fortunately kept their patients on the drugs, even after achieving non detectable viral levels. So, that's another positive. Also, according to my investigators, who have been in the field interviewing and working tirelessly since this thing began, doctors across the country are of unanimous consent, that RD-221, and RDX-214, are still the best viral suppressants in the industry. That is going to help us a lot on the legal front. So, we have some positives here. And if we're really fortunate, since no harm was actually done to any of the patients, we may be facing a case of false advertisement. This is the best case scenario."

"False advertisement?" Damian asked, nodding slowly. "I can live with that."

"That's our legal strategy," Paula Lynch chimed in. "And just a reminder. Everything that is discussed in this room, stays in this room. Especially our legal maneuvers and strategy."

"So, what are we looking at, if we can get it to boil down to false advertisement?" Cherin King asked.

"We're not sure," Kayla told her. "It depends on the jury. Juries in Texas are conservative, and fortunately, we were able to get into a federal district court located within the state. So, that was another plus. But even with a Texas jury, you never know. We're banking on their attorney's being afraid of a Texas jury. So, we're using that as a bargaining chip. If we can get this thing to a billion dollars or less, I say, we settle."

Again Damian nodded. "I can live with a billion dollars."

He knew that Bio One had a few billion in its cash

reserves, and would happily give up a billion in order to keep the company on solid ground. If the plantiff's attorneys would take a billion, he would gladly sign the check tomorrow.

"The good news is, Bio One's medical equipment supply side is booming," Helga Strasser told them. "We have some two hundred million in research grants under contract on our research side of the business. And on the pharmaceutical side of the business, we still have numerous other very successful drugs. So, those are some other positive things that we can build on."

"From a purely numbers standpoint, if we can get this thing to a billion or less, then the company will survive," Cabot Van De Groot declared. "The sticky point, is anything over two billion. Over two billion, and we are struggling. Over three billion, and the company is bankrupt."

"And, three billion is the sweet spot," Kayla Marin told them. "My preliminary conversations with some of the attorney's on the other side, tells me that that's what they are shooting for. Anywhere between three to five billion."

"They are trying to bankrupt us?" Damian asked.

"It's based on the company's valuation, not based on the company's cash reserves," Cherin explained to Damian. "They feel like we can pay that out easily. And what we don't have in cash, we can borrow."

"Borrow?" Damian lifted an eyebrow. "They expect me to walk into a bank and just borrow two billion dollars, after just coughing up three billion? Have they forgotten about payroll? Do they have any idea of how much money it requires to run a level four bio safety lab? Do they know how much it cost to maintain all of the facilities and operations that we need to function as a business?"

"That's not their concern, Damian," Thomas Voight chimed in. "They just want their money.

"And if they bankrupt us, they lose RD-221, and RDX-

158

214, two of the best drugs on the market!" Damian said forcefully. "Don't they realize that?"

Kayla, Paula, and Diane exchanged knowing glances.

"We've made them aware of that," Diane declared. "I don't think any of them want to go back to their clients and tell them that they can no longer get the best drugs on the market. The benefit of both drugs, is that the patients don't get sick from them. So, they'll have a choice. They can go back to the old drugs which made them sick, or they can keep taking RD-221, or RDX-214. It's up to them. Have no doubt, we're pulling out all of the stops on this thing, and we're playing hard ball with those attorneys."

"I have no doubt about that," Damian said with a smile.

The others around the table laughed.

"You hired us, because you know we're some mean, vicious, attack dogs in the courtroom," Diane laughed.

"Okay, so, just to recap on the legal front," Damian started off. "We're trying to get this thing down to a false advertisement case. We've got the lawsuits joined into one class action suit, and best case, we're looking at a billion dollar settlement. Worst case?"

"Three billion dollar judgment," Kayla told him. "Which in Texas, I don't think they are going to get. Especially once the jury hears that no one has died, and that most of the patients, if not all, are still on the drugs because they're the best thing out there. We're in a fucked up position, but the plaintiffs are also in a fucked up position. They are suing us, over a drug that helps them control their illness, and that causes them less pain and nausea than the alternatives. It makes them look like greedy bastards."

Nods went around the table.

"There is also another element to consider," Paula told them. "This is another tool in our legal arsenal, and the reason I've invited some of your scientist, biologist, and researchers

159

here. It has to do with future research into similar drugs."

"Future research?" Damian peered around the table. "The FDA won't approve an aspirin coming from Bio One, with these lawsuits. We took a big hit to our credibility on this one. Our people at the FDA who helped us get the initial drugs through expeditiously, are running for cover. They aren't going to lift a finger to help us out again, no matter how much money is on the table."

Adrian Andrew, Damian's criminal defense attorney place his fingers in his ears. "I didn't hear that!"

Laughs went around the table.

"I'm going to let Dr. Judith Bernstein take over from here," Diane told them.

"Good morning," Judith said in her British accent. She was born in Great Britain to a Jewish parents, who eventually immigrated to Israel, and then to the United States. Her accent however, remained distinctly British. "I am Dr. Judy, or D.J., as Diane calls me, and I am the head of Bio One's Level Four Bio Containment Lab. As you all know, we work with some particularly nasty viruses over at the lab. Well, over the last few years, we come across some very interesting findings, and my researchers applied them to some of the HIV virus strands that the main lab sends over to us, and the results have been astounding."

Damian lifted his hands and made a referee signal for 'time out'. "Hold on D.J., before you even get started, lets set some ground rules. I consider myself an egg head, and so do many others. But you guys are a completely different level of egg head. A lot of us here aren't scientist, in fact, we have a lot of lawyers around the table who need to understand exactly what all of you scientist are going to be talking about. So, I'm going to ask you to please speak in layman's terms as much as possible, so we none scientist can follow you."

Laughter went around the table.

"Got you!" Dr. Bernstein said nodding. "Okay, here's the deal. I'm going to let Dr. Levi explain his part first, and then I'll discuss my findings, once we've established a base."

All eyes at the table turn to Dr. Y'honathan Levi.

Dr. Levi shrugged. "Well, it's really simple."

"No its' not!" Damian interrupted. Again laughter went around the table. "It's simple to you guys. "Give it to me in English, Yoni."

"Before I was interrupted," Dr. Levi started off with a smile. "I was going to explain what's been going on in the world of HIV research and treatment. What has happened of late, is that we have found that several patients who received bone marrow transplants, along with anti retroviral drugs, have been what we called, 'clinically cured' of the virus."

Damian leaned back in his chair and whistled. "Are you shitting me?"

"No," Dr. Levi said shaking his head. "The emphasis is on clinically cured. We are not using the term 'cured' just yet. However, as the marrow transplant results in a new immune system for the patient, and as no traces of the virus can be found in the patient, the outcome appears to be very promising."

"So, some one has beat us to a cure?" Damian asked.

"No, " Dr. Hannah Rosenthal chimed in. "Bone marrow transplants are not a cure, so to speak. These transplants are extremely painful and risky, including the danger of the patient rejecting the marrow. And there is also the risk of what is known as graf-versus-host disease, where the marrow actually attacks the recipient."

"And that's even assuming that the patient can even find a matching donor," Dr. Benjamin Klein told them.

"Right," Dr. Levi nodded. "Bone marrow transplants for every patient with HIV is not possible. So, this is where the fun begins."

The scientist around the table laughed.

"I'm lost," Damian told them.

"Let me try to explain," Dr. Klein said. "What we have found is that there is also a group of patients who have been on anti retroviral drugs for so long, that after we have finally taken them off, they have developed a natural ability to suppress the virus. These people are known as Elite Controllers. And even after being off of anti retrovirals for seven years, their body still maintains very low levels of the virus. And then there is another discovery. We have found that certain people have a rare genetic mutation that blocks HIV from entering into their cells. So, there are in essence, three methods, all of them promising, and all of them natural."

Damian lifted his hand to his face, and stroked his trimmed goatee. "So, the trick is to develop a cure along the lines of what the body is already doing naturally?"

"Exactly!" Dr. Bernstein said joyously. "And that's where we are at!"

"What do you mean where we are at?" Damian asked.

"We never stopped working on different avenues or different cures after RDX-214 and RD-221 came out," Dr. Levi told him. "We continued to push forward, breaking new ground, making new discoveries."

"Really?" Damian asked, perking up. "And where are we at?"

"We are further along than anyone else," Daniella said with a smile.

"Okay, so we can't give everyone bone marrow transplants, and making them an Elite Controller allows them to live without medication, but the virus is not gone," Damian mused. "So, the third way, the genetic mutation. Is there a way to mimic that?"

Dr. Levi clapped his hands. "I think you missed your calling, Damian. You are a very fast learner. Perhaps you should have gone into the bio sciences."

"Yes," Dr. Klein joined in. "Being an Elite controller only suppresses the virus. And, because the virus is still present, there is the fear that pockets of the virus can awaken and re-infect a person. This is why a person with HIV usually has to be on medication for their entire life."

"The trick is to wake up the sleeping pockets, and then target them with drugs to destroy them," Dr. Levi explained. "It's tricky, because the pockets are found in a type of white blood cell, called the Memory T-Cell. And so you have to be careful about crafting a drug that attacks a person's white blood cells."

"And so the third method, the people who are naturally resistant to HIV," Damian stared off. "That appears to be the most promising? Is that what I'm hearing?"

"Even that is not a cake walk," Dr. Bernstein declared. She peered around the table at the lawyers, making sure she had everyone's attention. "Only one percent of the Caucasian population has the right HIV-resistant genetic constitution."

"What?" Damian shouted, sitting up. "Only white folks have a natural genetic resistance to HIV? You mean you folks have done it to us again?"

Laughter shot throughout the room.

"We paid for that with millions of deaths," Dr. Levi said with a smile. "What genetic researchers believe, is that several epidemic events throughout history, resulted in this phenomena. The Plague, is the biggest example of this. It wiped out millions, and caused a genetic mutation to resist the deadly virus. And so, only the people with this mutation were strong enough to survive. Eventually, they mated with none holders of the mutated gene, and so on and so forth, until present day. Now, only one percent of the Caucasian population has this resistance."

"Ain't that a bitch!" Damian said. "White folks crowded

up in England, drinking out of the shitty, contaminated Thames River, and now, centuries later, you people are the only ones that can fight off HIV. History is a motherfucker, isn't it?"

Laughter went around the room.

"So, how do we mimic this genetic mutation in the one percent?" Damian asked. "Can it even be done?"

"Yes," Dr. Bernstein told him. "To make a long story short. We all have a gene in our body called the C-C Chemokine Receptive Type 5, or CCr5 for short. The CCr5 protein is the gene that let's HIV into the key immune cells that it destroys. The trick is to cut off CCr5, or to basically shut it down, remove it, or close it."

"How?" Diane asked. "And what if the virus just goes to another gene?"

"It can, but it doesn't," Dr. Klein told her. "In all the test we've conducted, CCr5 has proven to be its receptor of choice. It just simply won't go anywhere else. And if the virus can't get in to destroy the immune cells, it's just floating around inside, susceptible to destruction."

"As for the how, we can target CCr5 using a restriction enzyme, or restriction endonuclear to basically mutate the genome sequence and cut it out of the picture," Dr. Levi explained.

Damian shook his head. "You went a little egg headish on me there, Doc. You were all doing just fine until them."

Dr. Levi smiled. "We can mutate the gene so the virus can't get into the immune cells and destroy them."

"And then we can just kill the virus?" Damian asked.

"This is where I come back in," Dr. Bernstein told them. "We are going to kill it, by using short chains of amino acids known as antibiotic peptides that we extracted from leucocytes, or rather disease fighting white blood cells that we've managed to synthesize."

"Synthesize?" Damian asked. "Re-recreate, you mean? A

fake version of amino acids from?"

Dr. Bernstein nodded and smiled. She leaned forward. "This does not leave this room. Is that understood?"

Nods went around the table.

"We've managed to synthesize, boost, and even control the white blood cells of the Western Australian Alligator."

"Alligators!" Diane, Kayla, Paula, and Damian all shouted in unison.

"In repeated test, we subjected human serum, and crocodile serum to a host of bacterial strains," Dr. Bernstein told them. "The human serum, managed to destroy only eight bacterial strains. The crocodile serum, killed all 23 strains, including drug resistant bacteria such as MRSA. It even managed to kill a good amount of the IIIV virus. And this was in its natural state. Once we sequenced the peptides, we created a chemical structure that we were able to boost and control, and this synthesized version of the peptides attacked and destroyed every trace of the virus in such a quick and brutal fashion, that it didn't stand a chance."

"And in humans?" Helen Strasser asked, turning up her palms. "If it destroyed the virus that violently, what damage will it do to other cells inside of a human body?"

"None," Dr. Bernstein told her.

"How soon can we be sure?" Helen asked.

"We're sure right now," Dr. Bernstein told her. "Ladies and gentlemen, we have performed this test several times on monkeys that were infected with SIVs, and on mice that were genetically engineered to have human immune systems. In all trials, the virus was destroyed, with no traces, no pockets, and without the use of anti retrovirals. I believe that we've actually done it."

Damian leaned back in his seat, and contemplated what he had just been told. This time it felt right. This time, it felt real. The science had a solid foundation behind it. If only he could get approval to start human trials. The U.S. would never grant it, even one they were presented with all of the documentation. The alternative, would be to set up human trials in a third world country. Which was something that he had always stayed away from. He didn't want to experiment on people just because they came from countries way down the economic ladder. They were still people. And to experiment on them first, only to make billions of dollars later, and cure everyone in the first world, was something his conscience wouldn't allow him to do. He had to find a way. If Bio One survived the lawsuits, he would find a way to make it happen. But the key to it all, was survival. It was for all the marbles now. His company was either going to survive, and blow the fuck up on a cure for HIV, or he was going to go bankrupt, in which case his entire family would be wiped out by their many enemies who were waiting to swoop in and gun them all down in the streets. Something had to give.

Chapter Sixteen

Darius strolled through Princesses living room and out into her lush backyard, where he found his sister by the swimming pool. Lying on a lounge chair next to her, was Julian Jones. Darius was taken aback a little. His sister was engaged to marry Emil, and her business was her business. It wasn't that he was accusing her of anything, but Julian lying next to her, just didn't look right. He would mention that to her later, but right now, he was here on another mission.

"What a pleasant surprise!" Princess said, upon Seeing Darius. "To what do I owe the pleasure of a visit from my baby brother?"

"Nothing," Darius told her. He walked up to her, leaned over and kissed her on her cheek. "Just dropped by for a visit."

"I ain't got it right now," Princess said, shaking her head.

Darius laughed. "Why you think I always want something?"

"Cause that usually when you come to see me," Princess told him. "And you kissed me on the cheek too?"

"Why can't I just be coming for a visit?" Darius asked with a smile.

"What do you want, negro?" Princess asked. "Ain't nobody crazy."

"What's up, young buck?" Julian asked.

"Chilling," Darius said, shaking Julian's hand. Darius took

a seat on the lounge chair on the other side of his sister. He leaned back on the lounge chair and kicked off his white Polo sandals. He pulled his Ralph Lauren sunglasses out of his white Polo shorts, placed them on his eyes and reclined.

Princess stared at her younger brother for several moments, before finally reclining once again. "Um-hum."

"So, what's been happening, young buck?" Julian asked.

"Nothing much," Darius answered.

"Where you gigging at right now?" Julian asked.

"No where. Getting ready to go to work at Energia Oil," Darius told him. "But enjoying my time until it's time to go to work."

"Putting that Harvard business degree to work, huh?" Julian asked.

"He should go back to law school," Princess interjected. "He's actually been accepted to Harvard Law."

Darius rolled his eyes.

"Oh, yeah?" Julian asked, lifting an eyebrow. "Congratulations!"

"I think I'm done with school for now," Darius told them.

"That is so stupid!" Princess said, frustrated about her brother's decision. "You have a golden opportunity to go to the best law school in the country, and you're throwing it away."

"I'm not throwing anything away," Darius told her. "My grades are always going to be the same. My score on the LSAT is not going to change. If I change my mind, I'll go then. But for right now, I'm done with school."

Darius didn't want to have this conversation with his sister, so he decided to change the subject and throw her a curve ball. "So, where's Emil? Haven't seen him in a while."

"Why are you asking about Emil?" Princess asked.

"He's going to be my brother-in-law, so I was just wondering what he's been up to," Darius told her. "Haven't seen him in a while. Julian, you seen him?"

Julian shook his head. "Naw, haven't seen that cat. You know, he's always busy doing other things."

"Like what?" Darius asked. "Not skirt chasing. Not Emil. That brother is as faithful as any I've ever seen. Real good dude."

Princess frowned. "Since when did you fall in love with Emil?"

Darius shrugged. "I'm just saying. I haven't seen the brother around. He needs to come around more often. Check up on everybody."

Princess frowned even more. She knew her brother. He could be an asshole, just like her other brothers. He had a mean streak in him like Dante. The little bastard, she said to herself.

"Speaking of coming through, I came through the other day looking for you, sis," Darius told her. "You weren't here."

"I had to go out of town for a meeting," she told him.

"Yeah, a little chick told me that. She said she was visiting from up north."

Princess thought hard for a few seconds.

"Yeah, old girl," Darius continued. "She was tatted up. Real high yellow, with a gold grill top and bottom. Hair all the way down her back."

"Peaches?" Princess asked. "Is that who you're talking about?"

"Yeah," Darius nodded, trying to be nonchalant. "What's up with old girl?"

"Peaches?" Princess asked again. "You're talking about Peaches? What do you mean what's up with her?"

Julian laughed.

"You know, what's up with her?"

Princess squinted her eyes, taking her brother in for a few moments. "Oh, *hell no*. Don't even think about it. *Put it out of your mind.*"

"Put what out of my mind?" Darius asked.

"Put *her* out of your mind, bro," Princess told him.

"What are you talking about?"

Princess shook her head. "Seriously, she's not for you."

"What makes you say that?" Darius asked.

"Darius, she didn't come up like you, she came up really rough," Princess explained. "She's been in the streets since she was thirteen. She's been dealing drugs, and going from one big time drug dealer to another. She is really fast when it comes to the the streets, and when it comes to dealing with men. She is really rough, and that's the kindest word that I can use to describe her."

"What, you think I'm some kind of simpleton or something?" Darius asked, offended.

"Have you ever killed anyone?" Princess asked flat out.

"No."

"Well, she has," Princess told him. "She's killed quite a few, with her own hands, and had many more killed. She's rough, and ruthless, and cold. She's not for you."

"Rough, and ruthless, and cold," Darius smiled. "Hmmm, sounds like someone I know. Are you sure she's not a relative."

Julian threw his head back in laughter.

Princess frowned. "Don't play with me. *She is not for you!* She's not. Just stay away from her."

"I'm a big boy," Darius told her. "I can take care of myself, and I make my own decisions now. I'm a grown man now, in case you've forgotten."

"Yeah, well remember that the next time you walk in here wanted some money to buy a Ferrari or Porsche, or the latest Benz, or a new condo."

"I'm going to add my two cents in, Big Dog," Julian said. "Your sister is right on this one. Peaches is about to become a member of The Commission. Which means she is going to be in charge of the entire state of Ohio. You don't get to that position, and especially in a state like that, without having left plenty of bodies behind. You have to have done plenty of dirty, underhanded, conniving shit, to have climbed to the top of that violent shit hole. A woman like that, is worst than a black widow. She don't just eat her man when she gets tired of him, she tortures his ass first, and then kills him in the worst kinda way. Leave her alone, young buck. And when she joins The Commission, if people think you're her man, that makes you an even bigger target that she is. They'll kill you, to send a message to her. It ain't worth it."

Julian shook his head. "There's plenty of bitches out there. You pull up in that new Ferrari, and they'll drop their panties for you."

Darius looked off. He wasn't trying to hear either of them. He was a grown ass man, and he knew what he wanted. And right now, he wanted a piece of that dangerous ass pie from Ohio. She was a fly ass bitch, and the fact that she was super ghetto, and really dangerous, only added to his desire. He was going to get that one.

Damian's Mansion

Cherin King and Thomas Voight strolled into Damian's home office. Damian was seated behind his desk. Cherin and Thomas seated themselves in the Queen Anne chairs on the opposite side of his desk.

"What's the deal, dude?" Cherin asked.

"What did you think about the Bio One meeting the other day?" Damian asked.

Cherin shrugged. "If we can survive the lawsuits, then it sounds like Bio One could be onto something big."

Damian leaned back in his chair. "That's a big *if* though. What's your take on the situation?"

"Attorneys always have to be cautious, and they have to give you the worst case scenario," Cherin told him. "However, since I am not the attorney for this case, I can give you my unvarnished opinion. However, do *not* hold me to it."

Damian laughed. "Lawyers, and your disclaimers. Just give it to me raw and uncut. You've always been right on the money, and you've always kept me out of prison and protected me and my businesses. I trust you."

"In my opinion we are going to survive this thing," Cherin told him. "I don't see a jury giving them money for a drug that is keeping them alive, and that's is still the best on the market. Whether it cured the disease or not, no one has died from it, and it's still helping them to suppress their viral levels and live a normal and fulfilling life. I just can't see it. And those attorneys are looking at the same thing."

Damian leaned back and exhaled. "You have just made me feel a whole lot better, and lifted a ton of weight off of my shoulders."

"Well, here is another bit of good news," Thomas told him. "Oil prices are through the roof. We are climbing back up over $100 dollars a barrel again, and Energia Oil is set to rake in record profits."

A huge smile spread across Damian's face. "That's good news. We were cutting it really close for a minute."

Thomas held up his hand. "I'm not finished yet. I have some more good news."

"What's that?" Damian asked. "The more good news, the better. Especially if it involves money."

"Another one of Energia's oil rigs in the gulf just came on line a full two months ahead of schedule," Thomas told him.

172

"It is now operational, and pumping oil. And the pipeline to take oil from the oil rig *Mantis Six*, is up and running as of this morning. Bio One is becoming the cash cow that you always wanted it to be. It's going to give you the breathing room that you desperately needed."

"Wow, that is great news," Damian told them.

"I thought you would like it," Thomas told him. "If oil prices keep rising the way they are, Mantis Six is going to be virtually shooting money across the bottom of the ocean into one of your brand new refineries in Louisiana."

Damian snapped. "Say that again."

"What?" Thomas asked, turning up his palms. "About the oil prices?"

"Shooting money across the bottom of the ocean into a refinery!" Damian leaped up from his seat, raced around the desk, and kissed Thomas on the top of his head. "Damn you, Tommy! That's why I fucking love you!"

"What?" Thomas asked. He and Cherin exchanged glances. Both of them were lost.

"Where in the hell is Dante!" Damian shouted. "Tommy, you just saved my ass, you know that?"

"If you say so," Thomas said shrugging.

Damian lifted Cherin out of her seat, wrapped his arms around her, and spun her around. "Did I ever tell you how fucking beautiful you are?"

"Damian!" Cherin said blushing.

Damian kissed her on her lips. "I love both of you!"

Thomas held up his hands. "Just don't kiss me!"

"I won't!" Damian released Cherin, and ran out of his office and down the hall shouting for joy. Thomas Voight had just given him a brilliant idea.

Deadly Reigns IV

Chapter Seventeen

Daniella strolled across the travertine floors of her luxurious apartment dripping wet. She had just enjoyed a nice steaming hot shower in her rain head shower stall, and was now heading into the kitchen for the second part of her relaxing evening. She made her way to her massive stainless steel Sub Zero refrigerator, opened up the freezer, and pulled out a pint of her favorite Ben and Jerry's ice cream. She had loved Neapolitan ever since she was little girl. Her father used to take her to Baskin and Robbin's every Friday after work, and since she could never make up her mind which flavor she wanted, she would always opt for Neapolitan, that way she could sample them all.

Daniella pulled loose the damp towel she had wrapped around her waist, and re-tightened it. She also pulled loose the towel she had wrapped around her wet hair. Today had been shampoo and conditioning day. Her beauty shop appointment was for tomorrow. And that was the *only* time she wet her hair. Other than the day before her weekly appointment, she kept it dry and looking fierce. Her position as a Bio One department head mandated it.

Daniella tossed the wet towel on her kitchen island, pulled a spoon from a nearby drawer, and headed into her family room with her ice cream. She had a massive flat screen mounted over her fireplace, and it was time for her to sit down and catch up on some of the shows she recorded on her DVR throughout the week. First up, was *Love and Hip Hop*. She wasn't a fan per se, but she loved the drama and foolishness that went on in the show. She watched her first episode out of curiosity, and afterward, she was pretty much hooked. She found it amusing, like so many of the other reality shows on television these days. Besides, after working in a boring, pristine, sterile lab filled with White and Asian people all day, she found it relaxing to unwind and watch some foolery on television.

Daniella plopped down on her creme colored leather sectional, lifted her remote, and switched on her television. An episode of *The First 48* was on. She decided to watch this instead. She loved *The First 48*. She loved the investigation, the hunt, the chase, and especially the forensic side of it. It was the scientist in her. She especially loved the *After The First 48* episodes, where they revisit the cases, show the trial, and show how the family or families have coped since the loss of their loved one. Those were the most heart breaking ones. She even found herself shedding a few tears on a couple of episodes. She was a softy for sure. It was one of the reasons she went into the field of bio science. She wanted to help people, she wanted to cure disease, she wanted to cheat death and spare families the heartache and pain of having to say goodbye to a loved one prematurely. She was a do-gooder, as her brother used to call her. but it was a title she relished.

Daniella leaned back on her sofa, and began to indulge in the creamy goodness of her Ben and Jerry's ice cream. Their Neapolitan had chunks of real strawberries in it, and she relished each chunk of the frozen red fruit that made its way onto her spoon. A hot shower, some delicious ice cream, and one of her favorite shows; life *almost* didn't get any better than this. Plus, she was off the next day, and she could hit the malls and shop after her beauty appointment. Perhaps she could even meet Damian for lunch, and even a secret rendezvous and get her a little bit. Damian hadn't swerved up inside of her in quite some time, and she definitely could use some weenie, she thought. She would call him tomorrow and see if she could hook that up. If not, tomorrow night would be another date with her bullet and her rabbit.

A knock came to her door, and Daniella sat up. She placed her ice cream down on one of the end tables next to her sectional, and rose. She wasn't expecting anyone, and guest usually didn't drop by unannounced. It wasn't like she had many friends to began with, and even fewer who actually knew where she lived, or felt comfortable enough to come to her house. And even weirder, was the fact that the desk downstairs didn't buzz her and let her know that she had a guest. She was definitely going to point that out to the building manager the next time she came across him.

Daniella exhaled, and headed for her door. She didn't want to be bothered this evening. Not unless it was Damian, with a really hard dick. She would definitely excuse the intrusion then. Daniella took a few more steps toward the door, and then the unthinkable occurred. A thunderous boom echoed throughout her unit as her door was kicked in. A secondary crash echoed as well, once the door swung full course and struck the wall. Five large Hispanics rushed into her penthouse.

"C'mere, bitch!" the first one shouted.

Daniella turned and raced for her bedroom. The men chased after her. She managed to make it into her bedroom, close the door, and lock it before they could reach her. The bedroom door was solid. Not as solid as her front door, which told her that it would only be seconds before they breached that door as well. She panicked and froze.

"Phone!" she shouted. Daniella willed her frozen feet to move. She raced for her dresser where her cordless phone was resting in its base. And then another thought hit her. She quickly raced to the side of the dresser, and pushed it in front of her bedroom door. At least that would surprise them on the initial kick. They would have to adjust their strength and re-kick, or at least have to use a couple of kicks to get in. She peered around the room for more furniture. Her king sized bed was the largest and heaviest object in the room. She raced to the side of her bed, and using every ounce of her strength, pushed the massive bed up against the dresser.

Daniella lifted her cordless phone and to her surprise, it still had a dial tone. The fools hadn't cut her phone lines. That told her a lot. This had to be some idiots doing a home invasion, and they picked her at random. Perhaps the fact that she had made it into her bedroom would scare them off. They didn't know if she was armed or not. Maybe they would think that she had made it to a gun that she had hidden in her closet or something. She decided to play up that bluff.

"I have my gun, you assholes!" Daniella shouted. She dialed 911 as quickly as her panicking fingers would allow. The operator came on line. "Hello! I need the police! Some men, they just kicked in my door."

"Are you safe, ma'am?" the operator asked.

"Hell no I'm not safe!" Daniella shouted. "I just told you, some assholes just kicked in my front door."

"The police are in route," the operator told her. "Are you in a separate room. Is there a safe place that you can hide until the police arrive?"

"I'm hiding in my bedroom!" Daniella shouted. "I've barricaded the door."

"Good," the operator replied. "Is there a window where you can escape if you need to?"

"No!" Daniella snapped. "I'm in a building! In the penthouse! Just tell them to hurry!"

The first kick at her bedroom door did little.

"I'm going to shoot!" Daniella shouted.

The second kick splintered her door jamb and only managed to move the furniture a couple of centimeters. Daniella raced to the bed post, and pushed it, which in turn pushed the dresser, and caused the door to shut. But the lock was ineffective. They intruders had splintered the door frame near the lock. Another solid kick came, and this one moved her, the dresser, and the bed back a couple of inches. And then her attackers got wise. She hadn't fired. And their heavy kicks where moving things and causing an opening. All five men rushed to the door and began to push.

Daniella weighed one hundred and fifty pounds, and despite her most ardent effort, she was unable to make a difference. Slowly the gap in the bedroom door grew wider and wider, until finally, she had to abandon her efforts, and race into the master bathroom and lock herself inside.

"I'm warning you!" she shouted through the door. "I don't want to shoot, but I will if I have to!"

A solid boom announced the arrival of her intruders. The bathroom door flew open, and the five men rushed inside. One of them grabbed her by her hair and she screamed.

"Why didn't you shoot, *Puta*?" Amiguel asked.

"What were you going to shoot us with, your finger?" Benito asked with a smile.

"Please, don't hurt me?" Daniella told them. "Take whatever you want. Please, I won't call the cops."

"You've already called them, *Puta*," Carlos told her. "That's why we can't stay long. We were going to have a little fun with you, but now, we just have to get it over with and leave."

"Get what over with?" Daniella asked nervously. Surely, they weren't going to rape her, she thought. The police would catch them before they could finish that dastardly act.

Carlos nodded toward Diego, the fourth man in the crew,

who pulled out a plastic bag and wrapped it around Daniella's head. She tried to kick and fight, and tear a hole in the plastic. Eduardo, the fifth man, along with Amiguel, and Benito, grabbed her hands and held them, while Carlos suffocated her. Daniella kicked and struggled as violently as she could, but to no avail. Soon, her body wimp limp.

"Get the balloon," Amiguel told Diego.

Diego handed Amiguel a fully inflated red balloon, along with a black permanent marker. Amiguel scrawled the words 'WAIT' on the balloon, and tied it around Daniella's neck. He also scribbled the word "WAIT" across her forehead, and then again on the bathroom mirror. He wanted to make sure that the Reigns family got the message. The Northern Mexican Cartels were serious about The Commission waiting for the border to re-open, and about The Commission not taking its business elsewhere. Billions of dollars were at stake, and they needed to send a very serious, attention getting message. They were not playing about their money.

WEST TEXAS

Desire could not believe the size and scope of the Double R ranch. Being a native Texan, she was used to large ranches, and could even ride of a horse with the best of them, but the ranches back in East Texas were nowhere near the size or complexity of the Reigns family's operation. Desire grew up in a suburb of Houston, or at least, that was the place she claimed as home. Being a military brat she had traveled the globe and lived on practically every continent with her parents. And despite her worldly travels, she was still impressed by the man who was riding beside her at that moment.

"This place is so beautiful, Dante," Desire declared. She peered into the sunset, shielding her eyes from its rays with her hand.

"I forget how beautiful it is sometimes," Dante admitted. "I get so caught up in the hustle and bustle of business, and travel, and city life. Coming out here was good for me. It reminded me of how important it is to slow down and enjoy some of life's simple pleasures. My wife used to do that for me. We had a dream. She used to say that we were going to just leave everything behind, move to Africa, and travel the continent."

"Doesn't sound like a bad plan," Desire said with a smile. She reached out, and placed her hand on top of his. "I'm glad that you came out here as well. I'm glad that I met you. I'm sorry about the circumstances under which we met. I want you to believe me when I say that. From the bottom of my heart, I wish that Angela had been here to help you with Lucky."

Dante nodded. "I know."

"Dante we've been hanging out for a couple of weeks now, and well, there's something that we haven't discussed," Desire told him. "It's like there is this enormous elephant in the room, and we're both trying to ignore it."

Dante dismounted, and clasped the reigns of his horse. Desire did the same.

"C'mon, let me show you one of the most beautiful parts of the ranch," Dante told her. "The river."

Desire nodded, and she and her horse followed just behind Dante and his horse.

"I can only guess what the elephant in the room is," Dante continued. "But you know what? Whatever you feel it is, I want to get it out. And I'll give you my word, that I'll tell you the truth. I don't want there to be any lies between us. But remember this, Desire, don't ask a question unless you really want to know the answer to it."

Desire smiled. "I'm a reporter, remember? I'm nosey by career choice. Any question that I ask, I definitely want to know the answer to."

Dante led the horses to the river, and allowed them to drink. "Okay, so shoot."

"Tell me about the rumors, Dante," Desire said flatly. "You can just as easily say that it's none of my business. I mean, we're not married, or engaged, or anything like that. And your business, is your business. It's just that with something that big, going unspoken between us..."

"I understand," Dante said nodding. "So, let me ask you this question first."

"Shoot."

"When we met at the grocery store, was that by chance?" Dante asked.

Desire nodded. "I'm not calculating like that. It was completely by chance. I would never use your little girl to get to you. Never."

"Are you doing a story on me or my family?" Dante asked.

"No," Desire told him. Tears began to well up in her eyes. That such thoughts could cross Dante's mind, disturbed her deeply. She hoped that he'd thought better of her. But it was she who brought up the elephant in the room, and these subjects were also enormous elephants. She couldn't start the game, and not want to play it.

Dante nodded. "Okay, your turn."

"Are the rumors about you family true?" Desire asked. "About them being involved in organized crime?"

"Yes," Dante told her. He was unsure the moment he answered. He didn't know if his answer would cause him to have to kill her later. He didn't want that. But for some mysterious reason, he wanted her to know the truth.

"Yes?" Desire repeated, stammering out the word. "You said... yes."

Dante nodded. "I did."

"Organized crime? Like, the mob?"

Again, Dante nodded.

"But, you're Black," Desire said, still shocked at his admission. "I mean, that's like Italian, or Sicilian type of stuff. And you're from Texas. When someone thinks of the mafia, they think of New York, New Jersey, The Sopranos."

Dante laughed. "I'm not Italian, or Sicilian, and I am from Texas. And no, we're not the mob, or the mafia, or anything like that."

"Then what is it?"

"A long time ago, my parents started several businesses," Dante explained. "And they were successful businesses. And over time, those businesses grew and expanded. And then one day, my father's business partner, screwed him out of a lot of money, and left my father, and my family in a lot of debt. We were facing ruin. I was in college at the time. And my sister, who had graduated, went out, and started making some moves that were not exactly legal. She got involved with some really tough people, and she did what she felt she had to do, to raise the money to save our family, and keep us off the street, and keep my father out of prison. She did what she had to do, to save her family. And she did it. And once I graduated from college, I went to work for her and helped her to protect my family from all of our business enemies. Legal, and illegal. It was never about the money, or the power, or anything remotely like that. It was always about protecting the people we love. I vowed that I would never let anyone hurt my father or mother, or take advantage of them like that again. When you see your mother sitting at the kitchen table in tears, worried about losing her home, worried about being tossed out on the street, worried about the IRS taking her husband to jail, it stays with you. That feeling, it's a feeling deep down inside of you, it's a feeling that no one should ever have to feel. It makes you feel worthless, like less than a man. And so I made a vow, that my mother would never cry because of something like that, ever again. It's always been about family. Do you understand?"

Desire peered into the distance. She understood completely what he was saying. She felt the same way about her father. He meant the world to her. She could still see him walking through the door in his Army uniform, and she could still see herself racing into his big strong arms. Her father was her life, and still was to that very day. So she could understand Dante's emotions, and his reasons for doing whatever it was that he did. But what exactly was it, that he had done for his family? Had he murdered? Or ordered the death of other men? Who was this man standing before her, she wondered? Who was this man who loved his daughter, loved his mother, loved his father, loved his sister, who loved horses, and sunsets, and ranching, and the simple things in life? Who was he? Her feelings for Dante were strong, and growing stronger with each of their encounters. They had been virtually inseparable for the last three weeks, with the exception of a few business trips on each of their ends. And she knew that she was falling hard for him.

"I understand," Desire said nodding.

"So, I guess we got that out in the open?" Dante asked.

Again, Desire nodded. He was a family man, and that was that. What real man wouldn't step up and do what was necessary to help his family? That didn't make him bad, it made him human. People were always quick to label others, particularly when it fit their narrative, or their own agendas. They labeled this man's family as having dealings with organized crime. But they ignored Joe Kennedy's bootlegging until long after he and his sons were long gone. At least Dante had given her a reason for his family's venture into the underworld, and it was for something a lot more noble than money. The question was, how deep in the underworld were they, and whether or not they even still delved into illegal activities. Those were things she would find out in time. But for right now, she was satisfied knowing that the man in front of her, wasn't some evil crime lord. He was a loving son, a good brother, and an even better father.

"So, I guess there is only one other thing that we need to get past then," Dante told her.

"What's that?" Desire asked.

Dante stepped to her, lifted his hand to her face and moved her hair back over her ears. He pulled her close, and kissed her. Their kiss was soft and gentle at first, but slowly built to one of passion. Their tongues intertwined, and Dante pulled her bottom lip into his mouth sucking gently, tasting it. He wanted to taste her. He wanted to sample her entire body. And Desire was ready for him. She had been without a boyfriend for more than a year. Her last boyfriend, turned out to be a two timing major in the Army, who had two different sets of family back East. Her career had kept her too busy to rebound quickly or to even go out on a single date. She was fortunate for the story along the border, and to have some downtime while covering it. She owed her boss a bottle of Krug for making her take the assignment. It was an assignment that everyone back at the headquarters tried to avoid. She now considered herself fortunate for having drawn the short straw during the straw pull. Standing next to a beautiful river and kissing one of the sexiest, richest Black men on the planet, beneath the rays of a beautiful sunset, was like a fairytale come true. She had found her beautiful Black Knight, she thought. And it all happened on a humbug trip to the supermarket, during a bullshit assignment to a boring ass desert. The Man Upstairs surely had a twisted sense of humor, Desire thought. She silently thanked Him, for bringing Dante into her lonely life.

Deadly Reigns IV

Chapter Eighteen

"Ahhhhhh!" Damian shouted. He raked everything off his desk onto the floor.

"Boss, calm down," Nicanor told him.

Damian stared at the balloon he held in his hands with the word 'WAIT' scrawled on it. His brown skin turned copper, as the blood bled into his face. His expression was one of sheer fury. He squeezed the giant red balloon until it popped.

"Damian, calm down," Nicanor repeated.

"I will not calm down!" Damian shouted. "Where the fuck is Dante?"

"I've sent a message to him," Nicanor said calmly.

"What the fuck is he still doing in West Texas?" Damian shouted. "His fucking ass should have been here! I need him here!"

Nicanor nodded toward the other men in the room, and they hurried out, closing the door to Damian's office behind them. He turned to Damian. "It might be a good thing that he's still in West Texas."

"Why the fuck is that?" Damian shouted. "He's fucking around out there, and I have fucking cartel members roaming around the city killing off my scientist!"

"Because, that puts him closer to Mexico, and it puts him in a better position to retaliate," Nicanor explained.

"Tell him to get on it!" Damian shouted. "I want those

motherfuckers dead! Tonight! I want them to feel it!"

"Damian, you are too close to this thing," Nicanor said calmly. "Don't let your relationship with Daniella cloud your judgment. We have to think this thing through."

"What is there to think through?" Damian asked, through clenched teeth. "I've got enemies roaming around my backyard, Damian is fucking around in West Texas, who the fuck knows where Princess is, Angela is dead, Bio One is near death, and the feds have shut down my other operations. I have motherfuckers trying me right and left, Nick. It's time to send those motherfuckers a message back."

Nicanor nodded. "I understand. Like I said, I already sent a messenger to brief Dante. I'll send another out, telling him to get to Juarez, and to let the Cartels know we got their message, and to show them how we felt about it."

"Make them bleed, Nicanor!" Damian said forcefully. "I want them to feel it!"

"Damian, Nicanor is right."

Startled, Damian and Nicanor quickly shifted their gaze toward the door to his office. Stacia was standing in the doorway. She was looking fierce in a black Ferragamo pants suit, with a black brim tilted slightly to the side.

"Stacia!" Damian's eyes flew wide. "What are you doing here?"

"I'm here to help you," Stacia told him. "And apparently, it's a good thing that I'm here. Damian, Nicanor is right. I want you to calm down. Now is not the time to get yourself all worked up."

Stacia strolled into the office. "I want you to calm down. Don't work yourself into another stroke."

"I'm not." Damian wrapped his arms around her and hugged her tight. "It's good to see you."

"It's good to see you too," Stacia said, kissing him on the cheek. "You need to take care of yourself, Boo."

"I'm taking care of myself," Damian told her. "It's just that these son of a bitches are pushing me. They think that we're weak, because of Bio One's problems."

Stacia wrapped her arms around Damian, and gently kissed him on the top of his head. "Let them think that. That's okay. And just when they think that you're at your weakest, and they've lowered their guard, you strike. We never strike when we're angry, have you forgotten that. That's what they want. When you're angry, and you're reacting to their actions, then they are in control. We are smoother than that. We are colder than that. We are smarter than that. We are Reigns. And that means, that they know it's coming. Once they pull the tiger's tail, they know they're in trouble. The trick is to not let them know when it's coming. We torture them, we make them suffer by waiting. And waiting is worse than actual death. You know how we do it, baby."

Damian smiled. Stacia's cool, calming voice soothed him. She reminded him so much of the glory days of the Reigns family. Those were the days when they felt like they could do anything. She reminded him of who they really were, and how they really did things. That was the one thing that he missed the most. The cool, calm, calculating touch of a woman's presence. Especially a Reigns woman. And although he never married Stacia, she was more of a Reigns than any of the other women in his life. They had grown up together, and they had loved one another through it all. Through the years, the time, the distance, their other relationships, through all of the other ups and downs, challenges, and adversity that life had thrown their way. If their ever were two people who were soul mates, it was them. Stacia had born Damian many children, and he loved her from a distance.

"Have you taken your blood pressure medicine today?" Stacia asked.

Damian nodded.

"Good. Now don't work yourself into a frenzy. I'll find Princess, and Nicanor has already sent word to Dante. We'll handle it."

"The way I want it handled?" Damian asked.

"You want them to get the message, then we'll make sure that they get the message."

"They can't come into my front yard and kill my people," Damian declared.

"Understood," Stacia said, crossing her arms. "And you should let them know that something like that is a no no. They killed one of your bitches, you kill one of theirs."

Damian shook his head. "They won't give a fuck. I want one of their main men to take a hit. I want this to be more than just a hard slap on the wrist. I want them to feel it."

"Is this going to escalate the situation?" Nicanor asked.

"What are they going to do?" Stacia asked. "Not sell us any dope?"

Nicanor laughed. She was right. But then again. "What if they feel the need to hit back even harder?"

"And war with us?" Stacia asked. "In the States? They couldn't. Cartel members running around killing American citizens left and right, would earn them the wrath of the American government. Two, they can't afford to piss off The Commission. Three, they are already at war with one another. The winner of this little power struggle they're having, will still need to do business with The Commission. No, this message was sent from Juarez, I suspect. And they should be reminded who the fuck we are."

Damian smiled. He missed Stacia's strength. She reminded him of who he was. She made him feel invincible. He decided to tell her.

"I miss you, Stacia," Damian said softly. "I miss having you around here."

Again, Stacia kissed him on top of his head. "I know.

And I miss being around here. But what was I supposed to do? Sit around all day, or shop all day, and play the roll of a spoiled baby momma? That's not me. After my divorce with Michael, I had to get a change of scenery. I needed to get away, and luckily, my career advancement allowed me to do just that."

"And you and Michael both ended up getting transferred to D.C.," Damian smiled. "Life is funny isn't it?"

"I got transferred to Washington," Stacia corrected him. "That asshole got transferred to Baltimore. I think he did that shit on purpose."

"And how is dear old dad?" Damian asked.

"Rising higher and higher," Stacia said with a smile. "And still wanting you dead."

"Dead?" Damian lifted an eyebrow. "Wow. That's an escalation. I thought he only wanted to see me rotting in prison?"

The three of them shared a laugh.

"So, what really brought you into town, Stacia?" Damian asked.

"Our son," she said, allowing her laughter to trail off slowly. "I heard that Dallas was involved in an incident."

Damian shook his head. "I'm sorry. I should have told you. I just didn't want you to worry, and I didn't want you to get upset with me."

"I'm his mother," Stacia told him. "I have a right to worry. Yes, you should have told me. And no, I wouldn't have blamed you. They went after my baby, and I have a right to know who, and why, and all of the other details."

"Cedras..."

"I know," Stacia said, stopping him in mid sentence. "I know who did it. And now, that son of a bitch, is going to have to feel my wrath. No one, goes after my baby."

"He was trying to send a message to me," Damian told her.

"I understand that," Stacia said, rubbing Damian head.

191

"But somebody should have told that motherfucker who was who, so that he could get at the right motherfuckers. He went after my baby, and so now, I'm involved. I have the ear of the Attorney General of the United States of America, and my father is the third highest ranking member of this nations Federal Bureau of Investigations. He has fucked up royally. I am personally, going to spend every waking moment, putting his name and organization in all of the right people's ear. I am going to make sure that the DEA, and The State Department, and The Department of Defense, and The Colombian government, crawls deep up his ass. I am personally going to either walk the Presidential Finding for his assassination over to the Department of Defense, or I am going to personally put the handcuffs on his ass when he his transferred into the custody of The Justice Department. Either way, my new mission in life, will be to fuck him up."

"Wow!" Nicanor said, whistling.

Damian pulled her into his lap. "You are so fucking sexy when you're pissed."

"What's that?" Stacia asked.

"You made my dick hard," Damian whispered.

"Well, we need to take care of that," Stacia whispered back. She leaned over and kissed Damian passionately on his lips.

Juarez, Mexico

Gregario Munoz was the number three man in the Juarez Cartel. He was the brains behind the cartels operations. Galindo was the undisputed leader, Antonio was the accountant and money man, while Nuni was the muscle. Gregario was the strategist in the organization. And he not only planned the Cartel's business strategy, but was also the chief architect of its wartime moves as well. He was the chess master for the Juarez Cartel, the one who saw six moves ahead.

Gregario had been brought up on the streets of Juarez. He lived next door to Galindo. And while Galindo had been a B and C student while growing up, Gregario had made straight A's. He went on to study at Mexico's prestigious Universidad Nacional Autonoma de Mexico, where he majored in mechanical engineering. He had planned to spend his life working for the oil company as an engineer, before Galindo's rise through the ranks of the underworld. His childhood friend pulled him into his organization with the lure of more money, and all of the woman he could stand. It was his appetite for women that sealed the deal. It was Gregario's weakness. It was also what had him out shopping today. He was leaving the jewelry store after buying a ten carat diamond bracelet for his favorite mistress.

"She's going to love this!" Gregario said, lifting the bracelet into the air and examining it. "Daddy is going to get much pussy tonight."

Gregario's chief bodyguard broke into laughter. The armored Escalade limousine that they were riding in, made a left, and ran smack into traffic.

"Dammit!" Gregario shouted. "I knew you should have taken the other way home! I hate this fucking traffic."

"It's downtown, boss!" the driver said shrugging. "You know how traffic is this time a day."

"Make a left at the next light, and take the back streets," Gregario ordered. "I don't want to be stuck in traffic all day."

"Yes, sir," the driver told him.

Gregario bodyguards peered around the streets, taking in their busy surroundings. They weren't worried, as they were in their own territory, and the Escalade they were riding in had

Level IV+ armoring. It could stop a fully automatic fifty caliber machine gun firing armor piercing rounds. It would shrug off grenades, RPG's and anything short of a anti-tank missile, or a damn tank itself. They were checking out the scene, simply because they were professionals.

Dante peered down at the armored limousine and smiled. Gregario was smart, and he had gone to the best to get his armored Escalade. Dante knew that unless he had an anti-tank missile, that he wouldn't be able to penetrate the limo. And although he did have a few of them in his inventory, firing one in the middle of a crowded street in Juarez would only serve to get a couple of his men caught, tortured, and killed. So he had to think of another way.

Dante had paid a pretty penny to get men into the city's public works department. The Juarez Cartels had the police department on lock, so he had to get men inside wherever he could. The public works department was one place where he found low paid public servants who the cartels had ignored, and who were more than willing to get on the Reigns family payroll. Today, they came in handy.

Dante had the public works department suddenly have to do repairs on certain streets downtown, in order to channel traffic into certain bottlenecks. He wanted to make sure that traffic ran past certain streets, and this was one of them. If he couldn't use an anti-tank missile in Juarez, then he would use something that would deliver just as much force. He just had to make sure that his target was in the right place.

Dante lifted his walkie-talkie. "He's in position right now."

"Roger that, boss," the voice on the other side of the communicator acknowledged.

Dante peered down at the armored limo stuck in traffic thirty stories below and smiled. It had all become too easy for him. Motherfuckers planned for the expected, not the unexpected. They planned to counter bullets, and grenades, and rockets, and ambushes, and even land mines. But they never thought outside the box. He would never allow Damian or himself to travel downtown, especially anywhere near a construction site. People thought of security as protection against an oncoming enemy, and very few of them ever planned against an enemy from above, unless it was a sniper in window. In this case, it was going to be a four thousand pound reinforced steel beam, dropping thirty feet through the roof of a limo. No armoring company armored the top of their vehicles. No one expected major attacks from above.

"Let the beam fall," Dante told him.

"Roger."

The top floor crane released the steel beam, and Dante watched as the monstrous beam picked up speed as it fell toward the street below. A few people on the ground saw the beam coming, screamed, and ran for their lives. Inside of the limo, they never knew what hit them.

The massive beam struck the limo with the force of a small atomic explosion. The SUV was completely obliterated, and what was left, was pancaked beneath a four thousand pound, six foot wide, thirty foot long piece of steel. A single Escalade wheel could be seen rolling down the street out of the cloud of smoke and dust. Dante hit the button on the construction lift, opening the door. He walked out onto the top floor of the building with a huge grin on his face. He could see one of his family's black vertical take off and landing aircraft in the distance, making its way toward the building. He wanted a quick exit for he and his men, and couldn't risk a getaway through the traffic jam that he had created.

Dante peered down at the wreckage once again and smiled. Damian wanted to send a message, and he had just sent a helluva message. He had just taken out the Juarez Cartel's chief strategist. It would be a devastating blow. It was also going to prolong the war in Mexico between the cartels, and perhaps even turn the tide. Without Gregario's brain to strategize, it was anyone's guess who would now come out on top. Things were about to get even bloodier in Mexico, because instead of a smart strategy, it was just going to be about killing. The game was now about who could kill off the other guy's men faster than they could recruit new ones. Damian's message would fuck up the drug trade in Northern Mexico for an extended period, but they didn't give a fuck. They had a deal with the Yucatan Cartels, and if Damian's new plan worked, they wouldn't need to fuck with those Juarez boys ever again.

Chapter Nineteen

Energia Oil Platform # 11, AKA, *The Great Explorer*, was a massive semi-submersible offshore oil production platform. It was the flagship of Energia Oil, and currently the largest oil platform in existence. *The Great Explorer* displaced some 140,000 tons, carried a length of some 450 feet, a beam of some 370 feet, a draught of some 100 feet, and a crew of 300. It was a state of the art oil facility, with the ability to drill, extract, process, and store several metric tons of oil. It was currently deployed in the Gulf of Mexico, off the coast of Louisiana. It was because of this proximity to Louisiana, that Anjounette was now on board. She lifted her cell phone and called Damian.

"Hello?" Damian answered.

"Hey, D," Anjounette greeted in turn. "I'm here with the engineers now. We just finished up the meeting. According to the engineers, what you're proposing is feasible."

"Feasible?" Damian asked. "I need a straight up answer, and no scientific mumbo jumbo. This isn't a study in some esoteric engineering theory, I need a straight up, yes or no. Can it be done?"

"It can be done," Anjounette told him. She turned to the engineers standing next to her. "I have Dave Ngomo, the Offshore Installation Manager, and Charles Oghenero, The Offshore Operations Engineer. They can speak to you about the engineering part of it a lot better than I can."

"Put Charlie on the phone," Damian told her.

Anjounette handed her cell phone to the offshore ops engineer.

"Hello, Boss?" Charles said, greeting Damian.

"Charlie, how's it going?" Damian asked.

"Everything is going well."

"Good," Damian said. "So, what's the deal with my proposal? Can it be done?"

"It can be done," Charles told him. "As long as there is proper containment on the other end. The offshoot gasses are going to be highly toxic, and highly flammable. They are going to have to be bled from the room, before it can be safe to walk into. As long as the facilities are in place to bleed off the gasses and store them until they can be processed, then it shouldn't be a problem."

"And the pressure in the pipe?" Damian asked.

"The pipe will be able to withstand the pressure without a problem," Charles told him.

"Are you sure?"

"I can guarantee it," Charles said, with a toothy grin that displayed the wide gap between his front teeth.

"Get your team working on the plug, and then catch a chopper to the refinery and get to working on the room we'll need to bring the plugs in and remove the gasses," Damian ordered. "I want this project up and running yesterday. Use whatever money, manpower, and resources you need to get this thing going ASAP. This is a priority one project. You have any problems, you contact me directly. You got that?"

"Yes, sir."

"You pull this off, you get a big ass bonus on your next paycheck, Charlie."

"Yes, sir!"

Night - San Antonio, Texas

The Candy Shop was Dante's premiere night club. It was where the youngsters hung out, and because of the beautiful exotic cars that he always kept at the club, either out in front, sitting in the lobby, or spinning around on an elevated turntable in the middle of the dance floor, the club stayed hot. After five years of going strong, it still remained the hottest club in the city.

"Y'all ready to bounce?" DeMarion asked.

"Where we going to eat?" Darius asked.

Peaches rubbed her stomach. "I could use some IHOP."

Darius peered down at his Rolex. "It's 3 O'clock."

"So, IHOP stays open all night!" Peaches told him. "At least it does in the rest of the country. Don't tell me y'all shut it down about 11 down here."

"Ha, that's real funny," Darius told her. "Naw, we keep it open. And the good thing about restaurants staying open down here, is that they don't have to worry about niggaz running in and robbing them all hours of the night."

"Oh, so you got jokes about Ohio, huh?" Peaches asked with a smile.

"You got jokes about Texas," Darius smiled back. "You been cracking on my state since you been here. Like we just down right country or something."

"Y'all niggaz is country," Peaches told him.

"Y'all niggaz is country," DeMarion repeated, mocking her.

"Oh and you don't even wanna start, pretty ass motherfucka!" Peaches shouted. She was highly inebriated. "You come to Columbus, and you'll be everybody's bitch."

"You got me fucked up!" DeMarion told her. "Don't let these handsome looks fool you!"

"Nigga you ain't handsome, you pretty!" Peaches said, bursting out in an alcoholic laugh.

"Let's get the fuck outta here!" Darius said.

"Who's driving?" DeMarion said. He peered at his cousins. They were fifteen deep. "I got a two seater."

"You can roll with me and Peaches," Darius told him.

"Cool."

DeMarion followed Darius and Peaches out to the parking lot, where they climbed inside of Darius's white Porsche Panamera GTS.

"Damn, nigga, scoot your seat up!" DeMarion protested from the back seat.

"Oh tall ass nigga," Darius said, motoring his power seat forward.

Peaches climbed inside, and ran her hand over the leather stitching of the dashboard. "I wish my brother could hook me up."

"This old spoiled ass nigga get's everything he wants," DeMarion said, slapping Darius across the back of his neck.

"Quit playing, soft ass nigga!" Darius told his cousin.

"I got your soft!" DeMarion replied.

Peaches leaned back in her seat. Her head felt like it weighed a ton, and she could feel the warmth of the alcohol radiating throughout her body. She lifted her hand and ran it across the side of Darius's cheek.

Darius had been trying hard since Peaches' arrival back in town. He had taken her out to dinner twice, he had taken her for a walk along the River Walk, he had taken her on a horse and carriage ride through the center of town, and he had even taken her to Six Flags Fiesta Texas amusement park, where he won her a Teddy Bear. Peaches thought that his advances were lame at first. He was a soft ass rich kid, who didn't know how to mack. He was used to dating little girls, and he wasn't ready for a real woman like her, she told herself. And then, as time went by, she realized that his game wasn't lame, it's just that she was used to a different kind of guy. She was used to gangsters and thugs, and had grown used to their idea of what a date was.

Once she had rose in the dope game, even before, as a matter of fact, niggas always showered her with gifts. They gave her gold, or platinum, and showered her with Dom P., or showed off by ordering bottles of Crystal, and tables full of lobster and shrimp, and by taking her to the VIP sections of whatever event they were attending. They threw money out like it grew on trees, and as a young girl she equated that with love. No man had ever won anything for her. No man, had ever taken her on a carriage ride, or offered her his jacket when he thought she was cold. No man, had ever taken her on a roller coaster ride, or to an amusement park for that matter. Men treated her like she was a trophy, while growing up. They took her beauty, and they put gold teeth in her mouth, they put tattoos on her body, and they made her look like the hood chick that they wanted. And she had gone through quite a few dope boys while growing up. And all of them had ended up either going to prison, or getting killed. Not one, not two, not some, and not a few, but all. And after one would get taken out, she would find comfort or security in the arms of another one. It was how she grew up on the streets. Find a dope boy to take care of you. She went from one to another, until she decided to learn the game on her own. It was from her last few dope boyfriends that she learned the game. And it was from her last boyfriend that she was able to gain control of a bomb ass cocaine connection, and all of his contacts and crew. That's how she finally broke the cycle of being dope boy arm candy, and being a boss herself. She had been on the streets since the age of thirteen, and she had seen it all and done it all. She was damaged goods, of that she was certain. But somehow, Darius saw past all of that. She knew that he had to have known about her past, and yet when he touched her, or held her in his arms, he treated her as if he were handling fine china. His eyes spoke volumes about his feelings for her. He was like a puppy dog, who had finally found a child that he could love. And that's what scared her more than anything.

Darius was not her type. He was a spoiled little rich kid, who had always had money, and everything else that he wanted. He wasn't hood, he wasn't street, and his brother was Damian Reigns, head of the most powerful drug family in the country. Darius was twenty two, and fresh out of Harvard. What could he do for her? He was soft as cotton. What could come out of a relationship with him? She could use him to get close to his brother, but what would that do? The Reigns family was already backing her for a position on The Commission. They were going to help her consolidate her power on all of Ohio. She was about to become even richer than she was right now. Rich beyond her wildest dreams. She wouldn't need Damian's money or power pretty soon. And, once she was on The Commission, she would be a full member in her own right. She would have full control over everything that happens in her state. She would have the money to recruit thousands of cats from Dayton, Cleveland, Cincinnati, and Columbus. She would be able to crush most of the other members on the Commission once she got her bread up enough to pay for that many soldiers. So, needing to get close to Damian, wouldn't be a reason to hook up with Darius. And shutting the door on him right now, wouldn't hurt either. She was already set to become a member of The Commission, and Damian wouldn't change his mind because she didn't want to fuck his brother. So, why keep this little lost puppy around, she wondered? He couldn't come back to Ohio with her. They would eat him alive the moment she left his side. Niggaz in

Ohio were vicious, and ruthless. He would be hanging from a telephone pole within hours. So what would be the purpose of this relationship?

Darius pulled up to IHOP and pulled into a parking spot. DeMarion was snoring in the back seat.

"I ought to leave his ass in here," Darius said.

Peaches laughed.

Darius and Peaches climbed out of the Porsche, and Darius opened the back door, and shook his cousin's leg.

"Wake up, fool!" Darius shouted.

DeMarion peered around his surroundings, He wiped some drool from the right corner of his mouth, and then stretched and yawned. "Where we at?"

"We at the IHOP, nigga!" Darius told him. "C'mon. I hope you didn't pee in my back seat."

"Fuck you!" DeMarion told him.

"You know how you used to do it when we were kids," Darius said smiling. "A nigga used to have to wear a scuba suit when he spent the night at your house."

"I'll pee on you right now, nigga!" DeMarion told him climbing out the back seat of the Porsche.

Darius walked to where Peaches was standing, and reached for her hand. It was something else that she wasn't used to. She still thought it was corny.

A beige Chevy Silverado crew cab pickup rolled up, and the windows slid down. DeMarion was the first one to see the barrel come out of the window.

"Kinfolk, gun!" DeMarion screamed. "Get down!"

The shotgun blast went off, causing sparks to fly through the air, lighting up the early morning darkness. Darius threw Peaches out of the way, and fell on top of her. DeMarion whipped out his nine millimeter Sig Sauer pistol, and returned fire. Peaches pulled out her nine millimeter Glock, and while lying on the ground, returned fire as well. Darius rolled off of

203

her, pulled out his nine millimeter H&K pistol, and also opened
fire. A chopper came out of the rear window of the truck, and
opened up. The sound of the AK-47's 7.62 millimeter rounds
ripping through the air and bouncing off of cars filled the area.
Darius crawled behind the tire of a nearby vehicle, and pulled
Peaches behind it with him.

"What the fuck, man?" Peaches screamed. Sparks were
flying off of the ground near her, as the bullets struck close.
"That chopper is going to tear our ass up!"

"D!" Darius screamed. "Are you alright, man?"

"I'm here!" DeMarion shouted. "They fucked up my high
though!"

Darius smiled. The sound of AK bullets penetrating the
door of the car they were hiding behind, caused his smile to
quickly dissipate. The car then shifted and went lower, as the
tires went flat.

"We're sitting ducks out here!" Peaches told him. "When
that truck pulls around, and that chopper starts singing, with
that gauge going off as well, we're in trouble. And no telling
what else they got in that truck. I'm sure that there's a third
motherfucker who going to be waiting for us to take off
running from that AK. That's the one who's gonna get us."

"How do you know this?" Darius asked.

"Been through it before," Peaches told him. "Twice as a
matter a fact. Lost my boyfriend Nikko like that. They popped
him right in the back. Use the AK to herd him right to the
pistol that popped him."

Darius shook his head. "Well, I ain't Nikko, and I ain't
waiting for them to whip around here and pop us."

Darius scooted back, while crouching down.

"Where are you going?" Peaches asked. And that was
when she see the wet spot on his shirt. "You're hit?"

"So what," Darius told her.

"How the fuck did you get hit?" she asked.

The bullets from the AK raked across the top of the hood of the car near her head, causing her to scream. Darius disappeared around the rear of the car.

"Come back here!" Peaches shouted. She saw the lights from the truck as it backed up, and then started pulling forward. The truck and the AK was coming for her. She heard the sound of gunfire nearby. "Darius!"

Nothing.

"Darius!" Peaches shouted. She crouched and scooted back to the rear of the car. The truck was almost upon her. Getting caught between two cars, while an AK lets loose was not in the plan. It would be easier than shooting fish in a barrel. It would be like shooting fish in a cup. She ducked behind the car, just as the truck pulled up and stopped. The AK let loose at the spot where she had been. Sparks flew up off of the concrete. And that was when she heard the other gunshots. And then she heard men shouting and screaming in Spanish.

Peaches peered over the rear of the car, and spotted DeMarion and Darius standing in front of the truck letting loose. It was her opportunity to step up and let loose as well. She rose, and started dumping on the passenger side windows, while walking toward the truck. It was now or never. She was going to kill or be killed. The dudes inside of the truck were ducking down now, and they were either wounded or dead. She was pouring too many bullets through the windows and doors to not have hit someone, and so was DeMarion and Darius. Darius raced up to the vehicle, stuck his gun inside, and started executing the men who were still alive. DeMarion did the same.

Peaches covered them from where she was. Darius raced toward her, with DeMarion just behind. Darius hopped in the passenger side of his Porsche, while DeMarion hopped in the driver's seat. She quickly climbed in the back. DeMarion raced the engine of the Porsche, backed out, and the pulled away.

"Hit the highway," Darius told him.

"I know, old square ass nigga!" DeMarion told him.

"Quit driving all sexy, you pretty motherfucker!" Darius said with a smile.

Peaches leaned back in the seat and smiled. They were cousins, who were as close as brothers, and she could tell by how they played with one another, how much they loved each other. And to top it off, they were straight up killers. She had discovered the secret of the Reigns family, she thought. They were rich, they were educated, and they were also straight up killers. Most niggaz would be in shock after getting ambushed like that. But these two fools went right back to playing and ribbing on each other like nothing had happened. She realized that she had been wrong about them. She had been wrong about all of them. She thought DeMarion was just a spoiled pretty boy, once she learned that he was a male model. And she had thought Darius just a spoiled little rich kid, living off of his brother's money. She thought that he would be dead meat if he ever left Texas. She realized just how wrong she had been.

"Hospital?" DeMarion asked, lifting an eyebrow.

Darius shook his head. "Princess's house."

"She's gonna be pissed," DeMarion told him.

"Pissed at us for going to IHOP and getting shot at?" Darius asked.

"She's going to blame us," DeMarion laughed. "She always blames us."

"She'll get a doctor over to the house to take a look at it," Darius told him.

"You're jinxy as a muthafucka, you know that?" DeMarion asked with a smile. "Second time in less than a month. Every time I go somewhere with your jinxy ass, I get into a shootout, and you always get fucked up. Learn how to duck, muthafucka!"

Darius laughed.

"How the fuck did you get hit?" Peaches asked.

"That first blast from that gauge," Darius told her.

Peaches thought about the shootout. Her mind replayed each moment, step by step. Darius had pushed her out of the way, and jumped in front of her when that first blast went off. The realization of what happen really fucked her mind up. Darius had taken a bullet meant for her? Had he actually saved her from the full blast of that gauge, she wondered? Had he actually saved her life?

Peaches slumped in the back seat of the Porsche, her mouth fell slightly open, and her eyes grew watery. She was harder than that, she told herself. What the fuck was she getting all misty eyed for? She was pissed at herself. She had driven all of the softness out of her body a long time ago. But the more she thought about the situation, the more she realized that Darius had saved her life. Sitting in the front seat, was a man who thought the world of her, who she had laughed at for looking like a lost little puppy dog. But it was that same man who had jumped in front of a shotgun for her. It was that same man, who had taken a bullet for her. Niggas talked a good game all of the time, but this one actually did more than talk, he acted.

Peaches didn't want the guys in the front seat to hear her, or to know what she was doing. She folded her head down into her lap, and balled as quietly as she could. Luckily, DeMarion had turned up the stereo on the Porsche, and they were busy looking out for cops. As much as Peaches didn't want them to, her tears flowed. It wasn't just that she had found a man who was willing to take a bullet for her, but one that thought that she was *actually worthy* of taking a bullet for. So many people throughout her life had judged her, and so many had condemned her and thought of her as being trash. She was hulled out, she heard someone say one time. Her pussy had been busted by every dope boy in Ohio, another cat had remarked. And now, she had a guy who was really feeling her, who had put his life on the line for her, and who thought that she was something special. He had shown her that he thought she was special enough to die for. She had wondered why she would even consider fucking with Darius Reigns, someone who couldn't do shit for her. She had even considered putting the brakes on his little overtures. But now, she had her answer. Why would she fuck with Darius Reigns, youngest brother of Damian Reigns? Because he thought that she was worth dying for. She would fuck with him, because tonight, with guns blazing, she had fallen in love with him. She didn't know how Damian would take it, or how Princess would take it. But at this point, she really didn't give a fuck. No one was going to get int the way of what she had. No one. And if Princess tried to stop it, then Ohio and Texas would just have to fall out. Darius had went to battle for her, and now her heart was willing to go to war for him.

Chapter Twenty

Nathan strolled into the room and the room went silent. He seated himself at the head of the conference table.

"We all know one another, and we all hate meetings just the same," Nathan told them. "So, let's make this thing short and sweet. I have to brief the Attorney General directly, and he'll be going straight to The White House afterward, to brief the President. They want an update on the situation in Mexico, and they want to brief the President on Liz's plan to use this as an opportunity to cripple the drug infrastructure in this country. With that, I'll turn to Agent Hector Villa, our point man in our embassy in Mexico. Hector."

"I'm going to make it short and sweet," Hector said, peering around the FBI Agents and Department of Justice officials gathered around the table. "The cartels in Northern Mexico are hurting. They are hurting from the border being closed, and they are reeling from the war they are fighting amongst themselves. Right now, there is no clear leader, or favorite to win amongst them. Which means, that the violence is going to continue for the foreseeable future."

"Which means that the border will remain closed for the foreseeable future," Nathan added. "And we are already seeing the effect of the squeeze on the streets. Mike."

Micheal Rogers cleared his throat. "Nathan asked me to put together a small task force to gather data from all of our field offices across the country. I can report to you all, that we are seeing an upward tick in the price of cocaine on the street. And this is across the board, all over the nation."

"A slight tick?" Deputy Attorney General Warren Williams asked. "I would think that the prices would skyrocket with no supply."

"There was plenty of supply in the pipeline," Micheal answered. "And the various drug organizations had plenty of supply stored up. What we are seeing is a slight tick, that is a reflection of dwindling inventories, and nervous organizations. They don't know when they'll be able to resupply, so they are being very careful and extremely judicious with the amount they are passing out. You buy twenty eight grams, you're getting twenty eight grams. You buy a kilogram, you're getting exactly one kilogram. And the price per kilogram is creeping upward."

"The last time we met, there was discussion about corresponding levels of violence once a shortage ensued," FBI Deputy Director Phillip Gray said, joining in. "Have we witnessed a corresponding level of violence as of yet?"

Nathan shook his head. "Not yet. As Micheal was explaining, there was still a significant amount of supply in the pipeline and in warehouses across the country. Once that supply dwindles, however, there is no doubt in my mind, that things are going to get extremely violent, and very bloody."

"So, what do we do?" Warren Williams asked.

"We move forward," Nathan answered. "The President has approved Liz's plan. Operation Interdicting Fury is a go. Coast Guard, State Department, DEA, NSA, DoD, CIA, NRO, and every other acronym this government has, are all in. We have intelligence assets from CIA who are going to be tasking satellites from The National Reconnaissance Office, the DoD is going to be assigning elements of the Coast Guard, Justice and Homeland Security are bringing in all of their relevant agencies. We are going to do what we should have done in the Eighties. We are going to interdict ships coming into our ports, we are going to search every vessel, no matter how large or small. We are going to have satellite surveillance on every port in Colombia, and we are going to know every single ship that leaves each and every port. We are going to shut them down this time."

Brooke Army Medical Center - Ft. Sam Houston, Texas

Damian pushed open the door to the hospital room, not knowing what to expect. To his surprise, Grace was sitting up in bed. She smiled when she saw him.

"Hospital food is the nastiest shit on the planet," Grace declared. She dropped her spoon back onto her plate. "Please tell me you brought me something to eat."

Damian's heart rejoiced. He was happy to see her alive, he was happy to see her eating, he was happy to see her with a sense of humor, but most of all, he was happy that she was happy to see him.

"Same old Grace," Damian said, stepping inside of the room and closing the door behind himself. "How ya feeling, champ?"

"Not like a million bucks," Grace told him. "But I'm still breathing."

"Well, that's something," Damian said with a shrug. "A lot of people wish they could say that."

Grace shrugged. "My aches and pains, have aches and

pains."

"Hit the button," Damian said with a smile. "What the hell are you saving the morphine for? You better get juiced up and fly high."

Grace laughed. It felt good seeing Damian. She had thought about him a lot while in the hospital. The boredom had given her plenty of time to reflect upon her life. And in her life, he was her biggest 'what if'. There had been so much that had happened between them, so many things left unsaid, so many things left undone, so many what if's involved in their relationship. She met him while on assignment as an FBI agent trying to bust him. And somewhere along the way, they had both fallen in love. They had even gotten engaged, and even had a son together. Despite all that had happened, she still managed to hang on to her FBI career, thanks to Liz, of course. Going that deep undercover, was something unheard of before September 11, and all of the deep penetrations of terrorist organizations that came afterward. In a way, she had set the blueprint for those deep cover operations. The lessons she learned had been invaluable in setting up the agent training and protocols. That was on the career side of things. And then there was the other side of the coin. The side that involved her relationship with Damian Reigns, major drug kingpin, and father to her child.

Grace never once doubted Damian's love for her. And she knew how she felt about him. Damian had come into her life at one of her loneliest points. And they found comfort in each other. It broke her heart in a way that was indescribable when she had to walk away from him. Damian was a good person, with a wonderful heart, but he did bad things. His organization was responsible for ruining the lives of countless families across the country. She couldn't be a part of that, she couldn't bring comfort and solace to a man responsible for such carnage. So despite how her heart felt, she had to walk away.

It was the hardest decision she ever had to make.

"I'm glad that you're okay," Damian told her. "When I heard about what happened, my heart stopped. I couldn't bear the thought of..."

"Of what?" Grace asked with a smile. "Of me not being around? I'm not around anyway. Or were you going to say that you couldn't bear the thought of losing me? You lost me a long time ago, Damian. You lost me when I broke into that warehouse, and I opened that crate, and I saw all of those drugs..."

"I don't want to talk about that, Grace," Damian told her. "That doesn't matter. None of that matters right now. The only thing that matters, is that you're alive, and you're safe."

"We never talk about it, Damian," Grace said smiling stoically, and staring at the wall. "Why haven't we ever talked about it? We have so much courage between us, and yet we're cowards when it comes to facing the truth of what happened. Why is that?"

"What do you want me to say?"

"I want you to say what needs to be said."

"Why would it matter at this point?"

"Because it does," Grace told him. "When you go through a situation like I just went through, it matters. Life matters. Reflection, matters. You think about things not said, things not done. You have a lot of 'what if's' in your life. And this is one that I need to face. This is one demon in my life that I need to confront."

"I am, who I am, Grace. I'm sorry. If it means anything to you, I'm sorry. That's the best that I can do. I can only apologize for being who I am, and for not being the man you wanted me to be."

"I'm not asking for your apologies, Damian!" Grace snapped. "I don't give a fuck about who you are, or what you do for a living. That's not what I'm talking about. I'm talking about us. Answer the question about us. And keep it real with me. Did you ever love me? Did you? Or was it all a ruse?"

"I fell in love with you, Grace," Damian said nodding. "I did. And it wasn't a ruse. It was real."

"How could you hurt me like that? How could you use me like that? You made a fool out of me! I went and I swore that you were innocent. I swore that you weren't doing anything. And you turned out to be a fucking monster, Damian. A fucking drug peddling monster! And I carried your child!"

"You're acting like the deception was all mines! If I recall, you were sent into the club that night to meet me, to make me fall for you, and to bust me. You went after me, with the intention of getting me a federal death sentence, or sending me to federal prison for the rest of my life, which is pretty much the same thing! So don't act like I was the only one involved in deception!"

"And after we fell in love? Why didn't you stop? Why didn't you pull out, or turn things over to your sister? Why didn't you do it so that we could be a family?"

"Are you talking about before or after you brought the FBI to arrest me?" Damian shouted. "You *must* be on morphine! And as for us being a family, we are a family, Grace! Little Damian and I have built a family together. You're the one running away from the situation."

"I'm an FBI agent, Damian! Are you stupid? Or are you *that* naive? You're a drug kingpin! What? I'm supposed to go to work, only to learn that my work is sitting in a van listening to my husband's phone calls?"

"Grace, it is what it is, so why are we even going there with each other? I had to do, what I had to do. And you had to do, what you felt you had to do. It is, what it is."

"And what about now, Damian? What is your excuse now? Why are you still pushing dope? Why haven't you gotten out? I almost died because of you!"

"Because of me?" Damian recoiled.

"Yes, because of you, and your got dammed Commission! I was in Mexico, because the people you deal with, the people your blood money empowers, kidnapped and beheaded American law enforcement officials! They killed hundreds of people, chopped off their heads, and threw them in a fucking pit! This is what they do! This is what your money supports! Without your money, they couldn't bribe Mexican officials. Without your money, they couldn't hire hundreds of soldiers. Without your money, they couldn't terrorize millions of their own citizens! This is on you, Damian!"

"I'm sorry you feel that way," Damian said softly. "But you know that I was trying to get out. You know that I've been trying to get out for the longest."

"And now? What about right now?"

"What do you want from me, Grace?"

"I want you to be a father that our son can be proud off," Grace said through clenched teeth. "I want him to be able to go with you on take-our-son-to-work-day. When they ask him in school what his daddy does for a living, I want him to be able to tell them."

"I own a major pharmaceutical company, and oil exploration company, and several other corporations."

"Then why are you still selling drugs?"

Damian shook his head. He didn't have an answer for her.

"I don't want the sins of the father, to come back on my child," Grace told him. "They've already come back on me. Promise me, that they won't affect him. Promise me, that he'll never have to pay for the evil that you have done. Promise me, that you'll always keep him safe. Promise me."

"You don't have to worry about that, Grace. You'll never have to worry about that."

"Good."

"He wants to see you."

215

"I've been thinking about that," Grace exhaled. "At first, I didn't want him to see me like this. Especially when things were really bad. But now, I think he can handle seeing me like this. I'm much better now."

Damian nodded. "I'll make sure that I bring him by. He's getting big. He's also getting curious. He's asking a lot of questions about us. About how we met, about when we got married, about why you have to work out of town."

"And what did you tell him?"

"I told him that his mother had a really important job, and that we are all really proud of her. He knows what the FBI is, and he's bragged to the kids at school that his mommy is a cool FBI agent."

Grace laughed.

"I also told him that I loved his mother very much. And that mommy and daddy met at a club, and that we fell madly in love at first sight."

"That's a lie," Grace said with a smile. "Tell him that I said that I fell in love with you on a horseback ride at his great grandmother's ranch. Tell him that I fell in love with you when we visited your grandmother's grave, and when I saw how much you loved her. I fell in love when I saw you kneel down beside her headstone, clear away the overgrown grass, and talk to her. I fell in love when you sang to her while walking into the family cemetery."

Grace closed her eyes, and her mind took her back to that moment. She began to sing the song that Damian sang at his grandmother's grave.

"I went, to the house, were she, used to live. A man, across the street, said I know, who you came to see. And she, she don't live here anymore."

Damian joined in, and they began to sing softly together.

"She's somewhere around God's thrown. She's somewhere around, God's thrown. So I'll keep searching, and searching,

216

until I find her. For she's somewhere around God's thrown."

"Wow, you remembered," Damian said softly.

"I remember everything," Grace said, with her eyes still closed.

Damian leaned over and kissed her forehead. The realization that Grace really loved him, hit him hard.

"You really loved me," Damian said under his breath.

Grace opened her eyes and nodded. "With every fiber of my being."

"You're not alone in your feelings. No matter what happened between us, or what happens between us in the future, you will always hold a piece of my heart in your hands," Damian told her. He lifted Grace's hands to his lips and kissed them softly. "I don't know if I ever said it to you, but I'll say it now if I haven't. I love you, Grace. Don't ever doubt that. No matter what I do, or what I am, or what I've done, I love you. I have so many regrets in my life, but you are not one of them. I too have plenty of 'what if's' that I have to contend with. And I wish that I could have been the man that you needed me to be. When I think about you, and I think about your career, and I think about what I've had to do, I keep thinking about parts of that song, 'Next Lifetime'. But it hurts. Because I don't want to give up. I don't want to have to chalk up this lifetime, or just write everything off."

Grace smiled. "I guess I'll see you next lifetime..."

Damian shook his head. "I'm not giving up."

"I'm not either," Grace told him.

Deadly Reigns IV

Chapter Twenty One

Amiguel peered out of the window of the motel room. He turned to Benito. "It's Carlos, open the door."

Benito uncocked his pistol, placed it in his waistband, and opened the door to the motel room. Amiguel sat his sawed off double barrel shotgun down on top of the cheap motel dresser, and returned to his bed. Carlos and Eduardo bounded inside of the room, carrying three boxes of Little Ceaser's pizza, and two cases of Bud Light.

"It's chow time!" Carlos declared. He sat the pizza's on top of one of the double beds, opened one up, and grabbed a slice.

"Fucking about time!" Diego said, walking into the room. He was still wet from his shower, and had a towel wrapped around his waist. "I'm starving."

Diego grabbed a couple of slices of pizza, while Benito tore open the a case of Bud. He tossed the beers around to his *compadres,* and then grabbed a couple of slices of pizza for himself.

"You eating?" Eduardo asked Amiguel.

"Go ahead," Amiguel told them. "I'll get some later."

"If there's any left," Eduardo told him.

Diego shrugged. "More for us."

The guys wolfed down the pizza, and tossed back the bottles of ice cold brew. Amiguel lifted the remote and changed the channel to the news.

"What the fuck?" Benito shouted. "I was watching that."

"Shut up, the news is on," Amiguel told them.

"What the fuck are you looking for?" Carlos asked.

"We just killed a bitch and tied a balloon around her neck, and there's been nothing on the news about it," Amiguel told them. "There should have been something."

"Relax, you worry to much," Eduardo told him. "Those fucking *Mayates*, they probably covered it up. Who knows. We know the bitch was dead. We sent the message, we did our job."

"And now we just sit here, fuck these fine ass Laredo bitches, and wait for our next assignment," Diego added, slapping hands with Eduardo.

Amiguel shook his head. They were young and stupid. And yet, they were probably right. The Reigns family had people everywhere. They controlled that fucking city, the police, the media, and everything else in Texas. They probably did have the news suppressed. But still, he had been in the business long enough to know when something didn't feel right. And this last job, didn't feel right.

Amiguel had never questioned orders before. And he wasn't about to start questioning them now. But killing that scientist, had left a bad taste in his mouth. Sure, he had killed innocent people before, but killing a scientist who was curing diseases didn't feel right with him. Yes, she worked for the Reigns family, and yes she was rumored to have been Damian's lover. But if she was someone who really matter to him, she would have been protected. Well protected. And that told him, that she hadn't been a target worth going after. She had been someone who was truly innocent. And even worse, she was a healer, someone who made the planet better. Growing up in the poorest shit holes in Mexico, had taught him the value of such people. It was Doctors Without Borders, the United

Nations Children's Fund, and the World Health Organization who had sent many doctors into his rural impoverished community over the years, and they had vaccinated the young and old, saved countless lives, treated numerous friends and neighbors, and had greatly improved the lives of his people. Killing that doctor, had given him a sick feeling in his stomach. We needed more doctors in this fucked up world, not less. Especially ones who were fighting to cure diseases. He had lost his father to cancer at age thirteen. And so he knew the value of her work.

The thunderous boom that nearly sent the motel door flying off the hinges caught them all completely off guard. It was immediately followed by a second, even louder boom, along with a bright flash of light. The flash bang grenade's light blinded them for several moments, while the thunderous percussion of the device caused massive disorientation to everyone inside of the cramped motel room. Amiguel flew off of the bed onto the floor, while the enormous pressure from the shock wave of the grenade tossed those standing around onto the floor. The acrid smell of gunpowder, burning metal, ammonia, and Pentolite blasted their nostrils. Once Amiguel was able to focus again, he saw numerous shapes inside of his motel room. His inner ear disturbance still had him off balance, but he knew that his room had gotten a lot more crowded.

"Fuck!" Eduardo screamed. He tried to rise, but his disorientation caused him to fall back down.

Carlos was rolling around on the ground screaming, with his hands cupped over his ears. Benito had been tossed back into Diego, and both were trying to get up off of the floor.

"What the fuck?" Amiguel shouted. He rubbed his eyes, and jiggled his fingers inside of his ears. He then opened and closed his mouth really wide several times, trying to use his jaw to help clear out the ringing sound in his ears.

"Hello, Miguel," a voice greeted him.

It was a voice he recognized almost instantly. It was soft, educated, female. It was the voice of Princess Reigns.

"Shit!" Amiguel shouted, again jigging his fingers in his ears. His hearing was slowly getting better, and his vision was returning. "What the fuck?"

"C'mon, now, Miguel," Princess said, standing in the doorway smiling. "I know you weren't about to ask me what the fuck I'm doing here?"

Princess was dressed in her best black Chanel suit. It was a skirt and jacket set, with a long skirt, and a matching black Chanel fedora that she wore slightly tilted to the side. On her feet, were a new pair of Chanel heels. She was dressed to kill.

"Did you think that you would be able to avoid detection for long?" Princess asked, stepping into the room. "Texas is mines. If a fly farts in Dallas, I know about it. If a whale shits in Galveston Bay, I get a phone call. I know every single fucking thing that happens in my state. Did you think a bunch of fucking wet backs sitting in a motel room in Laredo would go unnoticed? What? Did you think that you could blend in with the locals or something?"

Princess's men, grabbed Benito, Carlos, Diego, and Eduardo, and held them up.

"Galindo will pay," Amiguel told her. "He'll pay a hefty sum to get us back."

Princess laughed. "Oh, he'll get you back all right. I'm not sure that he'll be able to recognize who's who, but he'll get you back."

Eduardo broke into tears.

"*Cayete, Cavrone!*" Amiguel snapped, telling him the shut up. He turned to Princess. "He'll pay a shitload of money."

Princess shook her head. "I don't need his money. I'm not here to negotiate. I'm not her to bargain, or collect hostages for ransom. I'm here, to send him a message, just like the ones he's been sending to us. He wanted our attention, well, now he's got it. You don't pull the tail of a lion, unless you want to get your ass ate up. And Galindo, has pulled the lion's tail one too many times."

Amiguel shook his head and smiled. "You do this, where are you going to get your dope from? You'll never be able to buy a single gram again, if you step over the line, *Puta*."

"You think?" Princess asked with a smile. She began to slowly walk around the motel room, and examine it. "You motherfuckers were living like some filthy ass pigs here. But there's one thing that bothers me the most."

"You want me to ask what?" Amiguel sneered.

"There are five of you, and only two beds," Princess said with a smile. Her men broke into laughter. "You faggot motherfuckers."

Benito blew her a kiss. "I'll show you a faggot. Me and you, right now. In the bed."

Princess caressed the side of Benito's face. "I don't sleep with dead men."

Eduardo sniffled.

"Shut the fuck up!" Diego told him.

"Let me go!" Eduardo shouted.

"Shut up!" Amiguel told him.

"My brother will pay you!" Eduardo shouted. "He'll pay you a lot of money!"

He had Princess's attention.

"You're brother?" Princess asked, lifting an eyebrow. "And who might that be, young one?"

"Shut up!" Carlos shouted.

"Galindo Ortega!" Eduardo blurted out. "Just let me call him! He'll pay you whatever you ask for! I promise!"

"Shut the fuck up, Eddie!" Amiguel shouted. He knew that the eighteen year old had fucked up.

"Galindo's your brother?" Princess said with a smile.

"You're so young, so cute. You had so much potential."

"Leave him alone, Princess!" Amiguel shouted. "Don't do that to him. If you're gonna do it, just do it. Don't draw it out."

"Is that what you did to Daniella?" Princess asked. "You just handled it right away, or did you draw it out? Did she suffer, Miguel? Did she run panicking, scared, frightened, alone, into a bathroom, barricade the door, and plead for her life? Did she? How much mercy did you have for her, Miguel? Tell me that?"

Eduardo broke down crying again.

"Take this little crying one to my limo," Princess told her men. "I have a special way I'm going to kill him."

Eduardo tried to struggle, but two of Princess's enormous men lifted him off the ground and carried him out of the room.

"You've gone too far," Amiguel told her. "Once you kill him, it's over for you. The war in Mexico isn't going to last long. And once it's over, Galindo is going to come for you."

"Galindo can't set foot in Texas, without me knowing about it," Princess smiled.

"You didn't know about us," Amiguel smiled.

"It took me a little while to figure it out," Princess said nodding. "We kept getting little bee stings here and there, so after a while, I figured that there must be a hive somewhere. So I thought, where would I hide if I needed to set up a little place to operate from, and get to San Antonio and cause trouble. And then I thought, Laredo. And once I put the word out, it took my people exactly thirty minutes to get back to me. We had a bunch of idiots shacked up, ordering pizza and prostitutes, and not going to work in the morning. Usually when a bunch of guys are shacked up in a motel room, they're working on a construction project, or an oil pipeline, or something. They're not just blowing massive amounts of money, and hanging out all day and night. Luckily, the motel owner works for me. Most of the local cops are on my payroll.

Hell, the fucking pizza guy is one of my men. You should have known that it was only a matter of time before I caught up to you. You should have ran back across the border."

Amiguel smiled a sinister smile. "Couldn't. We were waiting on orders. I was hoping the order would come in to take your ass out."

Princess outstretched her arms. "I'm here."

"Yeah, you are," Amiguel said. He reached onto the bed, lifted a pack of cigarettes. His lighter was inside of the cellophane. He pulled his lighter out, lit up a cigarette, and blew smoke into the air. He knew that it was going to be his last.

Princess held out her hand, and one of her men placed a Beretta pistol with a long silencer attached to it, into her palm. She lifted the gun without hesitation, and put a bullet inside of Diego's forehead. He dropped instantly, with his eyes still open.

"Fuck!" Carlos screamed.

Princess shifted the weapon to Carlos, and the gun let out a muffled pop and silent whistle as she put two shots into Carlos' chest, and one into his throat. He fell clasping his throat.

Amiguel took a long draw on his cigarette. "You've stepped in it now. He was Nuni's nephew. His sister's son. There is nothing that's going to stop him from killing you. Not even Galindo."

"I wouldn't give a fuck if he was Nuni's left nut," Princess declared. "That shit means nothing to me. You people are afraid of Nuni. I eat motherfuckers like him for breakfast."

Without taking her eyes off of Amiguel, Princess quickly lifted the gun and put a bullet between Benito's eyes.

Amiguel closed his eyes. "Last chance. You let me and the kid go, and you win. You get big bucks. I stop the war between your family and Galindo, I smooth things over with Nuni and say the kid reached for a weapon, and everybody walks away happy. The other way, is not going to be good for your family."

Princess laughed.

"I'm telling you, we're going to win this war in Mexico," Amiguel said nervously. "And when we do, you'll be cut out. Galindo will make a deal with The Commission, and they'll gladly cut you off in exchange for getting the dope flowing again. Don't make a mistake you'll regret."

"We're not worried about dope," Princess told him.

"How is that?" Amiguel asked.

"Because, we've solved out little supply problems," Princess told him.

"Yucatan?" Amiguel sneered. "You think we don't know about that shit? They ain't gonna be able to get any drugs to you! They would have to come through our territory, and that shit ain't happening! Wake up and smell the coffee!"

Princess leaned in, and whispered into Amiguel's ear. His eyes went wide.

"Bullshit!" Amiguel told her.

Princess nodded.

"That shit ain't gonna work!"

Again, Princess nodded.

"Princess, let's be reasonable!" Amiguel shouted.

"I kinda thought Daniella was cool," Princess told him. "You didn't have to kill her."

One of Princess's men begin blowing up a balloon. Amiguel saw it, and a smile came to his face. He knew that it was over. The irony of the situation made him laugh.

"Can I ask, what you plan on writing on it?" Amiguel asked.

"Two words," Princess told him. "Fuck, *and* You."

The screeching sound of her silenced pistol pierced the air, as her first bullet found its way into Amiguel's testicles. He screamed. Princess's second bullet hit him in his right knee, causing him to fall. Her third bullet, hit him in his side.

"End this shit!" Amiguel screamed. "Please!"

Princess stood over Amiguel and smiled. One of her men knelt down, tied the balloon around his neck, and wrote 'Fuck You' on it in black permanent marker.

Princess fired again, striking Amiguel in his right arm, then left arm, and then his left knee.

"Don't do this!" Amiguel shouted. He realized what she was going to do.

Another one of her men, handcuffed Amiguel's hands around the legs of the bed. She was going to let him bleed out.

"I want you to suffer," Princess told him. "I want you to think about Daniella, and how she felt frightened and alone, knowing that she was going to die."

"Fuck you," Amiguel said weakly. His blood loss was already having an effect on him. He swallowed with great effort. His mouth was already dry. "Fuck... you..."

Princess turned to one of her men. "Cut his dick off, and stick it in his mouth. Galindo wants to send messages, then let's make sure he gets one he understands. Our answer, is for him to go suck a dick."

Princess turned, and strutted out of the motel room to her waiting black limo. Two Laredo police officers were sitting in their patrol cars outside. They waved to her, and she waved back, as she climbed inside of her limo. Texas, belonged to the Reigns family.

Deadly Reigns IV

Chapter Twenty Two

The JW Marriott San Antonio Hill Country Resort and Spa, was the largest Marriott hotel in the world. Set amidst more than 600 rolling acres of pristine hill country property, the hotel was an exercise in sheer luxury. The resort boasted more than 1,000 richly appointed guest rooms, and 85 luxury suites, seven restaurants, two PGA Tour, 18 hole Tournament Player's club golf courses, a 26,000 square foot world class spa, a six acre water park with multiple pools and a 1,100 foot meandering river, along with several water rides. And the suites themselves, were breathtaking.

Peaches maintained a three bedroom luxury golf suite overlooking the AT&T Canyons Course. Her massive suite included a luxurious living room with an equally massive stone fireplace, travertine tile floors, and gorgeous classical furnishings. It was a suite that was designed for the resorts wealthy, corporate, golf clientele.

"I don't want you to go," Darius said, wrapping his arms around Peaches and pulling her close.

"Boy, I have to go," Peaches told him, pulling away. She zipped her Louis Vuitton suitcase closed.

"Why?" Darius asked. "Just stay here an chill with me."

"I'm going to a meeting with The Commission," Peaches told him. "They are officially allowing me in. Do you know what that means?"

"Yeah," Darius said nodding. "It means that you'll become one of them."

"Your brother is one of them," Peaches shot back. "So, what's that supposed to mean."

"He's on The Commission, but he's not one of them. That's why they're always causing him grief."

Peaches shook her head. "I'll be back."

"No you won't," Darius told her. "Because after you become a full fledged member, then everything changes. You can't just fly into another Commission member's territory without asking them. They'll want to know why you're here. Plus, you'll be busy consolidating your hold on all of Ohio. Do you know what that means?"

Peaches nodded.

Darius shook his head. "I don't think you do. When you consolidate your hold on a territory, you get rid of all competition, and all potential competition. And when I say get rid of, you're not sending them on vacation to Disney World. Are you really ready for that? Can you do that?"

Peaches turned away from Darius. She didn't want him to see the smile on her face. Could she? She had already gotten rid of plenty of her enemies, and she was going to love getting rid of the rest of the bastards. She was personally going to put the vice grips around their nuts and squeeze until they exploded. She was going to torture them, and punish them for everything that they had ever done to her. She was going to find and kill all of her mother's ex-boyfriends, especially the ones who crept into her bed at night while her mother was passed out drunk on the couch. Revenge was going to be sweet. And what she was going to enjoy most of all, was the fact that she was going to be untouchable. The Commission was promising her virtual immunity from the police. If they could deliver on that promise, she was going to be unstoppable.

"Did you hear me?" Darius asked. He moved closer, and

rested his hands on her shoulders.

"What do you want me to say?" Peaches asked. "I can't back out now. If I do, then I'm dead. I have to do, what I have to do."

"I can talk to my brother," Darius told her. "I can tell him that you've changed your mind, that you want to leave it all behind. He'll understand that."

"Princess would still come after me," Peaches said with a smile.

"I'll tell them him how I feel about you," Darius told her. "He'll stop her. And I'll talk to Dante. You've made enough money. You can come to Texas and live, and we'll protect you from your enemies. Let someone else have Ohio."

"Ohio is my home," Peaches told him. "It's where I was raised. It's where I still have family. My grandmother lives in Columbus, who's going to protect her? You expect her to pull up roots and move someplace she's never lived? I don't think Nana's been out of Ohio before. Her husband is buried there, and she has a plot next to his. She's not leaving. I can't just pull up and leave."

Darius lowered his head. "I can come up there."

Peaches turned and faced him. She caressed the side of his face. "You think Damian would go for that? You living in Ohio with me?"

"It's not his choice."

"You would really pull up roots, leave everything behind, and move to another state to live with someone you haven't known longer than a minute?"

Darius stared into her eyes. "To be with you I would."

It made her close her eyes. Darius had her mind, and now, it was time to give him her body. He was right about them not seeing each other for a while. She would have to fly back to Ohio after the meeting and organize things. She had to consolidate her hold on Dayton, Cincinnati, and Cleveland.

Columbus was pretty much hers, and she had made inroads into the other places, but now it was time to take them over completely. She would have to re-organize, set up under bosses in those cities, get her legitimate businesses up and running to wash the money. There were warehouses to be bought, distribution routes to plan, officials to be bribed, and this was on top of eliminating all her rivals and completely taking over the states drug trade. She would be busy as hell. There was much to learn, and The Commission was going to teach her, and hold her hands until she got going. But for now, while she was here, she was free to not think about those things. She was free to be herself. Free to love, free to be a woman, free to allow herself a few moments of pleasure. Peaches wrapped her arms around Darius, pulled him close and kissed him.

"I don't want to think about those things right now," she told him.

Darius leaned forward, and they kissed once again. His kiss was tepid at first, but slowly, as he gained more confidence, it grew stronger. Soon, their tongues were wrestling, and then his tongue slowly found its way to her neck. Peaches leaned her head back and moaned. Her neck was her spot. It was the place that got her motor running quicker than any other spot.

Darius gently ran his hand over Peaches' breast. This was where she usually stopped his advances. Surprisingly, today she did not. He maneuvered his hand beneath her shirt and unbuckled her bra. She pulled her blouse over her head, and tossed it onto the floor, exposing her firm, nubile breast. Darius continued to shower her with kisses, slowly making his way down her neck to her chest, where he engulfed her right nipple. Peaches cupped the back of his head and gently moaned. She wanted Darius. She wanted to see if his love making was a warm and embracing as his words.

Darius moving from one breast to the other, licking her nipples and sucking gently. And then, he scooped her up into his arms and carried her over to the bed, where he laid her down softly. Peaches unbuckled her pants, pulled them off, and tossed them onto the floor as well. Darius kissed her stomach, slowly licking around her navel. He continued South, allowing his tongue to lead the way. Peaches held onto the back of his head and moaned. She was definitely ready for him.

Darius gently slid Peaches' panties off, and tossed them onto the floor next to her pants. He kiss her manicured toes, and the top of her tiny yellow feet, and slowly made his way up her thigh with his tongue. Soon, he found himself at her thick but firm thighs. She had tattoos there as well. A Chinese dragon, the name of her hood, the name of her street gang, and even the names of a couple of ex-boyfriends. Darius kissed those as well. Peaches felt what he was doing, and peered down at him as he kissed her tattoos. Quietly, tears began to fill her eyes. It was as if Darius was kissing away years of pain, years of scarring, and all of the years of a hurtful, destructive, and tortured life on the street.

After a while, Darius made his way up to her sweet spot. She was clean shaven, with a black rose tattooed over her womanhood. The stem crossed over her vagina, with the black bud ending at the top, just above her clitoris. Darius licked her rose bud, and slowly allowed his tongue to glide down into her sweetness. He took her clitoris into his mouth and gently sucked on it. This was now her favorite spot, and his sucking was driving her absolutely mad. Peaches opened her legs wider, pressed down on the back of his head, and began to gyrate. She moaned watery cries of pleasure, and Darius worked his tongue in and out, up and down, over and around her magical area. It drove her crazy when he sucked her lips, her vulva, and everything else that he could find down there.

He placed his mouth over her vagina, and sucked and licked like he was eating his last meal on Earth. No man had ever done that to her. It had always been wham, bam, thank you ma'am, and now I have to go and hit the cuts. Drug dealers were selfish lovers. It was all about pleasing them. None had bothered to kiss her, or caress her, or even remotely attempt to please her. And so now, for the first time in her life, she found a man who was giving her pleasure beyond belief.

"Oh my God!" Peaches screamed. She orgasm with the force of a locomotive hitting a brick wall. It was even beyond that. It was atomic. She could feel the cum flowing out of her. And to make matters worse, he had his mouth over her vagina sucking as hard as he could while she was cumming. It was causing her juices to stream out of her like a jet stream, which in turn was causing her to cum even more.

"Stop it!" Peaches said, exhausted. Her legs were shaking, and her entire body was trembling.

Darius ignored her pleas, and continued to lick and suck. Peaches found herself digging her nails into his muscular upper back. She also found herself in a position that she hadn't been in, in many years. She found herself in complete submission to a man, begging and pleading with him for mercy. Right now, he was in complete control. And the way he was sucking her pussy, he could have ordered her to rob a bank, and she would have done it.

Peaches found herself cumming again.

"Please," she said, pleading with Darius to stop.

Darius sucked the cum out of her vagina once again, and just for good measure, sucked her pearl tongue for a few moments, before making his way up to her navel. He kissed and licked her flat stomach, and made his way up to her breast, where he once again engulfed her nipples alternately. Peaches reached for Darius's manhood. She was desperate for him to entire into her.

Darius worked his way back up to her neck, where he kissed and sucked gently, and then back to her lips, where he devoured them as well. And then, something happened. He stopped, stared into her eyes for several moments. This was something that had never happened to her before. He stared into her eyes, and the feeling that his eyes were communicating, made her heart flutter.

Peaches kissed Darius passionately. She wanted him inside of her, but now, it wasn't about the yearning that she felt between her legs. Now, she wanted him inside of her, because she wanted to completely become one with him. She wanted him inside of her, while feeling his body pressed against hers, while kissing him passionately. Again she reached for his manhood, and this time she found it. She was surprised by what she felt.

Peaches placed Darius inside of her. He began stirring, and to her delight, he was stirring deep inside of her. He was a Texas bull, and he was fine as hell. Peaches caressed his ripped muscular back, and she could also feel the ripple of his hard, chiseled abs against her stomach. He lifted her legs, and went in even deeper.

"Ooooh!" Peaches cried out. Her hand shot to his stomach and she tried to lift him off a little bit, thinking that it would take some dick out of her. It didn't work.

"Oh!" Peaches cried out again. "Ooooh, boy!"

Darius worked her. He wasn't trying to pound her, he was just big by nature. He had been blessed to be long and thick, and so even his gentle motions were stretching her out and hitting bottom. And the fact that he was in a rhythm, made things worse for her. His stroke was hitting on all cylinders, and she didn't know what to do.

Peaches tried to grip the bed sheets, then she tried gripping his arms, and she tried to place her hands on his stomach, but nothing worked. He was simply going in deep. She bit his ear lobe, and then found herself biting his shoulder. Her nails were digging into his back, but nothing took away the pleasurable pain that she was feeling. She was breathing like she was in labor, and the only thing on her mind, was what had she gotten herself into. The country ass nigga had a Texas sized dick, and a stroke as deep and consistent as a Texas oil well pump.

"Oh, God!" Peaches cried out. "Oh, no! Oh, help me. Help me!"

Her moaning and her cries for help, only served to excite Darius even more. He knew that he was putting in work, and her cries only served to make him go harder. Soon, his deep stroke was not just stirring, but thrusting. It felt as if he were inside the middle of her stomach.

Peaches began to scream and moan and cry out.

"Damn, nigga!" she shouted.

"Are you on any protection?" Darius asked.

"You asking now?" Peaches cried out. She tried to smile, but his strokes quickly changed her facial expression.

"You don't tell me, I guess I'll just have to keep going," Darius told her. He lifted her legs a little more, and really started thrusting. Peaches screamed for dear life.

"I have an IUD!" she cried out. "I have the Mirena!"

Darius continued to punish her. And then, he placed his hands beneath her big, firm ass, and lifted her off of the bed. He held her up while still inside of her, bouncing her up and down. Peaches wrapped her arms around his neck. Darius held one of legs in each of his arms, which simply spread her apart even more. She couldn't use her hands to keep him from going deep. He was now going all the way up into her.

Peaches didn't know how many times she had came. She lost track after the seventh orgasm. But she did know that she was having another one. The fact that he was going deep up into her, and there was nothing she could do but take it, turned her on immensely. And the bonus came, when she felt Darius shooting his wad up inside of her. They came together, in one giant, cataclysmic orgasm. Her entire body was shaking.

Once Darius finally finished throbbing inside of her, he lowered her back onto the bed. Peaches was sweating immensely, and breathing like she had just run a marathon. Darius fell on top of her exhausted. Peaches could still feel him inside of her, and she could still feel his thrust. It was as if she was still cumming, without the ability to stop.

"C'mon, let's hit the shower," Darius told her. He rose, and Peaches rolled over on her stomach. She had an enormous black butterfly tattooed across her equally enormous ass. "That's fly."

"What?" Peaches asked, peering over her shoulder.

Darius rubbed her ass. Peaches made each of her ass cheeks jump independently of the other. It caused an instant erection with Darius.

"Damn, girl!" Again, he felt on her large, firm ass. "You gonna have to let me hit that from the back."

Peaches stared at him and smiled. She made her ass cheeks dance again. She saw the look on Darius' face, and noticed that his manhood was rising to attention once again.

"You're serious?" Peaches asked.

"Hell yeah!" Darius told her. "Let's hit the shower."

Peaches rolled her eyes. But she was just fronting for Darius. She had found her a cowboy with a horse dick, and she was going to enjoy her last day in the city. She climbed out of bed, and met her man in the shower.

Deadly Reigns IV

Chapter Twenty Three

The Palms Resort Hotel was a luxury casino resort hotel and residential complex. The Palms, as it was known, boasted more than 653 rooms and suites, a 95,000 square foot casino, a Michelin starred restaurant, and a massive recording studio that has been used by none other than Jay Z, Beyonce, Madonna, Katy Perry, Lady Gaga, Dr. Dre, Eminem, and 50 Cents, just to name a few. It was however, more known for its Sky Tower, which was home to its Sky Villas, which were some of the most expensive hotel suites in the world. It was inside of the $35,500 a night, two story Sky Villa where The Commission was holding one of its most important meetings ever. They were finally bringing new members into the organization.

Peaches stepped into the suite and marveled at her surroundings. The Sky Villa was a massive 9000 square foot, two story suite, with a glass wall to the rear of it, that provided unobstructed views of the Vegas Strip. A large poker table sat on the right side of the suite near a fully stocked bar, while just beyond the glass wall she could see a swimming pool sitting out on the terrace. One could literally swim while looking over the lights of the Las Vegas Strip. It was like nothing she had ever seen before.

"Peaches," Princess called out to her. She waved at a seat next to hers, and Peaches took it. "Hey, girl. How was your flight?"

"It was good," Peaches said nodding. She didn't know if Princess knew that her flight had originated from Texas, and not Ohio. But if Princess didn't mention it, she wouldn't either. No need to cause tension or to lose focus on the task at hand.

Other member of The Commission were milling about the gigantic suite. Many held drinks in their hands as they socialized and talked amongst themselves. After a while, Adolphus Brandt cleared his throat, and tapped on his champagne glass with a spoon.

"Attention," he said loudly. "Attention, everyone. It appears that everyone is present, so we can begin the meeting now. If everyone would be seated, we can get down to business."

The Commission members slowly migrated to the large conference table and began to seat themselves. Soon, the table was full with members, new and old. The entire suite was buzzing with excitement and energy. It was the first time that the new members were present, and it was the first time that many of the old members of The Commission were getting a look and feel for their new brethren.

"My name is Adolphus Brandt, and I am in charge of Colorado," he continued after they were seated, and the room had quieted down. "I guess it would be simpler if I went around the table and introduced everyone. I will introduce the original members first, and then I will have the new members introduce themselves. So without further ado, I'll start to my right. Next to me, we have Cesario Chavez of Arizona, while next to Ceasar, we have Barry Groomes of Arkansas. We have Dante Reigns of Texas and California, and Chacho Hernandez of New Mexico. Next to Chacho is Emil Douglas of Georgia, and then we have the lovely Rene Anjounette Tibbideaux-Reigns of Louisiana. Next to Anjounette is Raphael Guzman of Oklahoma, and then Mr. Julian Jones of Mississippi. We have the esteemed Jamie Forrest of Tennessee, and then my old friend, Steve Hawk of Kansas. Next to Steve we have Joshua Reigns of Pennsylvania, and Brandon Reigns of Maryland. We have my man, Malcom 'Baby Doc' Mueller of Alabama, we have Princess Reigns of Florida, and we have James Speech of Virginia. These are the original members of The Commission, along with the members from our first expansion. And now, I'll allow each of the new members from this expansion to introduce themselves. We'll start with the lovely lady to my right."

"My name is Peaches, and I'm from Ohio."

"My name is Rick Shorts, and I'm from North Carolina," the next gentleman told them. He was big and buff. He wore his hair cut short with waves. Rick was a former NFL football player who still ran with his old crew while in the NFL. He used his pro ball money to bankroll

his boys until they had risen far enough in the game to take over much of North Carolina. Rumor had it, that he betrayed all of the cats he grew up with, and had them executed under the guise of attending a meeting.

"My name is James Speech of Virginia," the next gentleman said, introducing himself. "I'm still considered a new member of The Commission, although I've been attending the meetings and running Virginia for a while. This is my official induction into the group."

"My name is Bobby Blake," the next gentleman told them. "I'm from West Virginia."

Bobby's introduction was short and sweet. It was no secret that Bobby was a Klansman, and that attending a meeting with niggers and Mexicans was something he detested. He was a heroine dealer, who turned to Ecstasy Pills, then Meth. And after taking over the Meth trade, he ventured into cocaine. Bobby was a part of the new Klan, he was a Tea Party man, and a shrewd politician. He not only hated niggers and Mexicans, but he also despised poor White trash as well.

241

Deadly Reigns IV

"My name is Vern McMillian," The next gentleman said,
rising slightly. "I'm from the great State of South Carolina, and
it is an honor to be amongst you."

Vern was another White Southerner. He was old school,
genteel, and could have been pulled straight from the pages of
Gone With The Wind. He was one of the types who referred to
The Civil War as The War of Northern Aggression, and who
called all Northerners Yankees. Blacks were okay to him, as
long as they knew their place. To him, all Black women were
cooks, nannies, or maids, while all Black men were simply
workers and hired hands.

"I'm Bo Henry, and I'se from Kentucky," the next
gentleman said, introducing himself with a thick Kentucky
accent. Bo Henry was a Klansman as well. But he was of the
old school, poor White trash variety. He was the white hood
and white robe type of Klan, the kind who still marched and
burnt crosses. He hated Bobby Blake, just as much as Bobby
Blake hated him. They were both Klansmen, but they were
two different types of Klan. Bobby Blake and his crowd had
traded in their white robes for black ones a long time ago.

"I'm DeAndre Micheals," the next gentleman told them.
He continued to brush his hair with his wave brush. "I'm from
Detroit. I run Michigan."

DeAndre was another who had risen from the streets. He
was from the mean streets of Detroit, and he had come up the
hard way. He started in the dope game when he was thirteen.
He stole fifty bucks from his mom's purse, and never looked
back. DeAndre was also a pretty boy who thought he was
God's gift to women. He also had a chip on his shoulder
against White people. He witnessed a White Detroit cop shoot
his father when he was twelve, and ever since then, he thought
them all devils.

"My name is MiAsia," the final new member of The
Commission stated. "I am from St.Louis, and I am here to

242

represent the wonderful State of Missouri."

MiAsia's story was a mystery to most on The Commission. They knew that she had managed to gain control of the entire state of Missouri, but no one knew how. St. Louis and Kansas City were filled with some of the most ruthless, violent, murdering drug dealers in the country. How this petite, half Black, half Japanese woman, with degrees from Oxford and Harvard Law, had managed to get control of that state, was an enigma to all. What they did know about MiAsia was that she was cover girl beautiful, and that she spoke with a very proper British accent. Rumor had it, that her father was a half White, half Black Englishman who married her Japanese mother, and raised her in England. But after that, everything else was very circumstantial. Some say that she was a high dollar criminal defense attorney, and that's how she built her empire. Others say that she was a Russian Mobsters girlfriend, and that she used him to wipe out all of her rivals, before finally killing him. What they did know, was that she hadn't fucked her way to the top like Peaches, and that she wasn't given a state like Anjounette was, after Dante killed her husband. She was high dollar, well bred, and well educated, with expensive taste. Her black form fitting Chanel jacket and matching black Chanel skirt were a testament to that. She also wore matching black Chanel heels, and coordinated Hermes scarf, and a matching Hermes Birkin Bag. She exuded Chanel No. 5, and looked more like a high dollar wife in Town and Country Magazine or French Vogue, than a member of The Commission. Princess and Dante were both fixated on her. Both thought that she was beautiful, and both of them wanted a piece of her.

"Well, that's about it for the new members," Adolphus said, peering around the table. "We welcome you to our little organization, and we hope that you stay with us for a long time. And with that said, I will turn the meeting over to my colleague. Princess."

"Welcome, everyone," Princess said, rising. Slowly, she began to pace around the large conference table. "I just wanted to give you some background, so that you fully understand what this organization is about. I know that many of you have questions, and we'll get to those in a moment. But for right now, let me tell you a little bit about The Commission. We were formed many years ago, in order to pool our resources, and to get better prices for our commodities. The organization was formed with the blessing of some friends from South America, who are no longer with us. At that time, it was our friends from Colombia who supplied our commodities, and they also maintained a representative at the table. We later parted ways with our friends from the South, and began to get our supplies from some groups a little closer to home. And that's where we are right now."

"I think that you glossed over the most important reason that this Commission was formed," Steve Hawk told her.

"Go ahead, Steve," Princess told him, while still pacing around the table.

"We formed this Commission primarily as protection," Steve told them. "Back in the day, before this Commission, we were all separate organizations, each with our own families, and that made us vulnerable. We were vulnerable to the bigger organizations anytime they decided that they wanted to muscle in on our action, or some of our territory, and we were also vulnerable to competing organizations within each of our states. The Commission changed all of that. It made us less vulnerable to outsiders coming in a taking over. We formed this organization, and we declared that an attack on one member, is an attack on all."

"Kinda like NATO," Rick Shorts laughed.

"Exactly like NATO," Princess declared. "The most important factor in regards to The Commission, is that we protect one another. At least from outsiders."

244

"And if someone on The Commission declares war on another member?" Bo Henry asked, staring at Bobby Blake.

"Then The Commission steps in and stops it," Princess answered. "We mediate the dispute."

"If only it really worked like that," Chacho Hernandez sneered.

"Chacho, don't start," Princess said, rolling her eyes.

"Theoretically, The Commission mediates disputes between members?" DeAndre asked. "It keeps the peace?"

Princess nodded.

"Unless one member gets so strong that they can just say fuck The Commission," Raphael Guzman said, shifting his gaze between Princess and Dante.

"Has that ever happened?" DeAndre asked.

"Are you fucking kidding me?" Baby Doc sneered.

"Don't fucking start that shit!" Princess snapped.

"The reason why there is no representative here from Vegas, or California, is because someone was allowed to get too strong," Cesario declared. "It's also the reason why one family controls Texas, Florida, California, Maryland, Pennsylvania..."

"Don't forget Louisiana, Georgia, and Virginia," Barry Groomes added.

"Hey, fuck you, Barry!" Emil shouted. "I control my state!"

"I control my state!" Anjounette shouted.

"Fuck you!" James Speech shouted as well.

"What the fuck is going on here?" DeAndre asked.

"They may as well know the truth," Raphael declared.

Dante held up his hands, silencing the group. "My family controlled Texas. My sister went to Florida, on her own, and took over Florida from a fat Cuban slob. The Reigns family had nothing to do with that, my sister accomplished that on her own, with her own men from Florida."

"Why didn't the Commission stop it?" Rick Shorts asked.

"Because they didn't think that I could win," Princess said with a smile.

"The Reigns family killed Frediano Ambrogiano of Las Vegas, because he betrayed this Commission over and over, time and time again, to The Old Ones."

"Who the fuck are The Old Ones?" Bo Henry asked.

"La Costa Nostra," Dante explained. "The old Sicilian families in New York, New Jersey, Chicago, Vegas... He kept giving them information, hoping that they would make him a made man within their structure. He had to be dealt with."

"I ain't got no problem dealing with a muthafucking turncoat!" DeAndrea said, brushing his waves.

"And as for California, I killed Marion Rook, because he betrayed us," Dante told them.

"Bullshit!" Baby Doc shouted. "You killed him, because he fucking insulted you, and because he stood up to you, and because he wasn't afraid of your ass!"

"Why wasn't his territory passed on to one of his under bosses?" Bobby Blake asked.

"Sounds like a power grab to me," Vern McMillian added.

"Yes, after killing him, I systematically began to destroy all of his under bosses who didn't bow down," Dante told them. "I systematically took over the State of California. And to this day, the Reigns family controls it."

"Are you planning on giving it back?" Vern asked. "I was under the impression that it was one member, one state."

"Put that out of your mind," Dante said, peering around the table. "At one time, the Reigns family controlled most of Oklahoma, most of New Mexico, chunks of Arizona, most of Arkansas, and all of Nevada. We gave all of that territory back to the people around this table. We are keeping California. Right now, the Reigns family controls only two states. Texas, and California. My sister controls Florida, because she rightfully took it. She was an under boss for Don Alemedez, and she went to war, and she won it. Florida is her business. Brandon was awarded Maryland and D.C. by this Commission, so I don't want to hear any shit about that. This Commission *gave* him that territory, because he took over and organized that territory on his own. Yes, he is my cousin. But his territory is his own business."

"So, if someone was to go to war and take it, you're telling me that all these other Reigns' around the table would sit on their hands and do nothing?" Bobby Blake asked.

Brandon frowned. Bobby was in charge of West Virginia, a state that bordered his own. He took Bobby Blake's question as a threat.

"The Commission would mediate the dispute," Princess said.

"The other Reigns around the table?" Dante asked, lifting an eyebrow. "Josh was in charge of Pennsylvania, he is however, pulling out. He is here today, because he hasn't pulled out all of the way as of yet. But he is restructuring, to restrict his operations to Philly, and only Philly. If he takes over all of Pennsylvania on his own, and this Commission eventually expands to include Pennsylvania, then I'm sure he'll be an excellent candidate to come on board."

"Why's he giving it up then?" Rick Shorts asked.

"As a gesture to the New York families," Dante explained. "Pennsylvania is full of unions, and is traditionally one of their bastions. We are pulling out as a peace gesture to them. This is also why we are not in New York, and why we are not in New Jersey."

"Also, the other Reigns at this table is Ajounette Rene Tibbedeaux Reigns," Princess said, jumping in. "Anjounette, as some of you call her, was married to Rene Tibbbedeaux. He was killed, and she took over the state. She later married my brother Dajon, and that's how she became a Reigns. But the state was hers, before she married my brother and became a Reigns."

"This is some bullshit!" Chacho declared. "Let's keep it fucking real. He wasn't killed. The Reigns family killed him! And then you gave his state to this cold hearted bitch, and she turned around and married into the family that killed her fucking husband!"

DeAndre whistled. "Cold blooded."

"We're all big boys and girls here," Princess said.

"I can explain for my self," James Speech told them. "I am not a Reigns, I'm a Speech. My great grandmother was a Speech, and Princess and Dante's great grandmother was a Speech. We share a great grandmother, and that's it. My great grandmother had a daughter, who got married and had a daughter, who got married to a Reigns, and shitted out Dante, Damian, Princess, Dajon, and Darius. They are not Speech's and I'm not a Reigns. It's just that simple. We don't see each other, we don't talk to each other, we don't fuck with each other. They're from Texas, and I'm from Virginia. So all of that shit that Chacho and Raphael was talking, is some bullshit, and they can both kiss my Black ass!"

"Okay, so if one member can kill another and take over his state, what's the point?" Vern asked.

"One member can *not* kill another and take over his state," Jamie Forrest declared. "That's the point of contention. This Commission will step in from now on. We will not allow that bullshit to go on any longer. And that's one of the reasons for bringing in you new members. We needed some diversity at the table. It started to feel like a Reigns family reunion whenever we met. But now, we have some new members, and you'll bring with you new voices, and plenty of soldiers, so we can prevent that type of stuff from happening."

"What about those of us who don't have plenty of soldiers?" De Andre asked, brushing his waves and chewing his gum.

"None of you have enough men to matter right now," Princess said with a smile. "One of the benefits you get from joining The Commission, is that we help you get to that point. We will help you completely take over your states, organize them, grow your legitimate businesses, recruit men, and consolidate your power."

"You'll help us get rid of our competition?" Bo Henry asked.

"Whichever member's state is closest to yours, will help you," Adolphus said. "They send you the men and provide the expertise that you need to win, to consolidate your hold, and to set up businesses to wash your money. We also provide you with political cover. That's where your ten percent goes. Once you take over your states, ten percent of your gross profits come back to The Commission. And it is used for operations that benefit us all. We used it to grease the pockets of federal officials, law enforcement and political ones. We use it for joint operations, like the one we are about to undertake. We are sending men into your states to help you take over. The 'Dime' as it's called, helps to fund this."

"Okay, so we get police protection, political cover, and you help us take over our states, organize, set up businesses to use as washing machines for our money," DeAndre said. "What are you getting out of it?"

"Besides ten percent?" Princess asked. "We get the strength that comes from adding a new state. More importantly, we get to control the prices of our commodities. The Commission set the prices across the board. And this benefits us all. A key in Ohio will cost the same in Florida, or Kansas, or Virginia, or New Mexico. This allows us to basically set the market price."

"Do you have any 'commodities' right now?" Bo Henry asked. "Because my state is dry as a fucking bone."

Looks were exchanged around the table.

"Well, who wants to explain this one?" Chacho laughed.

"Why don't you explain it," Julian Jones told Chacho.

"*No tres nada!*" Chacho declared. We don't have shit. "Right now, because of the situation along the border, nothing is getting in."

"So, y'all don't have any dope either?" DeAndre asked.

Head shakes went around the table. The original members had drugs, but weren't about to give up any of their dwindling supplies. They were all desperately clutching what they had left.

"So, what' they purpose of this shit?" Rick Shorts asked. "We could have had this meeting later! I was under the impression that y'all had supply."

"Nobody has any supply!" Raphael shouted. "Haven't you been listening?"

"Who the fuck you think you're talking to?" Rick shouted back.

"Enough!" Princess shouted. "We are working to rectify the situation."

"Which brings us to the next matter at hand," Adolphus declared. "Our old friends way down south, have supply. And they are willing to get it to us, if we agree to buy from them, and give them ten percent."

"I'll buy from anybody!" DeAndre said, brushing his hair.

"Wait a minute, ten percent on top of the ten percent that we have to give to this Commission?" Bo Henry asked.

"Correct," Adolphus said nodding.

"Twenty percent?" Bo Henry said excitedly. "Fucking grease monkeys, that' highway robbery."

"Twenty percent of something, is better than a hundred percent of nothing," Chacho declared.

"Once a dick sucker, always a dick sucker," Princess declared.

250

Chacho blew her a kiss and grabbed his crouch. "You would know, eh, *Puta*!"

"Chacho, you wish," Princess sneered at him. "Besides, you're too busy bending over so that Cedras can fuck you in the ass. I can't believe you want to go back to those son of a bitches in Colombia!"

"They have supply, Princess!" Steve Hawk shouted. "What do you want us to do? Sit here and go broke along with your family? This isn't a suicide pact, it's a business organization."

"Tell them the truth," Princess said. "Tell them that if we accept their terms, that they are going to send a big fat Colombian to sit at the head of this table, and they are going to have to approve every single move that we make. Our families won't be our own anymore! If you want to go to the bathroom and take a shit, you're going to have to get permission from Colombia!"

"We need dope!" Raphael shouted. "Why the fuck can't you understand that?"

"My answer is no!" Princess declared.

"No, Dante said, shaking his head."

"No," Peaches said, staring at Princess.

"No," Emil said.

"No," Julian said, staring at Princess.

"No," Anjounette said.

"No," Brandon told them.

"No," Josh said, shaking his head.

"Any one else?" Adolphus asked with a smile.

No one said anything.

"I vote yes," Chacho said.

"Yes," Adolphus added.

"Yes," Cesario said, staring at Princess.

"Yes," Barry Groomes told them.

"Yes," Raphael agreed.

"Yes," Jamie Forrest said, nodding.

"Yes," Steve Hawk said, also nodding.

"Yes," James Speech said.

"Yes," Rick Shorts voted.

"Yeah," Bo Henry added, with a toothy grin.

"Yes," Bobby Blake voted.

"Yep," Vern McMillian said nodding.

"If they got dope to sell, then my answer is hell yeah!" DeAndre told them.

A smile spread across Adophus Brandt's face. Their plan had worked. They knew that by expanding The Commission, they would have the votes to go back to the Colombian's as suppliers. And they were right. Adolphus exchanged knowing smiles with Chacho, Cesario, and Raphael. "It appears the yea's have it."

The Commission was now back in bed with the Colombian cartels. The new *El Jeffe* would now be sending a representative to sit at the head of the table. In one day, they had just diminished the Reigns family's hold on The Commission. And they also knew that the new *El Jeffe* would be in an unforgiving mood. He would want the Reigns family punished, and broken for its disobedience and disrespect. The end of the Reigns family had just taken a giant leap closer to being realized. And now, it was time for The Commission to put the second part of its plan into effect.

Chapter Twenty Four

Damian peered out of the massive clerestory windows of his family room, staring at the lake. Today, he was relaxing at his massive estate on Canyon Lake. He had planned a peaceful weekend to take his mind off of Bio One, off of Daniella, off of the FDA, the Juarez Cartel, the Colombian Cartels, and all of his other problems. He was desperate to unwind, in fact, his doctors ordered him to do so. And so, he packed his bags, and headed to one of his favorite places in the world, his beautiful mansion on the lake.

"I'm sorry, Damian," DaMina said softly.

"Are you sure it's her?" Damian asked, without turning away from the windows.

"I'm sure," DaMina said softly. "I saw it for myself."

Damian shook his head and peered down.

DaMina walked to where he was standing, and gently rubbed her cousin's back. "Just relax, okay. Go and lay down. I'll take care of everything."

Damian shook his head. "No. I want to see it."

"Damian, don't!" DaMina said forcefully.

"Mina, I have to!"

"No you don't!" DaMina told him. "Go lay down."

Damian turned to Kevin Reigns and nodded. Kevin quickly disappeared.

"Damian, don't do this to yourself," DaMina pleaded.

Kevin returned to the family room, followed by two of Damian's bodyguards. One of them was carrying a large box. He sat the box on the coffee table and stepped back.

"Damian!" DaMina said firmly.

Damian was fixated on the box. He walked deliberately to the coffee table, and carefully pulled open the lid. Inside of the plastic lined box, was the head of his estranged wife, Illyassa Malaika Reigns. Damian turned and vomited.

"Get a towel," DaMina shouted to the bodyguards. She grabbed Damian, and helped him over to a nearby sofa. "And get that damn thing out of here!"

"Wait!" Damian said, lifting his hand and staying the bodyguard. "Send it to her father."

"What?" DaMina said, recoiling.

"He needs to know," Damian said. "Just telling him that she's gone missing is not going to be enough. Especially if the body can't be found. And as a parent, a father, he deserves to know that she's really gone. Otherwise, he'll spend the rest of his life searching for her, thinking that maybe, somewhere, she's still alive. He needs to know that she's really gone."

"Damian, is that a wise move?" Kevin asked. "He's going to go ballistic."

"Wrap it up, just like it was delivered to my home, but include a note," Damian told him. "Let him know that it was the Juarez Cartel that did it."

"He won't stop until they are all gone," DaMina said softly.

"Good," Damian said. "They wanted to go there, so now we're going there. This is beyond sending a message. It's no longer about doing business. This was payback. And now, we're going to show them again."

"And it's never going to stop," DaMina said, lifting an eyebrow. "This is no longer about business. This is a war that neither side is going to walk away from. And pretty soon, it's going to get way out of hand."

"Fuck business!" Damian shouted. "This is personal! And this shit is already out of hand!"

DaMina nodded at the bodyguards. "Get it out of here. Get it to her father."

The bodyguards nodded, lifted the box, and left the room.

"I want Princess and Dante to go straight to Mexico from the meeting in Vegas. Tell them I said don't even bother coming to Texas. I'll have everything they need waiting for them when they get to Mexico. They want to send a message, then we're going to send an even louder message. Who the fuck do they think they are!"

"Cuzzo, calm down," DaMina told him. She turned to Kevin. "Has he had his medicine?"

Kevin shrugged.

"She didn't deserve that," Damian said, shaking his head and staring off into space. "She wasn't a part of this family's business. Hell, she and I weren't even together. They knew that. This was just some pure cold blooded, cold hearted, bullshit. They want to go after wives and girlfriends, then we can too."

Damian kicked his coffee table. "This was some bullshit!"

"Damian!" DaMina shouted. Again she turned to Kevin. "Find out if he's had his medicine."

"And now, now her father has to bury his other daughter," Damian said rambling. "He has to bury another daughter, because of the Reigns family. Because they chose to marry Reigns men, they died. That's not right. That's not fair."

Kevin ran out of the room.

"Damian, look at me!" DaMina shouted.

Damian continued rambling.

"Damian!" DaMina shouted again. She clasped his chin, lifted his face, and stared into his eyes. "Are you still on Phenobarbital?"

Damian continued to ramble.

"Get in here!" she shouted.

Several of Damian's suited bodyguards ran into the room.

"Get an ambulance!" DaMina ordered.

One of the men raced out of the room.

"Did he have his medication today?" DaMina asked.

"He took his blood pressure medicine this morning," one of the men told her.

"Is he still on Phenobarb?" DaMina asked.

The men all shrugged and stared at one another.

"Mina," Damian called out softly to her.

"Damian." DaMina said, as she quickly turned back to him.

"That was fucked up," Damian said, shaking his head.

DaMina nodded. "It was fucked up. Are you okay?"

Damian nodded.

"Did you take your medicine today?"

Again, Damian nodded. "I took it."

"Do you want me to get a nurse here to check you out?"

Damian shook his head.

"Are you sure?"

"I'm fine," Damian told her.

"Cancel the EMS unit," DaMina told the bodyguards.

One of them left the room to cancel the Ambulance.

"I just can't imagine having to bury one child, let alone two," Damian said softly. "And somehow, someway, it's all my fault. I am responsible for that man having to bury both of his daughters."

"It's not your fault, Damian," DaMina told him.

"Grace was right," Damian said. "Ultimately, I am responsible for what they do. It's my money that fueled their power. It's my organization that made them strong. And I am the reason why so many people are having to pay with their lives. Not just on this side of the border, but that one as well."

"That's bullshit, Damian," DaMina said, rubbing his back. "Daisalla married Dajon, because she loved him. And neither of them had anything to do with any of this. But people crossed the line, and they attacked them, and they killed an innocent woman. This is the exact same thing. Animals crossing the line, and killing people who have nothing to do with anything. They are killing busloads of innocent people in Mexico, and it's not your fault. They control their actions, not you. They are responsible for what they do, not you."

"I enable them," Damian said, shaking his head. He rose from the couch and headed for his back door. "I want out, Mina. I want out, like I've never wanted out before. I'm through."

Mina peered out of the window at the lake, and then back at Damian. "Where are you going?"

"I need some fresh air," Damian told her. "I'm going for a walk. I need to clear my head."

"Want me to come with?"

"No," Damian told her. "Take care of this mess for me. Get a hold of Dante and Princess, and let them know what the deal is. It's priority red. Use the new code. Make sure the message is not compromised. Don't want to have to deal with any extra unnecessary bullshit."

DaMina nodded. "Are you going to be okay."

Damian let out a half smile. "I'm not going to drown myself in the lake, if that's what you're asking."

Damian closed the door, and headed out for his walk. Kevin walked up behind DaMina.

"Is he going to be okay?" Kevin asked.

DaMina shrugged. "He's tired. He wants out."

"That might not be a bad thing," Kevin said.

"Remember the last time he wanted out?" DaMina asked. "This family fought a war amongst itself, because Damian wanted out, and Princess wanted to take over and keep us in.

We can't go through that shit again. Besides, I'm not sure if we can even get out at this point."

"Why? What do you mean."

"Bio One is not doing good," DaMina explained. "In fact, the lawsuits, combined with the drought, is killing us. If Damian's plan works, and we get the water turned back on, it'll be the only thing saving us from the poorhouse. And from our enemies."

"Damned if he do, damned if he don't," Kevin said.

"No," DaMina said, shaking her head. "Dead if we don't. We need that dope money now more than ever. We need to make payroll, and we need to get even bigger. We're headed down a path to war, and nobody is willing to pull back."

"That bad?" Kevin asked.

"Worse than you think," DaMina frowned. "Things are about to get bloody. Real bloody."

"Anything I can do to help?" Kevin asked.

DaMina turned to him. "Ever been on a ship?"

Kevin shook his head. "Does a yacht count?"

"Come with me to Louisiana."

"What for?"

"To pray that Damian's plan works," DaMina told him. "We have to make it work. We'll kill everyone we come across in order to make that motherfucker work, if we have to. You down?"

Kevin shrugged. "Whatever it takes, cuzzo. Whatever it takes."

Chapter Twenty Five

The RAPTR was a fully autonomous, vertical take-off and landing, small unmanned aerial system. It looked like an extremely large version of a child's model helicopter, with the exception of its sinister black paint, and equally large rotor blades. The standard RAPTR unmanned aerial vehicle, or UAV, had a rotor diameter of about seventy two and a half inches, and carried a payload of about ten pounds. This was no standard RAPTR, however. Dante had the manufacturer, Tactical Electronics, craft this one out of aircraft grade aluminum and titanium to lighten its weight and increase its strength. He also had them replace the air vehicle's tiny ten horsepower engine, with a significantly more powerful one hundred and twenty horsepower turbo engine. This increased the RAPTR's payload from a mere ten pounds, to a whopping one hundred and fifty pounds. And it was a weight increase that he would need, in order to carry out his current assignment. Slung beneath his modified RAPTR was a one hundred and fifty pound bomb.

"Okay, zoom in right there," Dante ordered the vehicle's controller. He and the unmanned aerial vehicle's pilot, were sitting ten miles away, inside of a air conditioned van. On the outside, the van had been made to look like a rusty old truck that sold tacos out of the back, while on the inside, it was a state of the art, computer geeks wet dream. Dante hovered over the operator's screen, as he controlled the joystick that controlled the camera on the air vehicle. The operator zoomed in on the front of Galindo's mansion.

Galindo's mansion on the outskirts of Juarez, Mexico, looked like a luxurious, and heavily guarded, Spanish hacienda style fortress. It was white stucco, with a combination of flat roofs, and red clay, mission barrel style tile roofs. It was a massive compound, consisting of a main mansion, and numerous other buildings. And all of it was encircled by an enormous stone and stucco wall that was heavily guarded. He even had guards driving around the perimeter in Chevy Silverados, while others patrolled on foot with German Shepherds. More guards extended the perimeter even further, by patrolling the acreage that surrounded the estate, on ATV's. Galindo's compound, looked like the home of a man at war with other cartels. It was virtually impenetrable.

"Okay, zoom out," Dante told the operator.

The camera on the RAPTR zoomed out, giving Dante a wider view of the compound. They had been in place for two days now, and had sent the RAPTR up half a dozen times after bringing it down for refueling and maintenance. They wanted it in the air, and ready for action, as soon as Galindo showed his face.

Soon, Galindo's armored Escalade pulled up to the front door. There were two more Escalades, a Jeep Cherokee, and a Jeep Wrangler with a fifty caliber machine gun mounted on its roll bars in front of Galindo's vehicle, and an Escalade, a Range Rover, another Jeep Cherokee, as well as a second Jeep Wrangler with a mounted machine gun behind it. It was a heavily armed caravan, and that meant only one thing. Galindo was leaving his compound.

"I think we have him, Boss," another operator in the van said, pulling off his head phones and turning toward Dante. "His wife's out of town on vacation, and he's leaving to go and pay a little visit to his mistress."

"Good," Dante said smiling. "Zoom in on the front door."

The drone operator zoomed in on the front door. Dozens of armed men poured out of the front door, and climbed inside of various vehicles in the caravan. Finally, Galindo himself emerged. He was talking on his cell phone, and Nuni was standing right next to him. Both men climbed inside of Galindo's heavily armored Escalade, and the convoy slowly pulled off.

"We got him!" the drone operator said excitedly. He zoomed in on the vehicle in which Galindo was riding in. "That one hundred and fifty pound high explosive is going to rip the top of that Escalade open like a sardine can."

"Switch to the targeting camera," Dante told him.

The operator switched the drone's camera, and was now staring at the black Escalade through an infrared targeting camera.

"Arm the bomb," Dante told him.

The operator lifted a red toggle cover on his control board, and then flip and toggle switch up, into the armed position. "The weapon is armed, sir."

"Good," Dante said. He reached over the operator, and moved the joystick controlling the drone's camera, so that it was now putting cross hairs on Galindo's mansion.

"Sir, the vehicle," the operator said excitedly.

"The Escalade is not our target," Dante told him.

"But Galindo!" the operator said. "He's inside of the Escalade! We can get him!"

"Galindo is not our target," Dante said. A grin slowly spread across his face. "I want Galindo to live. He can't feel pain, if he's dead. The target is the house. We were waiting for Galindo to leave, so that he could survive, and live with the pain of having to bury the people that he loves."

The drone operator's face went pale. He had been

watching the mansion for two days, and he knew that there were children in the house. Galindo's mother, and his children all lived with him.

"Lock on to the target," Dante ordered.

The drone operator turned back to his station, and locked the drone onto the target so that it would hover and stabilize. The bomb itself was unguided, but the drone could stabilize and hover, ensuring that the bomb would hit the target precisely. The one hundred and fifty pound bomb was a combination of a high explosive device, and an incendiary device. It was going to spread its highly flammable gel over over the structure once it exploded. It was not only going to collapse the structure, but burn it down completely, and with a level of speed and efficiency that would make survival virtually impossible.

"The drone is locked onto the target," the operator told him.

"Will Galindo be able to see the explosion from where he is?" Dante asked.

The drone operator switch camera's, and swiveled the surveillance camera around until he located Galindo's convoy. The video monitor split into two screens; one showing the house, and the other showing Galindo's moving convoy.

"He should be able to see it," the operator confirmed.

"Good," Dante smiled. "Drop the bomb."

The operator swallowed hard. He didn't want to do it, but he knew that he had to. He had been paid a lot of money since getting out of the Army and going to work for the Reigns family. And he knew that the Reigns family expected him to deliver. He also knew that he knew to much, and that Dante would either kill him, or have him killed if he hesitated. He pressed the red button on his control panel, releasing the bomb.

The camera on the RAPTR moved out of place for a few seconds, before the air vehicle readjusted itself to compensate for the sudden one hundred and fifty pound weight loss. The camera watched as the bomb made its way down to the center of the structure and exploded, sending a fireball high into the sky. The second camera showed Galindo's convoy coming to a screeching halt.

Dante laughed heartily. He turned to the second operator in the truck. "Get a hold of Princess. Tell her that it's a go. The code words are, 'Santa came early. He went right down the chimney'. Transmit the same message to Texas."

Dante peered down at the camera again, and watched as Galindo's convoy turned, and raced back toward his burning compound.

"Message that, muthafucka!" Dante said, staring into the camera.

Houston, Texas

Susie Ortega strutted out of the Houston Galleria Mall with shopping bag on top of shopping bag. She had two bodyguards with her, and both of their hands and arms were full as well. She loved these shopping trips to Texas. In fact, she wished that Galindo would finally give up his little business, relocate to Texas, and start some new businesses. That way, she could shop all of the time. In fact, she had her eye on a nice big mansion inside of The Woodlands. It was close to one of her favorite shopping destinations, The Woodlands Mall. It was also close to her secret lover, who worked at The Woodlands golf pro shop. She could shop, fuck, relax at the spa, and live the life she was born to live.

As much as Susie loved The Woodlands Mall, she loved

the Galleria Mall even more. The fact that it had 3 million square feet of shopping space, and was the largest mall in Texas didn't hurt. She loved the high end stores, of which, there were many. Macy's, Saks, Neimans, Gucci, Prada, Fendi, Escada, Versace, Prada, Chanel, Ralph Lauren, Louis Vuitton, Kate Spade, and Coach, as well as many others, were spaced throughout the mall. And these were just the clothing stores. She loved to hit the Galleria's expensive jewelry stores as well. And it showed.

Susie Ortiz was a walking Tiffany's display. She wore a couple of massive diamond rings on her fingers, an equally massive diamond bracelet on her wrist, and a diamond encrusted gold Piaget on her other wrist. There was a large diamond necklace, and sparkling diamond pendant around her neck, and these matched the massive diamond tear drop earrings dangling from her ears. She was also wearing Kate Spade from head to toe, with the exception of her purse, which was Nancy Gonzalez, and her shoes which were Louis Vuitton. With her diamonds blinding everyone within eye sight, Susie made her way to her waiting Cadillac XTS limo.

"Put it all in the trunk for me," she told her bodyguards. She sat her bags down on the ground behind the limo, walked to the door, and waited for her driver to open it. The trunk popped open, and her men began to place her numerous shopping bags inside of the trunk. Her driver opened the door, and she climbed inside of the limo. Inside, she was startled to find an unexpected guest.

"Who the fuck are you?" Susie asked, as the driver shut her door.

"My name is Princess."

Susie walked her eyes up and down Princess, who was wearing just as many diamonds as she was, but was Chrisitan Lacroix from head to toe. "I think you climbed into the wrong limo, bitch!"

A loud thud sounded throughout the car, and she could feel the rear of the car drop down for a few moments, before the Caddy's automatic load leveling suspension kicked it and raised the rear up again.

"Hey, watch my fucking bags!" Susie shouted, while banging on the rear window.

"They can't hear you," Princess told her.

"They can hear me!" Susie shouted. "And mind your own fucking business!"

The trunk closed. And it was Princess's men who were shutting it.

"I promise you, they can't hear you," Princess smiled. "Unless you know how to perform a seance."

"What?" Susie turned to see if she could spot her men. "What they fuck are you talking about, bitch? As soon as they get through loading my bags into the trunk, I'm going to have to pitch you out on your ass!"

"They're dead," Princess said calmly. She lifted a drink from the cup holder in the limo's window, and sipped. One of her men climbed into the limo, and forced Susie to scoot over.

"What the fuck is this?" Susie shouted. "Get the fuck outta my car!"

The limousine pulled away.

Susie pressed the intercom button so that she could communicate with the driver. "Where in the fuck are you going? Where's Nico and Richie?"

"Your bodyguards are in the trunk," Princess told her. "And your driver works for me."

"Bullshit!" Susie shouted. "*Get the fuck outta my car!*" Susie leaned forward and slapped Princess.

Princess smiled. And then slapped Susie back.

Susie clasped her cheek. "*Oh my god!* How dare you? Do you know who I am? Do you know who my husband is?"

"That's why I'm here," Princes told her. She punched Susie

with her fist, landing a right hook to Susie's left jaw.

"Aaaah!" Susie screamed. "My husband is going to kill you!"

"You husband is in mourning," Princess told her.

"Mourning? What the fuck are you talking about?"

"He lost his kids today," Princess smiled.

"His kids?" Susie gasped. "What the fuck have you done to my children? You bitch!" Susie reached for her cell phone, and again, Princess punched her.

"What the fuck do you want from me?" Susie screamed.

Princess's man, clasped Susie's arm, jabbed a syringe in it, and withdrew blood.

"What the fuck are you doing?" Susie shouted. She tried to struggle, but couldn't get her arm free from the hulking bodyguard.

"He's taking your blood," Princess told her.

The bodyguard withdrew the syringe, and then pulled the vile full of blood from the needle part of it. He held the vile in the air, shook it, and then tossed it to Princess.

"See this?" Princess asked, holding the vile into the air. "I'm sending this to Galindo."

"What for?" Susie asked, rubbing her arm. "Is that what this is about? Ransom?"

Princess smiled and shook her head. "I don't want or need your money. I'm sending this to your husband along with a note explaining that this is all that's left of you. Your husband loves to send messages, and so now, we have a really good one to send to him."

Susie eyes were wide. "What are you going to do. He'll pay you. He'll pay you whatever you ask. I'll call him and you'll see."

Again, Susie reached for her phone, and this time, Princess knocked the phone out of her hand.

"You're going to die, Susie," Princess said flatly. "You'd

better digest that information really fast, because the sooner you accept it, the better off you'll be. Get right with God."

The limo came to a stop, and Princess climbed out of it. She handed the vile of blood to the man who opened the limo door for her.

"Get this to Galindo with the note I wrote earlier," Princess told the man. She turned to another man. "When you're finished, take her body to the Sea of Cortez, and feed her ass to the White Sharks. I want nothing left."

Susie burst into tears. Princess turned back to her.

"Don't cry," Princess said. "The good news is, your children are waiting for you on the other side."

One of her bodyguards closed the limo door, just as Susie let out a loud wail. Princess walked to her waiting Infiniti QX 56 limo, and climbed inside.

"To the airport," she told the driver. She turned to another one of her men. "Get a message to my brothers. Tell them Shark Week is on the Discovery Channel."

Deadly Reigns IV

Chapter Twenty Six

Petroleos Mexicanos, or Pemex for short, was the world's second largest non-publicly traded company, and it was the second largest company in all of Latin America. Pemex, was a massive oil corporation, with over half a billion in assets, and it was wholly controlled by the Mexican government.

Brandon Reigns stood on the bridge of *The Bay of Campeche*, a massive 1,250 foot long, double hulled supertanker. *The Bay of Campeche* was more than 80 feet wide, and could carry more than 3 million barrels of oil. And it was owned by Pemex. Brandon lifted a pair of binoculars to his eyes, and peered at Energia Oil's massive oil rig, *The Great Explorer*. He focused the binoculars on the platform, and could see Anjounette staring back at the massive oil tanker through her own pair of binoculars. Brandon smiled, and turned to his cousin Kevin.

"Tell Damian that we're hooking up with the platform as we speak."

Kevin lifted his cell phone, and dialed Damian's number.

"Yeah, cuzzo?" Damian answered.

"Brandon says that we're hooking up with kinfolk right now," Kevin told him.

"Good deal," Damian told him. "Keep me posted."

"Will do," Kevin said, before hanging up.

The gigantic supertanker slowly, and carefully

maneuvered itself alongside of the equally gigantic oil platform, and then the ship dropped anchor. Several gun lines or pneumatic line throwers shot several lines from the ship to the oil rig. Lines were cast, as were hoses, and the two massive entities were lashed together in the middle of the Gulf of Mexico.

"You look like you're getting sea sick," Brandon told Kevin with a smile.

"This is not my cup of tea," Kevin told him. "Now I know why I didn't join the Navy."

"You didn't join the Navy because you're a pussy," Brandon said with a smile.

"We are ready," the Captain of the oil tanker told Brandon. "Follow me."

Brandon and Kevin followed the Captain out of the bridge, down the gangway, and down several flights of stairs, until they reached the ship's enormous deck. A walkie-talkie was handed to the Captain by his deck officer. The Captain handed the walkie-talkie to Brandon. The ship's Chief Mate approached.

"We're ready to begin offloading the cargo," the Chief Mate told him.

Brandon nodded.

The Chief Mate lifted his walkie-talkie. "Begin cargo transfer."

The men on board the oil tanker began loading crates onto the high lines that lashed the two vessels together. The crates were sent across the line from the tanker to the oil platform, where the crew on the oil platform took them off of the line, and then took them below deck. It was a manpower intensive operation, and the precision and repetitiveness of the operation made the hundreds of men involved on both vessels, look like worker ants.

Anjounette headed down several flights of stairs, until she

came to the lowest level on the oil platform. She strolled into the room where the crates were being stacked and began to observe the operation. Workers were stacking the crates, while others were taking the stacked crates, opening them open, and then removing the kilos of cocaine inside of them, and placing the drugs into special made, hollowed out, pipeline cleaning PIGs.

"It's called a pig," the engineer shouted over the noise.

"What?" Anjounette asked, cupping her hand over her ear.

"A pig!" the engineer shouted. "A Pipeline Inspection Gauge! We use them to clean sediment out of the pipeline! But not these!"

The engineer tapped at the round titanium constructed device.

Anjounette continued to watch as the men loaded the cocaine inside of the specially designed oil plugs.

"These are made from titanium!" the engineer explained. His grin was from ear to ear, showcasing all of the teeth that were missing, and he was beaming like a proud poppa. "Special built to withstand the high pressures of the gases that are going to be shooting them underwater through the pipeline to the refinery!"

Anjounette marveled at the brilliance of the entire operation.

The Energia workers carried the loaded PIG's to the pipeline, where they placed them inside one at a time, and then launched them using the high pressure gas that was a natural by-product of their oil drilling and production. One by one, the cocaine filled transports were sent off to an Energia oil refinery on the Louisiana coast.

The Oil Refinery

DaMina stood inside of a specially built control room at the refinery, staring through a thick glass window at workers inside of a room with yellow Hazmat suits and gas masks over their faces.

"On the way," Anjounette said over the walkie-talkie.

DaMina lifted her walkie-talkie to her lips. "Roger."

The wait felt like it was forever. DaMina began to pace back and forth once again.

"Relax," Joshua Reigns told her.

"I can't relax," DaMina told him. "This shit has to work."

"It will," Joshua said with an uncertain smile.

"It has to," DaMina reiterated. "If something goes wrong, if the pipeline gets clogged, or ruptures, then we're going to have oil plugs full of coke sitting at the bottom of the Gulf. And that's if we're lucky. If not, we'll have dozens of them floating in the Gulf, and the Coast Guard will be on to that shit quicker than we can blink."

"Mina, relax," Joshua told her.

DaMina knew the consequences of failure, and so did her cousin Joshua. She didn't understand how he could be so calm. Getting the dope flowing again, was the most important thing in the world at that moment. It was the only thing that was going to ensure the family's survival.

A slight rumble ensued, and then a banging. DaMina rushed back to the thick glass window and peered inside of the room where the workers were encased in Hazmat suits. One of them turned a valve, and the unlocked the end of a large pipe. To Da Mina's surprise, a PIG was was inside. The worker pulled the PIG out, and set it on the floor of the final delivery station, and then opened it. It was filled with bricks of cocaine. The worker lifted one of the bricks, turned it over and inspected it. It was dry and intact. He turned to DaMina and gave her a thumbs up.

"Yes!" DaMina shouted. She bounced up and down, and

hugged Joshua.

Inside of the final delivery station control room, the workers closed the first valve, and began to remove other PIGs from the other pipelines in the room. Other workers pulled the cocaine from the transports, placed the bricks on flat carts, and wheeled them into a separate room.

"Can I go in?" DaMina asked the engineer.

"Not into the final delivery room, unless you want to drop dead," he told her. "The reason they're wearing those suits, is to protect them from the gases that remain in the pipeline when they open them up. You can go into the storage room. I'll have them move some of the carts in there."

The engineer lifted his walkie-talkie. "Guys, send one of the carts into storage room alpha."

One of the men in the final delivery room nodded. He pulled a fully loaded cart into an ante room that served as an air lock. He closed the door to the final delivery room, allowing it to seal, and then pressed a large red button on the wall. A loud whooshing sound of air being sucked out of the ante room sounded throughout the building. After a few moments, and buzzer sounded, and a flashing red light on the wall went from red to green. The technician removed his mask, took in a breath of fresh air, and then opened the door leading into the storage area. DaMina raced around the corner and met the cart in the hallway. She lifted a brick of cocaine and examined it.

Joshua came up behind her. "Satisfied now?"

DaMina ripped open the brown packaging, and found a solid crystalline block of pure white cocaine inside. The brick had a bottle nosed dolphin stamped into it. It was the symbol of the Yucatan Cartel.

"Yes!" DaMina shouted for joy. Damian's plan had worked. The cocaine was flowing again.

DaMina sat the unwrapped brick back down onto the cart, walked back around the corner, and peered through the glass.

The final delivery room was now filling up with PIGs, and each of them contained dozens and dozens of kilos of pure Mexican flake. It was the most beautiful thing she ever saw. She lifted her iPhone.

"What's the word?" Damian asked.

"You're not going to believe this shit," DaMina told him.

Damian sat up behind his desk. "What? Don't tell me the pipe blew."

"Damian, I hate to tell you this, but your fucking plan worked."

"What?" Damian asked confused.

"Sorry to tell you this cuzzo, but the water is back on."

"Wooohooo!" Damian shouted. He stood. "Are you serious?"

"It's so beautiful, it almost brought tears to my eyes," DaMina told him. "You're an evil genius, you know that?"

DaMina, you're lucky you're not standing in front of me right now, because I would kiss you, girl!" Damian told her.

"Well, then I guess I'm the lucky one!"

"Keep doing what you're doing, and keep me posted!" Damian said excitedly, before disconnecting the conversation. "Hot damn!"

The Reigns family had just pulled back from the brink. If the pipeline held, he thought. The engineers had assured him that the pipeline could take the pressure of hauling PIG's filled with cocaine. And it appeared that it was holding. The Reigns family would be the only family with cocaine still flowing. He would be able to charge whatever he wanted, and he would be able to offset some of the losses because of the Bio One lawsuits. In fact, if the border stayed closed, and the price of cocaine continued to skyrocket, he would be able to cover all of his losses. He didn't know who he should thank more. The idiots in Mexico, or the President and Congress for overreacting and closing the border. But one thing he did know for sure, the tables had just turned.

Juarez had tried him to many times, thinking that he would need to bow down in order to keep the dope flowing once the borders re-opened. They were wrong. Cedras and the Colombian's had tried him as well, thinking that he would need to crawl back to them for his supply, because of the situation in Mexico. They had been wrong as well. And finally, The Commission had talked cash shit to Princess thinking that the Reigns family was weak, and that it was about to go broke and lose all of its power. They had been wrong as well. Soon, it would be time to let all of them know just how wrong they were. The water was back on. And now that the water was flowing again, he had no problem letting the blood flow as well. They were all going to learn just how deadly being wrong could be.

Damian sat back down inside of his seat, kicked his feet up on top of his desk, leaned back and relaxed. For the first time in a long time, he could really relax. His mind began to wonder, and he started to build the framework for a plan. A plan for each of them. Galindo had just learned a valuable lesson, and without a doubt he would be out for blood. And so now it would soon be time to let Galindo know who was really the master in there relationship. It was soon going to be time to spank Galindo, show the Commission that he was still the one motherfucker not to fuck with, and show the Colombian's a thing or two. Giving him time to think, was the most dangerous thing in the world. And now that the cocaine was flowing again, he had the time he needed to get things right. He was going to send Princess back to Florida eventually, and he was going to let Dante do his thing. And once again, after he spanked all of his enemies, he was going to set his family on a path of getting out of the drug game. But that was long term. Right now, he had to show all of the circling sharks who thought that they had smelt blood in the water who was really the predator, and who was really the prey. The great whites, were about to be introduced to a megladon.

Chapter Twenty Seven

Damian seated himself on the park bench and watched as his boys performed various maneuvers on their skateboards and rip sticks. He had an army of bodyguards in and around the park, but today, they were dressed casual, so as not to frighten the park goers. Getting out to the park was something that he hadn't done in a while. But today was a good day, and he felt invigorated.

"Hey, Boo!"

Damian turned in the direction from which the greeting came. He was surprised.

"Stacia! What are you doing here?"

"I can't be here?" Stacia asked. She leaned forward and kissed Damian on his forehead. "You're not happy to see me?" She seated herself on the bench next to him.

"I'm always happy to see you," Damian said with a smile. "Just wondering what the heck you're doing back here so soon. Are you trying to build up those frequent flier miles or something?"

Stacia waved her hand, dismissing the thought. "Oh, honey, I have too many of those already. They keep me in the air."

"And that another reason I was wondering what the heck you're doing back in town. You do have a job to go to."

"I'm just chilling," Stacia said. She turned toward the

park, and put her sunglasses on.

"Yeah, right. What's the deal?"

"The truth, or the bullshit I tried to make up on the flight out here?"

"Try the truth first. And if that sounds like bullshit, then give me the bullshit."

Stacia laughed. "Okay, I'm here because Mina called me the other day."

Damian rolled his eyes.

"She's just worried about you," Stacia told him.

"I'm fine."

"Damian, have you been taking your medicine?" Stacia asked. She pulled her sunglasses down on her nose and stared at him. "Seriously."

"I have," Damian nodded. "I have a nurse that comes to the house."

"Don't give me that shit," Stacia told him. "She works for you, and she's not going to challenge you if you tell her that you took your medicine."

"Stacia, I'm fine."

"Listen to me, little Black boy," Stacia said, putting her finger in his face. "High blood pressure is nothing to scoff at for a Black man. You already have way to many worries and responsibilities, and you love to take on more and more. You have to stop trying to put the world on your shoulders, and you have to get serious about taking your fucking medicine. I'm not going to fly down here and bury your ass, do you hear me? I'm not going to do it. If you're not going to do it for yourself, then do it for your children."

Damian nodded.

"Don't fuck with me, Damian, I'm not in the mood to be placated. I'm serious about you taking your medicine, do you hear me."

Damian lifted his hands in surrender. "I hear you. I'll get

on it a lot better."

"Okay," Stacia said. She lifted her sunglasses back over her eyes.

Dakari Reigns slid up to her and did a kick flip with his skateboard. "What's up, Ma? What are you doing here?"

"Just came to see you, baby," Stacia told him. "Where's your brother?"

"Coming up right behind you."

Dakota Reigns leaped over a curb, and landed right next to Stacia, startling her.

"Boy! What the hell is wrong with you?" Stacia asked.

Dakota leaned over and kissed his mother on the cheek. "I thought you weren't going to be back for at least two months?"

"I lied," Stacia told him. "What are you doing?"

"Getting my skate on," Dakota told her. He sped off just as quickly as he arrived.

"Gotta go!" Dakari said. He tossed his skateboard down, leaped on it, and skated off.

"What are you feeding my kids?" Stacia asked.

Damian shook his head. "Stacia, they're like vacuum cleaners. They inhale everything in the kitchen."

"They're enormous."

"They're not enormous, they're just tall."

"How's Dallas doing?"

"Good."

Stacia nodded. "Have you talked to him about Harvard?"

"He's not interested," Damian told her.

"Make him interested," Stacia said forcefully.

"Stacia, we've been pushing him since he started walking," Damian protested. "He's going to graduate from high school at the age of sixteen, what more can we ask? He just wants a break from school."

"What more can we ask?" Stacia repeated, leaning forward and staring at him. "We can ask him to not throw his life away. We can ask him to go to Harvard, or at least to some other Ivy League school."

"I got it," Damian nodded. "I'll take care of it"

"You just make sure that my son is safe, Damian. Do you hear me?"

"He's my son too. I would give my life to protect him."

Stacia peered off into the distance. She stood, and nodded. "Let's take a walk."

Damian looked into her eyes. He realized that she had something she wanted to tell him. He rose, and the two of them began to walk side by side through the park.

A trail of men in polo shirts and khaki pants slowly began to follow behind them. Some walked in front, while others off to the side. Pretty soon, they were being followed by three all white armored Range Rovers, and were flanked by more than twenty men.

"This is discreet? Stacia asked, laughing.

Damian had to laugh himself.

"This is ridiculous," Stacia said, shaking her head.

Damian shrugged. "You know, things are kinda heating up."

"Really?" Stacia asked, lifting an eyebrow.

"Galindo sends a message, and we send a message back."

Stacia nodded. "And in the meantime, no one is talking. All of these messages, and no one is actually talking to each other trying to resolve the situation. You know better than that, Damian."

"I know better than to try to play Mr. Nice Guy with Galindo and the boys in Northern Mexico. They take kindness for weakness real quick."

"The Feds have a new operation in place," Stacia said.

"Against me?" Damian asked.

"No, not directly. It's about interdicting drug supplies coming into the country."

"I thought they were already doing that," Damian told her.

"Not on this level," Stacia smiled. "They are bringing everyone to the table. DEA, NSA, DoD is contributing Coast Guard and Naval assets, ATF, Customs, FBI, everyone."

"Wow!" Damian said, whistling. "What the fuck's going on?"

Stacia shrugged. "They see this as an opportunity to really shut down the drug trade."

"What? The cocaine shortage?"

Stacia nodded. "The closing of the border. They have a damn FBI task force dedicated to gathering intel on the street level price of cocaine. They know that the border closing is having an effect. And so, they are planning on making sure that no other supply routes open up."

Damian stopped cold. "How?"

"They are tasking numerous assets to catch ships leaving Colombia," Stacia told him. "They know that with Mexico in shambles and shut out of the game, all of the drug organizations are scrambling back to the Colombians. They have satellites on every single port in Colombia and Bolivia, and they are going to inderdict every single ship headed from Colombia to a U.S. port."

Damian laughed heartily.

"What?" Stacia asked, turning up her palms. "What's so funny? I missed the joke. I just told you that the United States government is committing billions in assets to completely shut down the cocaine trade, and you break into laughter."

"Because, that is some of the best news I've had lately."

"Damian, what the fuck is going on? How is that good news? What the fuck are you up to?"

"I was trying to think of a way to fuck over Cedras, and now, you've just given me another tool to use."

"Yeah, but what about your supplies?"

Damian shook his head and smiled. "Not worried about

those."

"Damian, don't make me pull out my pistol and shoot you right here, right now, in front of all your bodyguards."

Damian laughed. "You would shoot me in front our kids?"

"They're in the park, they can't see us. What the fuck is going on?"

"I took care of my supply problem," Damian shrugged.

"How?"

"I made some new friends," Damian told her. "On the Yucatan Peninsula."

Stacia's mouth fell slightly open. "The Yucatan cartels? Damian, those boys are nothing to play with."

"We're not playing, we're doing business."

"And just how do they plan on supplying you?" Stacia asked.

Damian shrugged. "That's their problem."

"I'm sure they'll work it out."

"You seem too calm," Stacia said. She pulled off her sunglasses, and stared Damian in his eye. "I know you Damian Reigns, and you're full of shit. You've already figured out a way to get the shit here. Haven't you?"

Damian smiled.

"And while the government is busy watching South America, you'll be sneaking your shit in from Mexico," Stacia said, shaking her head. "You sneaky, slick, underhanded motherfucker you!"

Stacia wrapped her arms around Damian and kissed him. "And that's why I love your ass. You're a genius, and an evil one at that. If you ever decided to use that brain of yours for good, the world would be in trouble."

Damian laughed. He wrapped his arm around Stacia and pulled her close.

"I'll buy you some ice cream," he told her. And the two of them headed off to a nearby ice cream parlor.

Dante's Penthouse

"So, this is where you live?" Desire asked, while peering out of the wall of windows into the city skyline. "Not bad. Not bad at all for a bachelor pad."

"You expected clothes to be everywhere, old pizza boxes to be scattered around the table, and a nearly empty refrigerator with nothing but a couple of cans of Bud in it?"

"Yes!" Desire said, nodding emphatically.

Dante laughed. "I've been out of college for a long time. In my college days, yeah, that was me."

"And now?" Desire asked, lifting an eyebrow.

"Now, I'm all grown up."

"I guess you are."

Dante moved in and kissed Desire. He kissed her gently at first, and then let the passion fly. His warm tongue slid into her mouth, as he wrapped his arms around her and pulled her close. Desire wrapped her arms around Dante and moaned. Dante worked his way down her neck, giving gentle pecks. He loved the way she felt in his arms; he loved the way she smelled. She was beautiful to him. Everything about her, from her head to her toe, he thought perfect.

Desire melted in her new beau's arms. Growing up as an Army brat, she had an attraction to soldiers. And she had dated her share of officers after college. But within Dante she saw a different kind of strength. Within him, it was a strange brew of strength mixed with danger. Something in his eyes spoke volumes about his character. He was pure testosterone, with plenty of resolve, and a hint of gunpowder thrown in for good measure. Desire had no doubt about who Dante was. She was a reporter, and as such, she had done her research after meeting him. She knew what others said that he was capable of, and yet, it only served to increase her attraction to him. He was dangerous, but not in a wild, rebellious type of way. He was dangerous in a buttoned down, sophisticated, and intelligent way. He would do anything, and everything, to protect what was his. And so, she had no problem becoming his. It was within the circle of his protection that she found the safety that she had been yearning for since leaving her parent's nest.

Dante clasped the side of Desire's face, kissing her all over. He ran his fingers through her long, silky, dark brown hair. He kissed her eyes, her nose, her forehead, her cheeks, and once again, her lips. It was almost in desperation, as if he couldn't get enough of her sweetness inside of him fast enough.

Dante lifted Desire into the air, and carried her off into his bedroom, where he laid her down on his California king sized bed.

Desire caressed the side of Dante's face, and peered into his eyes. Her eyes told him, what she did not want to say with her lips. She thought that it was too soon to utter the words that she felt inside. She had fallen for him, and she had fallen fast. She was in love with Dante Reigns.

Staring into Desire's eyes, Dante felt a stirring inside. He could feel his heart fluttering. She was smart, beautiful, educated, but innocent. He had never fallen for a woman that was totally innocent, and not involved in the drug trade whatsoever. It was a weird feeling. How would she fit into his life? Could she? What could she actually be told, and how much could he allow her to know? And if she knew what he was, and the things that he had done, would she still want to be a part of his life? He knew that after she learned the horrors of his past, that he could not allow her to leave him. This was his greatest fear concerning Desire. He had fallen for her, and although he knew that he wouldn't hesitate to kill her, doing so, would certainly fuck him up for a while. And that was why he didn't allow women who weren't in the trade to get close to him. It was why he had fought a battle within to keep Desire at bay. But it was to late. He had lost that battle. He had lost that battle the moment she gave Lucky that medicine. He knew that he had lost the moment he seen her playing with Lucky, the moment he saw her braiding Lucky's hair, and the moment he saw his precious baby girl turn and give Desire a hug.

Dante leaned forward, and kissed Desire passionately once again. What did they really have in common, he wondered? She was a news reporter, the absolute worst person that he could be in a relationship with, besides a cop of course. But, if Damian could have a kid by an FBI agent, then maybe, just maybe, he could make it work with Desire. But then again, Damian was no longer hiding anything from Grace. How long would he be able to hide things from Desire? Fuck it, he thought.

Dante rose from on top of Desire.

"What's the matter?" Desire asked.

"I'm different," Dante said, staring at the floor.

"What?" Desire asked. "What are you talking about?"

"I'm a man of action," Dante told her. "I'm not one of those passive type of guys."

Desire lifted her eyebrow, and fixed her blouse. "I didn't think you were."

"I don't believe in beating around the bush, is what I'm saying."

"Okay?"

"I don't want you to go anywhere," Dante told her.

"I'm not going anywhere," Desire said, giving him a strange look.

"I want you to be my woman, is what I'm saying," Dante told her. "I want you to give me a chance. You know, to work things out."

Desire smiled. "Dante, if you give me a note telling me to check yes or no if I like you, I'm running out of here. We're not in elementary school. What are you talking about?"

"I'm not good at this relationship, dating, Mars and Venus type of stuff," Dante told her. "It's to bad you won't let me get away with giving you a note."

Desire laughed. "Okay, it depends on the note."

Dante walked to his nightstand, opened a drawer, pulled out a blue Tiffany's box, and tossed it to her. Desire caught it.

"What the fuck is this?" she asked.

"I told you I'm not good at this," Dante told her. "I didn't know when or how..."

Desire opened the box to find an enormous ten carat diamond ring, set on a six prong platinum base. She leaped off of the bed.

"What the hell is this?"

"It's something that I want you to wear as a commitment from me to you, until the time is right for the real deal. You know, like a promise ring."

Desire placed the ring on her finger, and lifted it to the light. It shown like the Star of Orion.

"Wow! You know, at first, I wasn't down with the elementary school thing, but yeah, I'll do the promise ring. Now where the hell is that note so I can check the yes box!"

Dante laughed. "So you like it?"

"Are you kidding me?" Desire leaped into Dante's arms and kissed him.

"Glad you like it," Dante said with a smile.

"One question though," Desire told him. "What does this mean? I mean, what does it really mean?"

"It means that I love you," Dante told her. "And that one day, I plan on asking you to marry me."

"Yes," Desire said nodding and tearing up. "Whenever

you do decide to pop the question, the answer is going to be yes."

Dante pulled Desire close again, and the two of them kissed passionately.

Deadly Reigns IV

Chapter Twenty Eight

The Commission meeting had been hastily called by Cedras who wanted to move fast. He now had The Commission begging for him to be their supplier again, and he wanted to assert his authority quickly, before the situation changed in Mexico. Dealing with the Commission, meant billions of dollars a year in drug profits, and he definitely wanted their business back. He put his new representative on the plane as soon as Adolphus Brandt called him. It was time for The Commission to kiss a little Colombian ass.

Cedras wished that he could be at the meeting himself, but was wanted by the International Criminal Court thanks to numerous Interpol warrants. Leaving the safety and security of his home country was really not an option for him. But technology would make it possible for him to get his message across, and for The Commission to feel his presence. He would vido conference in.

The hastily called meeting was to take place in Dallas, Texas, of all places. It was a thumb in the eye of the Reigns family. Cedras wanted them to bow down to him, somewhere within their own territory, figuring that it would send a powerful message to the rest of the Commission. This evening's meeting was being held at the ultra luxurious Rosewood Mansion on Turtle Creek. It was an iconic venue, filled with old world furnishings from around the world.

Princess strutted into the main parlor area to find most of the commission members present, along with Cedras's new representative, Richardo Echevario Delacruz.

"Late as always," Adolphus Brandt said, leaning back in his chair.

The members were arrayed around a hand carved Louis XV table, and were seated in silk covered hand carved Louis XVIII chairs, beneath a massive Swarovski crystal chandelier.

"I would think that you could be on time, since the meeting is in Texas," Cesario added.

Princess took a seat at the table. To her surprise, neither Dante, nor Damian were present. In fact, Brandon was not their either. And neither was Anjounette. She was the only Reigns present at the meeting.

"Glad you could join us," Delacruz told her. "Will your brother be joining us as well?"

Princess shrugged. "I don't know. I flew in from Florida."

"I sent him a message," Delacruz told her. "Well, perhaps he will grace us with his presence later. In the meantime, I suppose you can relay to him what was discussed."

Princess took in Delacruz. Unlike the other fat greasy Colombians that *El Jeffe*, and Cedras had sent before, Delacruz was different. He was in much better shape for one, and a little bit more seasoned, and significantly better educated. She had seen many like him before, and she knew how dangerous these types of men were. Behind their polite smiles, and gracious manners, lied sadistic, ruthless, heartless killers. She had no doubt in her mind, how heinous Delacruz really was. She also wondered where the hell her brothers were.

"I suppose that we can begin now," Delacruz told them. "First, I would like to thank you all for coming. Next, I want to convey the boss's enthusiasm for working with you once again. In fact, he will be addressing you personally in a little while, via secured video conferencing. In the meantime, I would like to tell you all, new members and old, that things will be a little different this time."

Nervous shifting in seats went around the table.

"First, the price of our little commodity will be set in Colombia, and not in The States, and not by this commission anymore," Delacruz said with a smile. "And I'm talking about the retail price per kilo, not just the amount that our commodities will cost you. Second, we feel, that to make up for lost time in our relationship, and also to help defray the cost of getting the products to you, a rate of fifteen percent is justified."

"Fifteen percent!" Chacho Hernandez shouted. "That's robbery!"

"Well, it's not the Eighties, gentlemen," Delacruz said with a smile. "It is a lot more difficult to get our commodities across the ocean to you. Besides, the percentage is non negotiable. In fact, so there will be no misunderstandings between us, let us get something clear up front. Nothing that I say today, or here on out, is negotiable. I'm telling you how things will be, and if you find these things to be disagreeable, you're always free to find another supplier."

Delacruz knew that he had them in the palm of his hands. There were no other suppliers. They could buy from them, pay the fifteen percent surcharge, or go to hell. It was that simple. He was going to teach them all a lesson. That was why Cedras had sent him. He wanted a iron fist to sit at the head of the table, and make The Commission pay for its past betrayal.

"Another thing, and this concerns your brother, more than anyone else," Delacruz told Princess. "That is why I wish that one of them would have showed up. Anyway, you can convey the message. The boss would like for the Reigns family to send a high ranking member to Colombia to serve as an ambassador of sorts, in order to help smooth over any miscommunication that may occur during the course of doing business together."

"I'm sure that we can find a Spanish speaking representative that Cedras would be comfortable with," Princess told him.

"No, I'm sorry, perhaps you misunderstood," Delacruz said with a smile. "We were thinking of someone along the lines of your brother Dajon, or even your youngest brother, Darius."

Princess leaned back in her seat. "You want a hostage."

Delacruz smiled like that cat that was about to eat the canary. "Hostage is such a hostile term. It connotes animosity, or hostility, no, no, no. Think of this as an ambassadorship. Perhaps even like a semester abroad. We have a fine university in Bogata. Perhaps your brother Darius would like to continue his studies?"

"I don't think so," Princess told him.

"It's not a request," Delacruz told her. "There have been many representatives that have come here in good faith, only to return to Colombia in a box. If they return at all, that is. So this time, we are requesting a little good faith on the part of the Reigns family. After all, if there is no good faith between us, then how can we do business? Choose an ambassador between your two brothers, and put him on the plane tomorrow, or there will be no commodities coming to America. At least not to this commission. And remember, while you deliberate, your enemies will be cutting deals, taking over your territories, and getting stronger."

"It appears we don't have a choice," Chacho said with a smile. "I say we send him."

"Easy for you to say, he's not asking for your brother," Princess told him.

"Fuck him," Chacho said. "There are enough Reigns in this world as it is."

Laughter went around the table. The only two who didn't laugh, were Princess and Peaches. The latter thought about options. She could warn Darius, have him run to Ohio and hide out with her. She could protect him. In fact, she *would* protect him.

Princess's cell phone rang. She lifted it, and peered at the screen. It was Damian calling.

"Hello?" Princess answered.

"Hey what's up?" Damian asked. "Where are you at?"

"I was just about to ask you the same thing," Princess told him.

"Why, what's the matter?"

"I'm at The Commission meeting," Princess told him.

"What meeting?"

"Cedras called a meeting," Princess explained. "His new representative is here. He said that he sent a message for you to be here."

"Maybe they reached Dante," Damian told her.

"Damian, they want us to send a hostage to Colombia," Princess said, cupping her hand over her mouth and speaking into the phone.

"What?" Damian asked. "Are you shitting me?"

"And they want fifteen percent, and they are going to set the street level price from Colombia. They are completely taking over The Commission once again."

"I thought Mina called you," Damian told her.

"About what?" Princess asked. "What's the matter?"

"The water is back on," Damian told her.

"What?"

"I said the water is back on."

"Now you're shitting me," Princess told him.

"I shit you not."

She could hear the smile in Damian's voice.

"Are you sure? I mean, really sure?"

"It's a fucking flood," Damian told her. "There's so much water in the basement, we're going to need a pump."

Princes threw her head back in laughter. "Oh my god! Why didn't she call me and tell me!"

"She's probably super busy," Damian said.

"Wow!" Princess exhaled.

"Do you mind?" Raphael Guzman asked. "We are trying to have a meeting here!"

Princess held up her hand silencing him.

"So, what do you want me to do about this meeting?" Princess asked.

"What do you want to do about it?" Damian asked. He knew his sister.

"Is there enough for everyone at the table to have a drink?" Princess asked.

"Yep."

"It's secure, reliable, continuous?" Princess asked.

"Permanent."

"Well, woah is the new representative," Princess declared.

Damian laughed. "Do you have enough men."

"Of course," Princess said. "We are in Texas, right? They're outside."

"Who leading them?"

"Khaleel."

"I'm going to call him, and tell him to get in there."

"Thanks," Princess told him.

"Have fun, but don't go crazy," Damian told her.

"I got this, negro," Princess told him. "See you soon."

"Love ya, sis," Damian told her.

"Smooches."

Princess disconnected. She turned her attention back to the others and smiled.

"Are you done?" Delacruz asked.

"Oh yeah, I'm done," Princess said with an enormous smile. "And so is this meeting. And so are you, for that matter."

"I don't believe you understood what was said earlier," Delacruz told her. "Although at one time you believed that you were in charge of this little organization, let me be perfectly clear. That, my dear, is no longer the case."

Princess's men opened the door to the suite and rushed inside. They completely surrounded the table.

"What is the meaning of this?" Adolphus demanded.

"All of your men are safe," Princess told them. "They've just been sequestered. Now, whether or not you remain safe, is up to you."

"You are finished!" Delacruz told her. "The Reigns family is through in the drugs business. You won't be able to buy a gram of coke, once I'm done with you. You are finished!"

"Here's where you're mistaken," Princess told Delacruz. "And let me be perfectly clear, you are the one who's finished."

"If you touch one hair on my head, this commission will never be able to buy an aspirin from South America ever again!" Delacruz shouted. He peered around the table. "If I were you, I would save myself, and not let this woman ruin your chances for getting your commodities flowing once again."

"Princess, what is the meaning of this!" Adolphus shouted.

"Shut the fuck up!" Princess told him. "Quit being a scary little bitch, Adolphus! You're so quick to run for cover. A little hiccup, and you're ready to jump back in bed with the Colombian's and start sucking their dicks. Grow a pair!"

Princess rose from her seat at the table, and walked to the head of the table, where Delacruz was seated. "I believe, you're sitting in my seat."

"You run nothing," Delacruz told her.

Princess held out her hand. One of her men placed a large silenced pistol in her palm.

"Don't be stupid," Delacruz told her.

"Princess don't!" Adolphus shouted.

"Don't fuck up our supply, *Puta!*" Chacho shouted.

Princess cocked the pistol, put it to Delacruz's head, and put a bullet through his temple. His body fell sideways, knocking over the chair. One of Princess's men brought her another chair, and placed it at the head of the table. She sat down.

"Get rid of that thing," she told her men, while peering down at Delacruz's crumpled body.

"Do you realize what you've done!" Chacho shouted.

"I'm tired of you, Chacho," Princess said, glowering at him. "Since you have a problem with the number of Reigns in this world, then perhaps I should just put you out of your misery. The Reigns family is here to stay."

"Princess, you just killed our only means of supply!" Steve Hawk told her. "Think about what you've done! You've just killed us all. I'll have people who actually have dope, moving in on my territory within weeks!"

"Stop panicking," Princess told him. "We will supply you."

"What?" Baby Doc asked. He was pissed. He had cut a separate deal with the Colombian's to use his ports in Alabama. His separate deal would have also cut his percentage down to seven percent. The only thing stopping him from getting up and strangling Princess, was the gun in her hand, and the room full of men she had surrounding the table. "How the fuck you gonna supply all of us?"

"Don't worry about how," Princess told him. "You give us the money and we'll fill the order."

"You can do this?" DeAndre asked. "You can really do this?"

Princess nodded.

Looks went around the table.

"We have to know how this is possible?" Adolphus told her.

"Don't worry about the how, just give us your order, and we'll ship it to you, as always, just like when the border was open," Princess told him.

"We'll see," Barry Groomes said nodding. "And if you can't..."

"If I can't you still won't be able to do shit," Princes told him. "You finish the sentence, and I'll be eating breakfast in Little Rock by Thursday morning."

DeAndre whistled and laughed.

"And for all of you new members of The Commission, allow me to formally introduce myself. My name is Princess, and welcome to my fucking table."

Deadly Reigns IV

Chapter Twenty Nine

The Holy Church of The Immaculate Conception was the traditional church for Reigns weddings and funerals. It was a massive white stone cathedral, with massive two story columns, dozens upon dozens of stairs leading to the entrance, and a giant stain glass dome in the center of the church. The church was the largest Catholic church in the state, and had benefited from tens of millions of dollars in Reigns family donations. The fact that the Reigns family was devoutly Catholic was well known, and the fact that they loved their church was also well known. The main church alone encompassed more than one hundred thousand square feet. And then their was the community center, the community kitchen, the hospice, the elementary, middle, and high school, the gym, the community recreation center, the youth center, the offices, the hospital, the library, a natatorium, the nunnery for the retired sisters of the church, dozens of other buildings and facilities. In fact, the entire complex had come to be known as 'The Little Vatican'.

Inside, in one of the private rooms, Princess was seated in front of a full length mirror, while an assistant placed a one hundred carat diamond necklace around her neck.

"You look beautiful," Anjounette told her.

Princess examined her ivory colored, custom made Vera Wang dress in the mirror. It contained more than thirty thousand tiny Swarovski crystals sewn in an intricate pattern throughout, and a train more than twenty feet in length. The gown was sleeveless, and the bodice form fitting, yet layered. The diamonds hanging from her ears and around her neck, complemented her gown to a tee.

Princess smiled at Anjounette, and thought about Angela and Daisalla. Although she and Anjounette had become close, she missed Daisalla dearly. Daisalla was a physician, and had nothing to do with the family's illegal activities, and yet she felt she had more in common with her than with Anjounette. She was still glad that Anjounette was there though. And as for Angela, she loved her dearly. Angela was the sister she never had. They had tried to kill one another a couple of times during the family war, but that was business. Angela had been her girl. If there was ever another woman she truly respected, it was Angela. She considered Angela her soul sister. She was the only woman she ever knew, who cold be as ruthless and cold heart and herself. The thought of Angela bought mist to Princess's eyes.

"Ah," the ladies in he room cried out in unison.

Anjounette handed Princess a tissue.

"It's your special day, girl!" Cherin told her. "You go ahead and cry."

"I miss that psychopathic bitch Angela," Princess said sniffling and blowing her nose.

*****

Darius pulled Peaches into another room, and began kissing her all over.

"Boy!" Peaches said through clenched teeth. "What if

someone sees us?"

"No one will!" Darius said kissing her.

"You're going to mess up my make-up!" Peaches told him.

"You look good," Darius told her. He stepped back and examined her. "You look really good. I've never seen you looking like this before."

"Don't laugh!" Peaches told him. She pulled her panties from between her butt cheeks. "This tight ass dress keeps riding up, and I had to wear these little bitty ass drawers, and they keep giving me a booty bite."

"They're panties," Darius smiled. "Girls wear panties."

Peaches smacked her lips. "Ha, ha, real funny. I don't! If I put on anything, it's gonna be a comfortable pair off boxers."

Darius shook his head. "How many times have you wore a little black dress before?"

"Never!" Peaches told him. "And don't plan to again. And I don't wear heels either."

"So what do you wear when you hit the clubs in Ohio?"

"Leggings, Jeggings, tight jeans, and whatever used to show off my ass!"

"Oh yeah?" Darius asked, stepping closer. "You don't be showing off my booty to nobody!"

Peaches shoved him back. "I said used to. I don't go to no clubs no more, too much drama."

"You better not be letting no niggas slobber all over you."

"Why?" Peaches asked with a smile. "You jealous?"

"You damn right!" Darius told her. He grabbed her butt. "This is mine. All mine!"

Peaches giggled, and Darius leaned in and kissed her.

*****

"When is it going to be your turn, Dante?" Father O'Connell asked.

Dante smiled and shrugged. "I don't know, Father. One day soon, I hope."

Dante wrapped his arms around Father O'Connell and hugged him tightly. Father O'Connell hugged him back, patting him on his back.

"Your mother would be so happy today."

"I know," Dante said nodding. "But not as happy as my father. You know, Princess was Daddy's little girl."

"I know," Father O'Connell said with a smile. "Oh, I remember the day she was born. We all raced to the hospital, and Davidian was so nervous that he was shaking like a leaf. The only time I ever seen your father afraid, was at the birth of his children. Oh, that man loved each of you, with all of his heart."

"He was a good man, Father," Dante said, smiling at the thought of his father.

"He was," Father O'Connell said with a nod. He poked Dante's chest. "And one thing I know for a fact, is that the apple didn't fall far from the tree."

"Who me?" Dante laughed. "Oh no, Father. This apple was catapulted as far away from that tree as humanly possible."

Father O'Connell and Dante shared a laugh.

"There is a good man inside, Dante Reigns. I know it. I see it. I believe it. I pray for you and your brothers and sister every night. The Lord has not given up on you. He's waiting on you to realize it. And once you do, He's going to use you for something great. You just have to have faith."

"Father, I have faith, but I gave up believing that I had even a remote chance of making to Heaven."

"Well, that's a shame, Dante," Father O'Connell told him. "Because The Lord has never given up on you."

Dante looked down and nodded.

"See you at Mass this Saturday," Father O'Connell said sternly. "And bring that lovely new prospect with you. Is she a hottie?"

Dante laughed. "She's a hottie, Father."

"I knew she would be," Father O'Connell said nudging him and smiling. "Is she a good Catholic girl?"

Dante nodded. "I believe she is, Father."

"Good! We can have us a big Catholic wedding!"

"That would be nice, Father."

"Dante," Father O'Connell said softly.

Dante peered up at the Father.

"It's never to late, son. It's never to late. You confess your sins, you repent, you change your ways, and believe me, The Lord can work miracles. All you have to do is meet him half way, son. Make an effort. You reach out to Him, and He'll take care of the rest. Don't you ever think that He's given up on you, you got that?"

Dante smiled and nodded. "Yes, Father."

What was my slogan when you played baseball for me all those years while growing up?"

"Kick their arse's?" Dante said, imitating the Father's Irish accent.

"Yeah, that, but more importantly, never give up," Father O'Connell said blushing. "We never give up. We are not quitters. Our faith is strong, our cause is righteous, and we are?"

"Warriors for The Lord," Dante said, finishing Father O'Connell's sentence.

"Don't give up, son. Because He'll never give up on you." Father O'Connell patted Dante on his shoulder and walked off.

*****

Lucky was inside of a playroom with several other Reigns children. She was dressed in a silk and lace taffeta gown, with crystal beads embroidered throughout. She was the flower girl for her Aunt Princess's wedding, and like the other small children who were participating in the wedding, she had been sequestered in a small waiting room, so as not to dirty up her beautiful gown. Her basket of flowers sat next to her on a Queen Anne end table, and she lifted them and then threw them back into their basket container repetitively. She was bored to death.

A hand reached out to her, and Lucky peered up at the familiar face, and took the hand. The wedding preparations had everyone moving too and fro, and no one paid any attention to little Lucky as she was led out of the cathedral, and placed inside of an old Chevy Impala. The hand that led her away had been a trusted hand. It had been a hand that was allowed to be around the wedding, and the children. It was the soft, caring hand, of a Mexican nanny who had been around the family for a few years.

Lucky's absence was noticed after a short while. Dante went in to check on his baby girl, only to find that she was gone. The other children said that she had been taken to the bathroom by a nanny. After the bathroom search turned up empty, more and more people were questioned. The last person that saw her, said that she was headed toward the front door with a Mexican woman. Dante quickly put two and two together. He raced out of the cathedral into the parking lot and peered around. She was gone. His baby girl was gone.

"*Lucky*!" Dante screamed at the top of his lungs.

Damian ran out into the parking lot.

Dante was in tears.

"*Lucky*!" he bellowed once again. It was the cry of a

304

wounded animal.

Damian placed his hand on his brother's back and rubbed him.

"We'll find her," Damian told him. "We'll get her back, bro. I give you my word."

Dante peered at his brother with his bloodshot eyes, and there was only one thing on his mind. He was going to kill everyone from San Antonio to Mexico in order to get his daughter back.

Princess raced out of the church. "I've alerted everyone. I've even alerted the local and statewide law enforcement agencies. We're going to find her, Dante."

Dante dropped to his knees and curled into a ball. He was in pain, and his tears were flowing. The only thing he wanted to hear was war. Damian told him what he wanted to hear.

"The gloves come off," Damian declared. "Everyone, and everything we suspect had anything to do with this, dies. If it takes every penny we have, pulling every soldier we have from wherever they are, I want it done. If we have to move mountains, then we'll move them. No one lives, no one gets mercy. We'll kill every drug lord, cartel member, and commission member from New York to Colombia if we have to. This is total war."

Deadly Reigns IV

Deadly Reigns V
Coming Soon!

Please follow me on Twitter for updates on Deadly Reigns V and other exciting novels at; Twitter.com/CalebAlexander.

Also, please like my Facebook author page CalebTheHitFactoryAlexander. You can also friend me on Facebook. One of my Facebook pages is full, so please connect with me on the other one! And don't forget to check out;

Boyfriend # 2
Eastside
Two Thin Dimes
Just Another Damn Love Story
Belly of the Beast
Baby Baller

Also be sure and check out **Peaches' Story, The Takeover,** and see how she and her girls battle to take control of Ohio, in order to insure her seat on The Commission.

Knight Memorial Library - PCL

CPSIA information can be obtained
at www.ICGtesting.com
Printed in the USA
LVOW12s1436290317

528916LV00001B/194/P